VISHNU SAKHARAM KHANDEKAR (1898-1976) is acknowledged as one of the all time greats of Marathi literature. In his literary career spanning nearly half a century he published eleven novels, thirty one collections of short stories, six collections of allegorical stories and fifteen volumes of critical literary essays. In 1941 he became the President of the Marathi Sahitya Sammelan and was later nominated a Fellow of India's National Academy of Letters, the Sahitya Akademi in 1975. His works have been translated into several languages, including English, Hindi, Malayalam, Bengali and Gujarati, amongst others.

Yayati remains his best known and his most critically acclaimed work. It won him the prestigious Sahitya Akademi Award (1960) and the Jnanpith Award, India's highest literary award, in 1974. He was conferred the Padma Bhushan in 1968 for his landmark contribution to Indian literature.

'Artistic maturity and a high seriousness of purpose make this work a significant contribution to Marathi literature.'

Sahitya Akademi Award Citation

LIBRARY OF
SOUTH ASIAN LITERATURE

Library of South Asian Literature is an ongoing endeavour to publish in English an eclectic selection of some of the finest writings from the rich diversity of South Asian Literature. It attempts to bring together books regarded as landmarks in their language, for having won literary awards or critical acclaim, or having been a major influence in their genre, creating a new narrative style or simply representing an outstanding writer's art.

Readers are invited to recommend books to make this more truly representative of the vigorous literary tradition of South Asia. These maybe sent by mail, fax or email to Editor, Orient Paperbacks, 5A/8, Ansari Road, New Delhi-110 002. Tel: +91-11-2327 8877, 2327 8878 Fax: +91-11-2327 8879, email: mail@orientpaperbacks.com

YAYATI
A Classic Tale of Lust

TRANSLATED AND ABRIDGED FROM MARATHI BY
Y P KULKARNI

V S KHANDEKAR

Orient
Paperbacks

DELHI | MUMBAI

ISBN: 978-81-222-0428-5

Yayati: A Classic Tale of Lust

Subject: Fiction

© Mandakini V. Khandekar, 1978

This Printing 2022

Published by
Orient Paperbacks
(A division of Vision Books Pvt. Ltd.)
5A/8 Ansari Road, New Delhi-110 002
www.orientpaperbacks.com

Printed and bound at Thomson Press (I) Ltd.

INTRODUCTION

The story of Yayati had been on my mind for 45 years before I got around to writing it. When I read it as a child, I must have been fascinated by the mysteries in it, specially, the interesting incident of the instantaneous exchange of youth and old age! But why Yayati, married to Devayani, falls in love with Sharmishtha or even after the birth of five sons from these two, says, 'My lust for pleasure is still unsatisfied.'

I just did not understand. On the contrary I was angry with Yayati for robbing his son of youth. I had by then read the story of Babar praying to Allah by his son's deathbed, to bestow the remainder of his life to his son Humayun. I had melted at such parental love. If at that tender age a publisher had asked me for a novel, it would certainly have been *Babar* and not *Yayati!*

The story of Yayati did not really interest me as a tale until I read *Shakuntala*. There, when Shakuntala leaves for her husband's house Rishi Kanva blesses her thus: 'May you be as dear to your husband as Sharmishtha was to Yayati.' These words stuck in my mind but I did not agree that Sharmishtha was dearer to Yayati than Devayani. When Shukra curses him with old age, in asking for his youth back, the mythological Yayati said, 'I am not yet fulfilled in my marital life with Devayani. I am yet unsatisfied. So have mercy and give me back my youth.'

The explanation that was offered did not carry conviction. I felt that the words, 'May you be as dear to your husband' conveyed much

5

more. In life all of us get married, but it does not follow that we love each other ardently.

Kalidas agreed that Sharmishtha was very dear to Yayati. Only a wife who successively treads the path of love by charming her husband through physical pleasure, by inspiring confidence, showing respect and through devotion makes him feel thus. But in the tale of Yayati as given in *Mahabharata*, there was no such indication.

I was on the side of Kalidas. I was unable to reconcile myself to the picture as drawn in mythology.

Sharmishtha had made a great sacrifice for her community. A woman, who could go through the ordeal of being maid to Devayani who hated her, must undoubtedly be uncommon. It was impossible that such a person would try to entice Yayati for gratification of sex or that she would endear herself or earn his respect by a clandestine love affair.

I got thinking. Devayani was married to Yayati in the presence of the sacrificial fire and before Brahmins. But did their marriage connote a union of hearts? It follows that Sharmishtha must have brought Yayati something which Devayani was unable to give. He must have found happiness beyond sex and lust from Sharmishtha. The tale of Sharmishtha being very dear to Yayati must have stemmed from this and Kalidas had put it to good use.

Following the trail of Kalidas's words I started constructing Sharmishtha's life on my own.

From the original story of Kacha and Devayani, with due regard to the essence of it, I pieced together the reasons why the married life of Devayani and Yayati was unhappy.

Devayani was really in love with Kacha. He was her first and ardent love. She married Yayati from ambition. She made Sharmishtha her maid to avenge herself. I have accordingly portrayed Devayani in this novel on the pattern of behaviour of a woman who is egoistic, ambitious, spiteful and disappointed in love.

This, in brief, is how the seed of the character sketch of the two heroines, Sharmishtha and Devayani, first took root in my mind.

Yayati's tale is a subsidiary part of *Mahabharata*. It is not the central theme. A writer of fiction would be guilty of transgression if he made any basic change in the character of Rama and Sita, or Krishna and Draupadi. But the same rule does not hold in respect of secondary characters. The writer of fiction may make changes in the subsidiary characters to suit his theme, even if based on mythology.

It is for this reason that the Shakuntala of Kalidas is a little different from that of Vyas. The Rambhadra of Bhavabhuti is not the Rama of the first poet. Following the footsteps of these great authors, I have drawn in this novel a Devayani as she appeared to me and have attempted to paint her in my words.

So it is with Kacha. Thus it is that *Yayati* the novel is different from Yayati the character in *Mahabharata*. The Kacha of *Mahabharata* who returns to heaven after taking away the power of Sanjeevani is never seen again in the original. But here I have drawn an imaginary picture of his later life. He is linked with Yayati, Devayani and Sharmishtha in different ways. Although one may think of Yayati to be the hero, this story really has two heroes like two heroines.

Sharmishtha, Devayani and Kacha engaged my mind for a long time for different reasons, but when I set out to write *Yayati*, it was not because of them. The final inspiration came from the character sketch of Yayati himself. I do not know if I would have written this novel, if in the decade 1942-51 I had not been witness to the happenings in the world and in our country — the strange spectacle of physical advancement and moral degeneration going hand in hand. If I had written it before 1942 it would have been a very different story. I would then have confined myself to Sharmishtha's love affair.

The original portrait of Yayati in the *Mahabharata* is very representative. Yayati is symbolic of the common man in the times gone by. Inspite of much varied happiness, he is always dissatisfied and blindly running in pursuit of new pleasures. He does not know the difference between happiness and enjoyment. Pleasure, momentary animal pleasure, is mistaken for eternal happiness and he is pondering over how to get it all the time. In his world of emotion there is no other principle.

The common man of today is groping like Yayati in the twilight of a world in which the old spiritual values have been swept away and new spiritual ones have yet to be discovered. Blind pursuit of pleasure is tending to be his religion.

In the case of the mythological Yayati the idea of pleasure was limited to that with a woman. Not so today. The whole world, made more beautiful and prosperous by science, machine and culture is spread before us. The various instruments of pleasure tempt us at every step, all the time. Every moment passions are being moved and roused. This is leading to a degeneration of social values and corruption of the human mind. The loss is society's which I feel very deeply about.

In this novel each character is complex. Devayani is not simply wife and mother; she has a lust for power which guides her thoughts and actions. Sharmishtha is more than a romantic interest of the King. She is always guided by devotion and symbolises sacrifice. Kacha is the spiritual guide whose actions more than his speech serve to set the philosophical tone of the novel, that personal relationships have at times to be subordinate to duty. Yayati is the scholarly, valorous king whose lust for pleasure overpowers all else. I would like the readers to keep this in mind.

A good work of art can at anytime rise to different heights ranging from artistic entertainment, the play of emotions, social education to exposition of life whether subtle or palpable. Only readers can judge whether or not I have been able to do so.

V S Khandekar

1959

8

YAYATI

A Classic Tale of Lust

Yayati	King of Hastinapur, married Devayani, the daughter of Maharishi Shukra, and her maid Sharmishtha.
Nahusha	King of Hastinapur, father of Yati and Yayati.
Yati	Elder brother of Yayati who became an ascetic.
Kacha	Friend of Yayati, Devayani's love and brother (by affection) of Sharmishtha.
Maharishi Angiras	Yati and Yayati were born by the blessings of the sage.
Devayani	Daughter of Maharishi Shukra, wife of Yayati and mother of Yadu.
Maharishi Shukra	Preceptor of the Asuras* and father of Devayani.
Sharmishtha	Daughter of Vrishaparva, the King of the Asuras, mother of Puroo.
Vrishaparva	King of the Asuras and father of Sharmishtha.

---

* In Indian mythology 'asuras' were the 'non-gods' or 'anti-gods' and feared as enemies of the gods. Sometimes they are referred to as demons, as in this story.

YAYATI

I do not really know why I want to recount the events of my life. Is it perhaps because I am a king? Am I really a king? No, I was a king.

The stories of kings and queens have a wide appeal, in particular the fantasies woven around their many loves.

My life is also a story of love but, one wonders about the content of the story. I realise that it is not great enough to attract a poet to it. At the back of this history there is no pride, no ego and no exhibitionism. These are the tatters of a rich brocade. What is there left in it to display?

As the son of King Nahusha of Hastinapur, I became a king after his death. That is neither to my credit nor to my discredit. People will stare with curiosity at even the crow sitting atop the palace dome!

How would life have moulded itself if instead of a prince, I had been born in the house of an ascetic? Would it have been as glorious as the starry night of autumn or like a dark cold night of late winter? Who knows?

Would I have been happier if I had been born in a hermitage? Much as I have tried, I cannot find the answer. It would not have had the overtones of the brightly coloured magnificent brocade fit for a king. Even with its rich overtones, not all the shades in that fabric of life please me.

Maybe I am obsessed with the story. I keep thinking of it. A passing pleasant thought says, my story may serve to show to some the pitfalls of life and warn them in time.

Who does not know the legend of the moon which, for the sin of being enamoured of the wife of his tutor, was branded with spots for all time? Does not the world know that Indra — the King of the Gods — was punished with a thousand sores for his infatuation for Ahalya's beauty? The world errs, even realises the errors, but seldom learns from them.

We are all a little wiser towards the end of our lives and the wisdom often comes from the pain suffered by oneself. A creeper has many flowers; some are offered to God in worship and so arouse devotion. Some adorn the lovely ringlets of maidens and are silent witnesses to the hours of love and pleasures indulged in. The same is true of humans born in this world. Some live to be old and some rise to honour and fame and some are crushed by poverty. But in the end, all these flowers fall to the ground and are lost in the earth. That is their common lot.

In my life's sojourn, a few things happened which are worth recalling. Maybe I am mistaken in believing so, but I honestly do think so. The infant Yayati, the adolescent Yayati, Yayati the youth and later Yayati the man were all of a piece. But the Yayati as I see him today is a little different. The physical identity is the same but he now perceives what the earlier Yayatis had failed to see. He cannot resist the temptation to dwell on his life, so that the world may come to see, however faintly, through his eyes what he himself had failed to see.

⌒

I have always been passionately fond of flowers, even from early childhood. I am told that for hours on end, I used to be window gazing on the blossoms in the palace garden. My mother was amused at my childish ways and fondly told my father that I had the makings of a great poet.

Father pooh-poohed the idea, saying, 'What ... a poet! And what would young Yayu get from being a poet? Poets can only draw pretty word-pictures of the beauties of the world. On the other hand, it is only the born soldier who drinks deep of the beautiful things of the world. Yayu must make a great soldier. Of our ancestors, King Pururava won the heart of the most beautiful Apsara, Urvashi, by his valour. I have defeated in battle even the gods and have had the honour of mounting the throne of Indra, the King of the Gods. Yayu must uphold that tradition.'

This was much later in life. There is one unforgettable incident of that time which haunts me. It is like the scar from an old wound. I did not understand its significance till recently — but now, I am convinced that what in the earlier stages of life are meaningless happenings, come to have real significance and a deep meaning towards the end of life.

Mother had, among her maids, a favourite, Kalika by name. I too was fond of her and sometimes dreamt of her. I never understood why. I was then barely six. Once in play, she caught me and took me in her arms. I struggled to escape, when she pressed my head to her bosom and said, 'My little prince, you are getting naughtier everyday. I fed you as a baby. You were then a sweet docile kid, who returned my loving care, but now... .'

Clinging to her I said, 'From now on, I am going to call you mother.'

She put her hand on my mouth and said, 'My little prince, the queen is your mother. I am nobody. I am only a maid.'

I protested in petulance, 'Why then did mother not feed me?'

For the first time that day I was angry with my mother. I did not speak to her all that day. At night she came to my bed and gently called to me. She stroked my head with the tenderness of a flower. I relented a little but did not speak. I would not open my eyes. In my agitation I kept thinking that if I had the powers of a great ascetic

13

to pronounce a curse, I would instantly turn my mother into a piece of stone.

The feel of a touch is more expressive than the spoken word, but it cannot stir the heart as tears alone can do. I felt hot tears on my cheek and broke down. I opened my eyes. I had never before seen mother crying and I was touched. I crept up to her and with my arms round her, sobbed, 'Mother, what is the matter?'

She did not speak. She drew me to herself and shed silent tears, stroking my head for a long time.

I pressed her to tell me what was hurting her. In my innocence, I asked her if her favourite bird had flown away to which she said, 'No,' and added, 'I am worried about my other pet flying away.'

'Which is the other pet, mother?'

In reply, she drew me closer until it almost hurt and said, 'Who else, my son?'

She was holding me so tight that it hurt but it was also thrilling. I wiped her tears with my little fingers and prattled, 'No, mother, I shall never, never leave you.'

She echoed, 'Never, never leave me?'

Childhood is conscious only of the present and I repeated, 'I am sure I shall never, never leave you.' I did not know why the thought should even have come to her and pressed her to tell me.

In the end she said, 'You have been cross with me all day. You have not spoken to me. Even now, though you were not asleep, there was no response to my calling. Why are you so cross with me? Yayu, my son, children cannot understand the grief of their parents. But I beg of you that you will not follow in his footsteps.'

'Whose footsteps, mother?'

Mother and I were alone together and father was some distance away. Outside the door, a maid slept and even the low flame in the golden lampstand was dimming. And yet, mother looked a little scared and shaken. She got up and closed the door.

She took me in her lap and said in a tremulous voice, 'Yayu, my son, I was not going to tell you till you were really grown up. But seeing you so cross today ... I fear you will leave me one of these days, like the other one.'

I still did not know who the other one was and asked her.

She said, 'Your elder brother.'

'And where is he?'

She did not know. The thought came to me that a brother for a playmate would have been great. With trepidation I asked mother his name. It was Yati. I asked her when had he left. 'Eighteen months before you were born,' she said, 'he went away all alone.'

I did not notice the utter distress in mother's voice as she spoke. All I thought of was that Yati must be very brave to have gone away all by himself.

I again asked mother, 'When did he go?'

'At dead of night and into the forest,' she said. 'I was awake till quite late in the night, trying to dissuade him. I was tired and must have dozed off. When I woke up towards the morning, Yati was not in his bed. The guards looked for him everywhere but he was not to be found.'

I said to myself, 'What a worthy brother!' Then the mystery of the occurrence struck me again and I said to mother, 'Where had you taken Yati?'

'I had taken him to see a great rishi. It was by his blessing that Yati was born to me and I used to take him to seek the rishi's blessings every anniversary of his birth. Once, when I was returning from the hermitage, Yati went away. He wanted to stay at the hermitage. I was angry about it and spoke very harshly to him.

'I brought him away by force. I did not heed him or pause to think of what he wanted... .'

In curiosity I asked, 'What did he want?'

Amid tears she said, 'I still do not know what he wanted. He was deeply religious and at home with rishis, hermits and yogis. He made friends with them immediately. We have looked for him everywhere but like the meteorite falling from the sky, my Yati is not to be found anywhere.'

Mother was narrating her grievous loss calmly but towards the end she broke down. In recalling the incident, she seemed to be experiencing again that cruel morning in the dense frightening forest. Suddenly she stuttered, the words ceased and she was trembling. It was like the plaintive note of a violin suddenly ceasing on a string snapping. I was frightened by the blank look on her face. Then she heaved a sigh, drew me to her and wept bitterly. I could find no words to console her.

'I was frightened that like Yati, you might leave us one day. Yayu, my son, a child is the apple of his mother's eye.'

I sobbed, 'No, mother, I shall not leave you as Yati did. I shall do nothing to hurt you.'

'Sure, promise you will not,' said mother.

I clasped her hand and swore to her, 'Mother, I shall never, never turn a hermit.'

I still remember that night, but cannot recall the effect that conversation had on my mind nor the thoughts that came to me. But one thing is certain. In that one single night I had matured. It was an awakening from a world of fantasy to one of fact. I had my first acquaintance with grief. I saw the flood of tears in the eyes of my mother whose mere caress was heavenly to me. Subconsciously I grew to hate what had caused her pain.

I did not sleep well. I still remember a pleasant dream in which as king of the whole world, I stalked with a whip in hand through every town and village. Every rishi, hermit and beggar that I came across I lashed with the whip.

Yes, I did grow up that night. I saw clearly the form and content of life in those few hours of pitch darkness. I had been kept in ignorance of the fact that my elder brother had run away to turn a hermit — why this concealment?

Until this revelation came to me, I had lived in a fantasy world of blooming flowers, gentle rivulets and cool breezes. I used to wake up in the morning fresh like the new blooms in the garden. I had no fear of an occasional storm. It seemed to me that like the other elements, the wind sometimes turned fierce. The ripples on the gently flowing rivulet I imagined hummed a tune as I sometimes did. My world contained a neat array of dreams and butterflies, flowers and stars, peacocks dancing at the sight of clouds and the clouds in turn purring at that gorgeous sight, the bright smiling mornings with fresh blooms and the eventides like the fading flowers, the fresh greenery of the spring and the rainbows of the monsoon, the resounding of the hooves of horses and the tinkle of the temple bells, the soft sand of the riverbank and the soft cushions on the divan. Until that night, nature and man had been one in my eyes.

Such had been my world till that night. It was like a beautiful dream. If I was upset at anything, all that was necessary was to go up a tree and think of God. Such was the faith that He would answer the call and instantly come down in person to punish the guilty.

No matter how sweet or mysterious it was, it was still the tiny world of a bud yet to blossom. That world had not yet awakened to the humming of the bees. The soft caress of the golden warm rays of the sun was foreign to it. The bud had not opened to look on the vast expanse of the sky. It had not yet known even in a dream the entrancing grace of the carved image of the Goddess or the lure of black tresses, the crowning glory of a beautiful maiden. A bud cannot forever remain a bud. Blossom it must into maturity.

Yes, I did grow up that night. I said to myself, someday I must find Yati and bring him to mother and say to him, 'As the elder brother, this throne is yours by right. Take it. At least now let us have the satisfaction of sharing what is ours, like children sharing sweets.'

~

I was now six and as a prince it was necessary for me to acquire the Letters and the Arts. Father arranged for my tuition. At first I did not take kindly to my tutors. My gymnastics tutor appeared to me an ungainly giant. His size and physique alone seemed sufficient to justify his selection. He would make me exercise hard a the crack of dawn. At first, the body ached all over. I appealed to my mother against all this. She consoled me with the words, 'The future king must bear with all this.' In the beginning, I invariably came off the worse in wrestling and I despaired of ever becoming proficient at it, but my tutor reassured me. He said, 'When I was your age, I was soft like butter. But look at me now. I am hard as steel.'

Once at the age of fourteen, standing before a mirror deeply absorbed in admiring the grace and beauty of my form, I impulsively, felt like shaking my strong well knit arm and resting my head on it.

It reminded me of the picture portraying Indra resting peacefully on the arm of his wife Indrani, after returning from the battle with Vritra.

Such thoughts are intoxicating like wine and I do not know how long I stood before the mirror in admiration. Someone was speaking and I looked round in surprise. It was mother saying, 'Men also love to look at themselves for hours ... do they? I had thought it was only women who were vain about their form.' She had apparently mistaken me for father and added, 'Yayu has grown up now. What would he think, if he saw this?'

On seeing me, she exclaimed, 'Yayu, my son, how you have grown overnight! I pray that I myself do not cast the evil eye! You were

18

standing with your back to me and for a moment I thought it was your father before the mirror... .' She said, 'I am now relieved of one anxiety.'

Mother stopped suddenly. Tears came to her eyes and I said, 'You are the Queen of Hastinapur. You are not the wife of a poor hermit or a wretched menial. What cares can you have?'

'You forget my son ... that I am a mother.'

'True, but you are my mother.' I said 'my' with pride and glanced at the reflection. Mother also saw it and smiled. In an instant she turned grave and said, 'That maybe, but for me, whose cup of nectar was once turned into poison, it is but natural that I should be nervous about the other.' Mother was obviously referring to Yati. I said, 'Mother, you get me the permission and I shall ransack the earth in search of Yati and bring him to you.'

She said, 'Child, how can you find Yati? If he suddenly returned and stood in person before me, even I may not recognise him. Then how will you who have never seen him. I wonder where he is, how he is, what name he bears, and, indeed, if he is there at all... .'

She could say no more — Yati's departure had left a deep scar. That scar she carried secretly and would not bare even to father. That I had an elder brother who had left in the aspiration of becoming a great rishi, I had almost forgotten.

She looked gravely at me and said, 'Yayu, my son, you have grown before your time into a man and acquired proficiency in the Letters and the Arts. We must now find you a bride. It will make me very happy ... I shall speak to father today.'

Except with regard to Yati, father always gave in to mother. She was never denied anything. Once, one of my tutors suggested to father that I should reside in a hermitage for a few days. Father agreed saying, 'You are right ... a tree needs both rain and sunshine for its proper growth.' This happened in my presence and I was stunned. My distaste for the hermit's life has grown everyday since understanding came to me. I was never able to fathom why God

19

Shiva was so impressed with the long years of penance of a hermit as to bestow on him the divine power to bless or curse. My education was mostly directed to the worship of beauty and strength. These have no place in a hermit's life. There, corporal suffering is an article of faith. Wild herbs and roots are to them a delicacy and the chanting of hymns is their only war cry. Peeling fruit and cutting vegetables is to them what hunting is to others and the lowly hut serves for a palace. The maids of the palace were apsaras* by comparison with their womenfolk. All these thoughts crowded in on me and I was uneasy at the prospect of going to a hermitage.

When father and the tutor talked about it again the next day, I listened in from behind a closed door. My heart was beating wildly. In the end father only said, 'I also think it would be better if Yayu went into a hermitage but his mother does not agree.' My mother saved me that day but was now putting me into new difficulties by planning my marriage.

I was unable to sleep in peace even on my soft bed, tired though I used to be in body and mind. I would wake up with a start. Dreams of valour in fierce battles between the gods and the demons disturbed my sleep. My great grandfather Pururava was a mighty unconquered hero. He had made Urvashi his queen after fighting the demon who had kidnapped her. I had in my childhood learnt by heart the epic in which his prowess was sung. My father King Nahusha was no less brave. Early in life he had vanquished the tribals known as Dasyus and given protection to the rishis. Later, it is said, he even defeated the gods and acquired Indra's kingdom. I was obsessed with a desire to emulate these deeds of unique and unparalleled heroism, and my mother was thinking of marrying me off, lest I emulate Yati.

'At your birth, a great astrologer forecast your life.'

'What then did the quack forecast?'

I could see from her face that she did not relish this remark. She was silent for a while and said, 'Yayu, my son, the astrologer said this

---

* The nymphs in Indra's heaven.

20

child is destined to great good fortune. He will be King and will come by all kinds of pleasures. But he will never be happy.'

I laughed at this nonsense of the astrologer. In the end I said to mother, 'Mother, later, if you wish, I shall marry a hundred times but today, I am not after love. I wish to show my prowess. I do not want to loll in a boudoir. I want to engage in battle. They say the gods and the demons are spoiling for a fight. Let me join it. If father so wishes, let him turn loose the victory horse. I will accompany it right round Aryavarta. When I return victorious after destroying the enemy I can think of marriage.'

I did not realise how much I had changed during my student days. Like a stream adapting itself to the contours of its surroundings, my mind had rapidly changed a great deal. In learning archery, I, for the first time, experienced the unique satisfaction of intense co-ordination of the eye and the mind. In childhood, the sight of the rich variety of colour in the garden used to thrill me. But the experience of sighting the target in archery was quite the opposite. Everything except the target ceased to exist. The purple of the hills, the green of the trees and the blue of the sky in the perspective were forgotten. There was only the black spot there. The small black spot, the target of my arrow was all that existed for me in that instant.

This new experience was also thrilling. I was soon adept at hitting, without fail, inanimate objects. It was naturally followed by live targets. That was so many years ago but the joy of that first shot, which unerringly found its live target, still vibrates in the mind. It was a bird quietly perched on the tall branch of a tree. It made a beautiful picture framed against the deep blue of the sky. Every moment one felt that in the next instant the picture would come to life and take to its wings. The sun was setting in the west. Somewhere in a nest her little fledglings, perhaps without their wings, must be waiting for her. But my tutor and I were hardly concerned with her brood or their fate. I wanted to be proficient in archery and the tutor's livelihood hung by his teaching. I suffered intense agony shooting at that innocent little bird and that shot snapped my intimate association with nature. Till then, at the bottom of my heart, I was a poet. That instant the poet in me was dead.

Mother herself cooked that meat and served the delicacy to father and me. Father certainly relished every morsel and was all admiration. But I had to make an effort to bring myself to eat it. At night I woke up three or four times and once, I imagined I heard the shrill cry of the bird in mortal agony; at another time hearing the chirping of her little ones. Mother was still brooding over the loss of her offspring many years ago but the same mother could cheerfully look upon the death of a mother bird. She had admiration for her son who had killed that innocent bird. She could partake of the dead mother's meat with relish.

I was baffled by this contradiction in life.

The next evening the elderly Prime Minister called and I put my puzzle to him. He pointed out that life is not sustained by mercy but by power.

He told me many tales from mythology and interesting stories of beasts and birds. The central theme of all was this: The world is sustained by the struggle for power, lives on rivalry and conflict and strives for sensual pleasure.

From that day I turned a devotee of power. To my mind cruelty and bravery were twins.

My bravery was soon to be put to the test. Tales of conflict between gods and demons often came to father, sometimes from Devarishi Narad and sometimes from others. The desire to fight on the side of the gods and to defeat and crush the demons, so as to demonstrate to people the prowess of their future king was strongly borne in upon me quite frequently. But father disliked the idea of siding with the gods or the demons.

I often tried to investigate the cause of father's aversion to both from the old Prime Minister but his stock answer was, 'Everyone gets to know things in their own good time. After all, trees do not grow leaf, flower and fruit all together.' I then thought I should satisfy my craving for the battlefield in other adventures.

The annual festivities of the deities of the town were approaching. People from far and near used to flock to the capital to witness the celebrations. The capital town of Hastinapur turned into a sea of humanity. There were so many attractions that the ten days of festivities were soon over.

For the last day of the celebrations that year, the army commander had innovated an attraction. The idea must have been to encourage the spirit of adventure among his men. A steed of fleetfoot was to be doped and let loose in the circular arena. When the steed broke into a gallop, the contestant was to catch and mount it. He then had to go around the course five rounds and dismount without stopping the steed. For every contestant a fresh horse was brought in.

I liked the sport but it was meant for the common soldier. Nobody would have liked the prince to participate in it. With a pang of disappointment at heart, I sat by my parents keenly watching the sport. Four riders had been thrown off before they could complete the course. I looked at the fifth steed cantering in. He had the appearance of a great and graceful giant. You could see in every eye fear, wonder and admiration. He was being led to the course by six attendants but was defiant and neighed loudly. He pawed the earth with his powerful hooves. Occasionally would throw up his head scattering and ruffling the mane, which then looked as fearful as the white unruly hair of an angry rishi, poised for pronouncing a curse.

Looking at him, a wild desire welled in me and my hands began to itch. Excitedly, I stamped the ground. Every atom in my body was thrilledly and acting like the dancing jets of a fountain.

I looked at mother and saw deep fright in her eyes. She whispered to father, 'Ask them to take this horse away. He is frightening. There will be an accident, spoiling the last day of the celebrations.'

Father smiled and said, 'The life of man is dedicated to prowess.' I closed my eyes to understand the implication of what my father had said. There was a terrifying scream from the spectators. When I opened my eyes, I saw that the contestant had failed. He had been thrown and the horse was galloping away. Two or three others tried but the horse was intractable. The entire arena was frightened. There was a deep roar in my ears urging me to arise and reminding me that the life of man is dedicated to prowess.

The voice said, 'Arise, Yayati. You are the future King of Hastinapur. A king may have no fear. Otherwise, it will be the talk of the town, that Hastinapur has been subdued by a horse. The gossip will reach the gods and the demons. You are the son of the brave King Nahusha.'

I was shaken. I stood up and was moving forward when I was held back firmly by two tender arms. I turned around. It was mother.

Roughly I pushed her hands away and jumped into the arena. A sea of men surrounded me but they seemed fixed like stone carvings and were soon out of my mind.

All I could see was the wild horse. It looked defiant and appeared to challenge the might of the Nahusha kings. Gradually I approached him. A feeling arose in me that it was no horse but a mere rabbit, and its mane looked like a rabbit's fur.

While I was thus focused a shrill voice seemed to warn me. 'You fool, where are you going? It is the Valley of Death.'

I shouted back, 'No, it is not. It is not the Valley of Death but the Peak of Fame. It is a high peak but I am going to climb to the top. See, I am already at the top.'

I have no recollection of the sequence of events except the next thing I distinctly remember is being firmly in the saddle and the horse was flying over the course like a hurricane. It was like riding a storm with the lightning firmly under control.

Two rounds were soon completed. The huge crowd was shouting with admiration and joy.

That spirited animal and the rider, young Yayati, were both intoxicated. Both were mobile statues. Both were travelling at a tremendous speed. Like the sin and merit acquired in an earlier birth, these two had become inseparable.

Four rounds had been completed and the fifth had started. This was to be the last. I was conscious of my unique achievement. The golden dream of my youth was about to come true.

These were the nuances of my wild thoughts. I did not even realise that the horse was foaming at the mouth and that his speed had slackened. My mind warned me to be cautious. The fifth was to end a little beyond where father and mother were sitting. I moved near their seats, I wanted to see the glow on my mother's face. The temptation was great and I looked back just as I was passing them.

That one instant of temptation was near fatal. My grip on the saddle must have slackened and before I knew what was happening, I had been thrown from the saddle. The bitter revenge of that dumb animal was concentrated in that one act. For an instant, while I was in the air, I could hear shrill but plaintive cries from the crowd. The next moment I was deep in the abyss of unconsciousness.

When I came out of that frightful abyss, all I saw was a mild solitary ray of light. I did not know where I was.

I was suddenly jogged into remembrance. Then followed pain coursing through the head and limbs. Like a dry leaf in high wind, I had that day been flung into the air. Was I perhaps maimed from the accident? Why otherwise can I not get up? I put my right hand to the forehead. There was a cold pack there. I must have been in fever. With all my strength I shouted, 'Mother!'

I heard the jingling of bangles. It must be mother coming to me. I strained my eyes to see, but it was not her. It was someone else. Was I mortally hurt in that accident? Am I in my bed or at the door of death? I could not make out. I looked steadily at the figure standing by my bed. Has death such a beautiful form? Why then is man afraid of death? I heard a voice calling, 'Prince?' It was Alaka.

Her voice was shaky. For eight days the sun had risen every morning and set every evening, but I was not conscious of it. Where was I those days? What did I do then? I was baffled. I thought I was

25

a different person but with the same form. But 'I' could not recall a single moment of those eight days.

I asked of my mother and Alaka said, 'Her Majesty is in her room. She has given up eating since that day. Yesterday with great misgiving she came to see you and fainted at the sight. The physician has ordered her to rest in bed.'

She added, 'The physician has been watching over you night and day. A little while ago, he danced with joy on feeling your pulse and said, "Alaka, earlier I had feared that my skill was going to fail me and disgrace my grey hair. But now the prince is out of danger. He will probably regain consciousness about midnight or early morning at the latest. You must keep awake till he does so. See that the pack on his forehead is kept cold." '

Suddenly, she remembered something. She quickly moved away and returned to the bed. By now, I could see a little better. Was it Alaka standing by my bed? — Perhaps not. It was a fairy standing by me.

I smiled at the thought. Is beauty also subject to tides like the sea? Who knows? But Alaka was every moment looking more and more beautiful. I was gazing at her. She was flustered and murmured, 'What is the matter with me? I brought medicine to put it on the pack and forgot about it. Please close your eyes.'

'Why?'

'This medicine is very strong. The physician has strictly warned me that not a drop must fall into your eyes.'

'But my eyes will not close.'

'Why?'

How could I tell her that I wanted to keep looking at her? She might not like it. Her mother had fed me at her breast. She had brought me up in her lap. Even father respected Kalika and as for mother, she looked on her as a near relation. Mother used to say Kalika took greater care of me than she herself had. With Kalika's daughter —

26

Alaka said, 'If you do not close your eyes now, I shall stop even talking to you.' Those childish words brought my childhood back to me. It was as if the waters of the river which had flown into the sea had receded again.

I quickly closed my eyes. Alaka was wetting the pack drop by drop. There passed before my eyes the gradual transformation in many forms, from the childish Alaka refusing to talk to me to the Alaka now in attendance on me, near my bed. The bud was the same but in blossoming everyday it assumed more attractive and pleasing forms. Every form of Alaka that I saw was attractive in a different way.

Alaka had grown up in the palace with her mother. But till today, she had not attracted me so much. Why should it be? I reminisced we were playmates till I was six. Then we parted. As prince, I strutted about the palace, the town, the court and at the festive celebrations. She was a maid's daughter and hung back. She ran little errands in the palace.

I was destined to be a king and a world renowned warrior. She was destined to be a maid in eternal service of somebody. That is why our ways parted.

A heavenly fragrance intoxicated me. My eyes were still closed. I slowly lifted my right hand. Alaka was bending over and carefully pouring the drops of medicine. One of her tresses was rubbing against my cheek. I felt that lock of hair with my hand and that soft touch sent a thrill through my whole body. I knew that Alaka would suddenly move away from embarrassment if I opened my eyes. Eyes closed, I said, 'Alaka, where is this delicious fragrance coming from?'

'It comes from the jasmine flowers in my braid.'

'Let me smell them where they are,' I said. Alaka did not reply. I added, 'If you do not let me smell them in your hair, I shall scream. Then, they will all wake up and... .'

'If you scream, they will all rush in panic and mother will take me to task saying, "You wretch, can't you even make a good attendant?" She will hang me for it.'

27

'Don't you think,' I said, 'it would be better to let me smell the flowers in your hair than be hanged? They say a good deed should be done on time.'

All the flowers in the garden of Eden must have contributed their share of fragrance to those jasmine flowers. I was intoxicated by the fragrance of Alaka's hair. Apart from the flowers, the feel of her hair on my nose and cheeks was the height of pleasure.

I forgot myself when I realised that Alaka was withdrawing. I opened my eyes. She was moving away. I said, 'I have not had enough. I must have more ... much more... .'

Before I realised what I was doing, my arms were around her and our lips met. Delicious is not the word — her lips were full of nectar. Like a traveller in the desert, my lips were dry. I was dying with thirst. I drank deep of that nectar. I kept demanding for more and more of it. I was only conscious of one fact. I was swimming in happiness but its waters were not deep enough.

The nectar of which I had drunk deep was burning me like poison. I had to have more nectar to quench it.

I was struggling to my feet. There was a shooting pain in my right leg and like a bird shot down, I screamed in agony and fell back on my bed.

It took me three or four months to get over my accident. But my piercing scream of that night brought joy to the palace. Everyone was happy that I had regained consciousness and had practically come to life from dead. The old physician, in fact, rushed into my room and wept like a child full of emotion.

I was soon rid of my fever. But, the injury to the bone was more intractable. The physician had, however, imported from East Aryavarta a tribal known for his skill in bone setting. He set it well and there was no defect left, but those three or four months were very difficult for me. I was irritated with my disability when I saw birds flitting outside the window. I felt like going out of the window in the manner of a bird without caring for the consequences. My hands itched at the sound of a horse and the thighs strained for a mount. I did not know where to get rid of my irritation at the disability. Frustrated, I would gaze at my limbs. I had spent every day of ten long years to cultivate a strong and beautiful body but it had failed me. There is no limit to a man's love of his body but the body does not reciprocate. Indeed, on occasion, it lets him down.

Lying in bed, I tried to discover what was it that the body was antagonistic to, but never succeeded. I often thought there was a Yayati in me, different and distinct from the body. But how was one to understand the nature of that other Yayati? I knew that mind, heart and intellect were not parts of the body but had their separate identity. In the eight days of my unconsciousness, when with the rare drugs administered, I would have quietly swallowed even poison, where was my mind? And the intellect? And the heart? There was no answer. I was completely in the dark.

When, in exasperation, I gazed at my limbs, something whispered into my ear, 'You are wrong. Has your body always been your enemy? What about the pleasure of that night, when you kissed Alaka? Was it not made possible by your body alone?'

That night was a sweet immortal dream. The thought of it made me forget all pain in my life. Even the bright sun outside was obscured in the memory of that night and it all came vividly back to me, like the indelible impression of a young maiden, setting out for worship with an oil lamp. That maddening fragrance of the jasmine flowers, the softness of Alaka's tresses, the sweetness of her lips — the memory of it all was thrilling.

Together with sweet memory of Alaka, there was another thought which served to bring me happiness. The tribal who set the bone had travelled widely in Aryavarta. He recounted enchanting tales of the caves, forests and towns, sea and hills, the old temples and the men he had come across. From those tales I conjured up a beautiful dream.

In my dream I was escorting the sacrificial horse let loose in challenge of supreme sovereignty. In the end I returned a victorious

29

hero, having conquered the world and at the head of the maidens waiting to worship me was Alaka with an oil lamp.

I was well again. I mentioned my dreams to the Prime Minister and my tutors. They all liked the idea and inspite of my mother's protests father announced the sending forth of the victory horse.

I still remember those days!

~

I was away for nearly eighteen months escorting the horse. Everywhere I saw the grandeur of this ancient sacred land. I was enriching my mind with the countless folk songs sung to her glory and set to the music of the elements. I stored in my eyes the ever new folk dances. We first headed north, then west, south and east. How exquisitely pretty was the countryside everywhere. With the changing seasons the land wore a new attractive garb and was bedecked with various ornaments. Sometimes I thought the motherland was standing before me in person with rivers and streams like jets of milk, flowing from her breasts, the mountains. The thought that it was this milk which sustained her children was thrilling and invigorating.

We were challenged in only a few kingdoms. Father had in his time put awe into the whole of Aryavarta by his bravery. It was the victory horse of that very King Nahusha who had defeated Indra. Who dared challenge it? Those who thoughtlessly threw a challenge soon learnt that Yayati was the worthy son of a worthy father.

I was extremely happy in all such minor conflicts. I was an adept hunter and bagged with ease most kinds of animals. But the joy of vanquishing an army which is as well armoured as your own, is quite different. It is on such occasions that a warrior is really inspired. Victory in war is more heady than hunting. It was that kind of heady victory that I was aspiring to. When I had risked my life during the festivities, it was because I had understood the intoxication of victory, but after all, that was only a victory over an animal.

30

I was often unable to sleep during the campaign. Not that I was restless thinking of mother or something important. It was an undefined worry that kept my sleep away. I was weary. Just as one lively horse of a chariot takes to gallop unmindful of his slow mate, so did my mind ignore the weary body and indulge in wild fantasies. It used to dwell on things like death, love, religion and God. It was difficult to free myself from that maze of such thoughts. Every atom of my body wanted above all, 'to live.' At this, the mind would intervene with the question, 'Why then are you escorting the victory horse? You maybe challenged, when there will be a fierce battle and you may fall on the battlefield. Why should you, who wants to live, go where death is disporting wildly?'

It was impossible to settle this paradox and at such times even a bed of flowers pricked like thorns. I would stroll out, gaze at the stars and be soothed by the cool fresh breeze. The mango trees in the adjacent grove would rustle in a whisper and the *charwak* birds in the pond nearby could be heard wailing for each other. The mind was enchanted with such soothing music.

Gradually peace and quiet would descend on me. The birds would have by then fallen into silence and there would be no sound of movement or flutter. In the peace of such surroundings I would utter words of prayer. I would say them softly. In the end with folded hands, refreshed in mind and contented, I would look around at the expanse of heaven and earth in front and fervently say, 'Peace and goodwill on Earth.' Then sleep would enfold me in her fine silken garb and sing a lullaby.

I valued this peace at night, just as much as the pleasure derived from the rough and tumble of the day. I could not, however, reconcile the two. While I was escorting the horse, time was moving apace. In this roving life I experienced in many different forms both peace and intoxication.

I cannot describe the many varied forms in which peace and exhilaration came to me during these wanderings. There was the luscious green grass which looked like fur standing up, as if in ecstasy, and the tall stout deodar trees proudly poised as if to uphold the sky. There was the gentle drizzle of rain which was like Ganges water sprinkled by the priest in blessing and there was also the downpour, like jets of water thrown up by an elephant. There was the tiny lovely butterfly which, descending on the finger, looked like a ring set in precious stones. There were lofty minarets of temples and the inviting houses of dancing girls. I also saw tall twenty foot statues of the warriors and the delicately carved figures of young maidens on the walls of caves.

I went to see one such figure of a lovely woman. My escorts were all outside. The figure was exquisitely beautiful. It was the figure of Rati, the Goddess of Love in mourning, when Lord Shiva had destroyed Madan, the God of Love. I gazed at it for a long time. Her sari had strayed a little. Her tresses were hanging loose. I forgot that it was a lifeless figure. And before I knew what I was doing I kissed that beautiful figure passionately on the mouth. If it were not for the cold feel of the stone which brought me to my senses, I would have gone on indefinitely.

The region was alive with many elephants and I decided to indulge in elephant hunting. I had heard that wild elephants go to the pond for a drink at night. Once at midnight, I penetrated deep into the forest all alone and climbed a tall tree by the side of a pond. It was an exciting experience. It was pitch dark and you could not see even a yard away.

There was great satisfaction in getting an elephant under these conditions. I pricked my ears for stray sounds. I had heard that while drinking elephants emit a bubbling sound. I was straining to hear this sound and gradually lost consciousness of all other sounds. Every moment was like an hour.

A vague sound came to my ears. I thought it was a bubbling sound and was electrified. You could see nothing and had to aim by sound. When hit, the animal would squeal. I had decided to shoot quickly in succession in the same direction on hearing the squeal.

I shot an arrow. The sound of its impact on the target and a harsh human voice came to my ears together.

'Who shot the arrow? You sinner, come forward. Otherwise... .'

Even a squirrel could not have got down as quickly as I did. I walked in the direction of the sound. The forest was thinner by the side of the pond and I saw in the faint moonlight, a human being. He seemed like a ghost. I hastened to fall at his feet without looking up. Suddenly the figure fell back with the words, 'I must not be touched by a sinner.'

'I am no sinner, Sire, I came for the love of hunting, thought I heard an elephant drinking and shot the arrow. I am a Kshatriya. Hunting is enjoined on me by my religion.'

'You dare talk of religion to me, an ascetic under vow. I am a Brahmachari. Tell me the truth. Have not your lips been sullied by contact with those of a woman. You can touch my feet only if you are pure in that respect.'

I dared not tell a lie. The memory of my passionately kissing Alaka that night was vivid before my eyes. This ascetic must be omniscient and he would at once know whether I was telling the truth. He would blast me with a curse. I hung down my head. The yogi harshly named me a profligate.

The yogi said, 'I have no time to waste on a degenerate person like you. In the early hours after midnight, I finish my morning ritual and sit in prayer.' I knelt before him, folded my hands and said, 'Sire, I crave your blessing.'

'I am not simple like Lord Shiva to bless anyone and everyone. How can I bless you without knowing who you are?'

'I am a Prince.'

'Then you are unworthy of a blessing.'

'Why?' I asked in trepidation.

'Because you are a slave to your body. The greater the status, the greater the degradation of the soul. Every moment he succumbs to

33

the animal pleasures. He enjoys to his fill the fragrance of flowers and the perfume of scents. He rules over his subjects but is ruled by his senses. A woman is the epitome of all pleasures, that is why we ascetics look upon her as utterly forbidden. Prince, go your way. If you wish to be blessed by me, renounce all worldly things and come to me. Then... .'

'But, Sire, I have promised that I shall never turn an ascetic.'

'Why?' asked the ascetic in curiosity.

'My elder brother ran away as a child to renounce the world. Mother has still not forgotten her grief.'

'You are... .'

'Yayati of Hastinapur.' 'Your brother?' 'Yati.'

'Follow me,' said the ascetic and started off. A little later when he looked back, I had not moved. He said a little softly, 'Yayati, your elder brother is asking you to follow him.'

Fear, like hope, prompts all kinds of ideas. I had met Yati for the first time. I should have been glad at the unexpected meeting. But I was chilled by his words. I did not know what to say to him in his cave.

We soon arrived there. It was a straggling cave with its opening covered by thorns. It was when Yati pushed them aside that I realised it was a cave. A tiger growled. I instinctively put my hand to the bow and arrow. Yati turned back and smiled. He said, 'No, that has no use here. He growled because he smelt your presence. Otherwise he lies here like a rabbit. I make friends of wild beasts wherever I go. They are purer than human beings.'

Yati patted the tiger's head and it started playing with him like a kitten.

We were now well in the interior of the cave. There was an unusual glow of light there. I looked round and saw masses of fireflies. There was a cobra quietly curled up in every corner, with the jewel in its hood sparkling. To the right, Yati pointed to his bed.

I looked down. A small stone served for pillow and the thorny creepers at the entrance served for a mattress. I shuddered that Yati slept in such a bed. He was my elder brother. Why had he renounced all the royal pleasures for this kind of life? What pleasure was there in it? What was Yati going to gain in the end? What was he in search of?

Yati picked up a deerskin lying near the bed and spread it on the uneven ground for me to sit on. He himself sat on his thorny bed.

Yati's philosophy of life and the cave had deadened my feelings. Otherwise, on my meeting him for the first time, I would have embraced him, wept on his shoulder and insisted on taking him to Hastinapur to meet mother. But as if aware that this was not possible, I sat there like a dumb animal.

Then for something to say, I said, 'Mother will be very happy to see you.'

'There is only one abiding happiness in life ... eternal happiness. Worldly pleasures end in unhappiness ... be it the pleasure of touch or sight. The body is man's greatest enemy. It is the prime duty of man to strive persistently for mastery over the body. Look at the fruit I eat.'

I took the fruit he offered and broke a small piece and ate it as a sacramental offering. It was bitter and the bitterness must have been reflected in my face. He said, 'Man loves sweet fruit. Indulgence in them leads to a craving. It is this indulgence which makes man the slave of his body. Man's love of the body deadens his soul. It is only continence that awakens the soul. I eat these bitter fruit with relish to attain that continence.'

He picked up one and ate it nonchalantly. The small piece in my mouth remained there. If I could have gone out of the cave, I would have spat it out.

Yati and I were brothers. But there was a deep chasm between us. I could see it clearly now. I was emboldened to ask, 'How did you turn to asceticism so young?'

35

'Renunciation dawned on me in the hermitage of the same ascetic by whose blessing I was born. Mother had taken me to him. She was fast asleep but I had dreams. I came out of the hut and stealthily stepped across to another one nearby. The disciples were talking and I heard them saying, "The children of King Nahusha will never be happy." '

I was startled by these words. I was also King Nahusha's son. 'Why should it be so?' I asked.

'There is a curse on him cast by a great rishi. I was warned by the words of those disciples and I decided to be a happy hermit rather than an unhappy prince. I wandered into the Himalayas and found a guru. Now, you had better go. It is past time for meditation. I shall show you the way out and... .'

I tried to persuade him to let me bring mother to see him, to no avail. We came out brushing aside the thorny creepers at the mouth of the cave. I had now to take leave of him. I said in a broken voice, 'Farewell Yati ... remember me.'

He had not even touched me since I went into the cave. My words must have touched him. With his hand on my shoulder, he said, 'Yayati, one day you will be king. You will be a sovereign. You will celebrate a hundred sacrifices. But never forget that it is easier to conquer the world than to master the mind... .'

I returned victorious to Hastinapur with the horse. The capital gave me a rousing welcome. The whole town was bedecked like a bride, immersed in dance and song like a dancing girl and showered me with flowers as if they were the glances of young maidens.

But I was neither excited nor aroused by such a grand welcome. It was like a beautiful garland of fragrant flowers, in which one's favourite flower was missing! Alaka was not to be seen among the maids who welcomed me with the sacred lamp.

The joy of my mother was evident in every move she made. She appeared to have grown younger. But even though I was bathed in the love overflowing from her eyes, one corner of my heart remained dry. In the end I pretended to have casually remembered her and asked, 'Alaka does not seem to be here?'

'She has gone to her aunt.'

'Where is her aunt's house?'

'It is very far way, at the foot of the Himalayas. It borders on the Kingdom of the Demons.'

All that night, I thought of Yati and Alaka. Gradually, in the celebration of *Ashwamedha*, I forgot all this. Almost before the end of the celebrations, the disciples of the ascetic who had blessed father with a son, brought a message from him.

It was the rule in our house not to mention the name of that ascetic. Whether it was from awe or anger nobody knows. But in recounting the story of my life, I keep repeating to myself that nothing is to be kept back. His name is Angiras.

It appeared that a fierce war was likely to break out between the gods and the demons. In order to prevent it, Maharishi Angiras had taken the vow of a sacrifice for peace. Kacha, his favourite disciple was the leading priest. It was feared that the demons would raise obstacles in it. As protection against any obstacles to the sacrifice Angiras had begged of the king for his son, the renowned warrior, to be there.

This was an honour even greater than the Horse sacrifice. Indra himself would send for me, as the young hero who defeated with ease the demons. I shall travel to Heaven and assure Indra thus, 'Oh, King of Gods, I shall ever be on your side in any battle with the demons. But there is one thing you must do. My father carries a curse that his children will never be happy. I wish to be blessed with a counter-blessing to nullify it.'

~

My bodyguard was following leisurely. My horse grew tired of jogging along at slow pace. He galloped like the whirlwind and I was near the cottage of Maharishi Angiras in no time.

It was evening. Black smoke from a cluster of trees ahead was coiling up to the bluish sky. Its movement up was like the graceful steps of a dancer. Birds returning to their nests were twittering sweetly. The west looked beautiful with a sacrificial fire like glow. It was as if pieces of cloud were being offered to the fire as oblation and the birds were chanting hymns like priests. Bird life was returning to roost. I had not seen so much colour even in the palace. I reined in my horse. I was enchanted by their song and colour in flight. A multicoloured bird flew past me. I was overcome by the temptation to shoot him for his lovely plume as a keepsake. I mounted the arrow when, in a harsh voice, someone said, 'Hold back.'

It was not a request. It was an order. Absorbed as I was in the beauty of the colours and I had not noticed my surroundings. To the left, on the branch of a tree, was perched a young ascetic, admiring the beauty of the twilight. The next instant he jumped down from the tree, came near and said, 'This is the sacred hermitage of Maharishi Angiras.'

'I am aware of that,' I retorted.

'Did you intend to kill a bird in the precincts of this hermitage? That would have been a sin.'

'I am a Kshatriya ... hunting is enjoined on me by my religion.'

'There is religious sanction to killing in self-defence or to subdue evil. How did this innocent dumb bird hurt you? What harm has it done?'

'I admired his plume.'

'You seem to be an epicure. But remember, He who gave you that quality also endowed that bird with life.'

I was annoyed and said, 'Such dry sermons sound very well in a temple.'

The boy smiled and said, 'You are in a temple itself. Look, there in the west, the lamp of this temple is getting low a little. Higher up, you will see oil lamps being lit one after another.'

In appearance he was a common young ascetic. But his talk would have become a poet more than an ascetic. In disparagement I said, 'My venerable poet, can you ride?'

'No.'

'Then you will never experience the pleasure of hunting.'

'But I also go hunting.'

'And pray, what do you hunt ... the sacred grass?'

He calmly said, 'My enemies.'

'Is it possible that an ascetic wearing a tree bark and living in a cottage has enemies?'

'Not one but many of them.'

'And, pray, what do you fight with?'

'A spirited steed faster than Lord Indra's and of the Sun... .'

'But you said you cannot ride!'

'Not your kind of horse ... no. But my own, yes. It is beautiful and fast. How can I describe its lightning speed? In an instant he can travel from earth to heaven. He can fathom fastnesses where light does not penetrate. Horses for the victory sacrifice pale before it. He has the power to make man a God and a God ... a greater God.'

In irritation I spurred my horse, saying to the insolent boy, 'Show me your horse.'

'I cannot show him to you. But he is with me all the time, eternally at my service.'

'Can you name it?'

'Yes ... the soul.'

I was taken aback when that night Maharishi Angiras introduced the ascetic to me. He was Kacha, the leading priest of the sacrifice for peace. He was the son of Brihaspati, the tutor of the gods. He looked my age or maybe a year or two more! I was surprised that a selfless great rishi like Angiras should make one so young the leading priest. Love is no doubt blind, be it of mother for child or of preceptor for disciple.

Kacha was also surprised when I was introduced. My mother had impressed on me the need to be humble at the hermitage. I had removed my royal attire and must have seemed an ordinary soldier to him. Just that evening we had had a clash of views in the forest.

'One must be truthful but in adhering to the truth, one must put it in agreeable words. This teaching of my tutor I have not yet imbibed. Please do not take offence. It is uncertain how and when one's mind gets out of control like the horse. Please forgive me,' he said.

We two were given separate huts at one end of the settlement. 'Prince, we are neighbours now,' said Kacha smilingly. 'Kachadeva, have you heard of the proverb ... there is no worse enemy than the neighbour,' I replied in jest.

'There is a half truth in every proverb,' he said with a smile.

Maybe because of my duty in regard to the sacrifice for peace or maybe because Maharishi Angiras kept flattering me with good words: 'The demons know that you are here and dare not interfere with the sacrifice.' Maybe the friendship of the learned philosopher Kacha did it, but the ache in my body was dissolved in some other happiness, like the drone of the insects of the forest in the chanting of hymns.

As the leading priest of the sacrifice Kacha lived on water alone for the day. As the principal guardian of the sacrifice, I should have done the same.

Maharishi Angiras chose six of my bodyguards and between the seven of us we had to live on water only one day each. That one day in the week was very difficult for me. Hunger gnawed at my insides and made me restless. It was not that, when out hunting or escorting the victory horse, I kept regular mealtimes, but then the mind was absorbed in something else. Hunger was not noticed.

I was all admiration for Kacha on fasting days and wondered how he had acquired the power to fast cheerfully all seven days of the week, when I found it so difficult to go through even one day. I never found an answer. I would console myself thus: I lead the life of a warrior. The body is my mainstay. I was taught to cultivate it, to make it strong and well nurtured. That is why I cannot prevail over hunger. Kacha is different. An ascetic may have thin limbs like dry brushwood. But the limbs of a warrior must be like steel. There is no derogation then, even if I cannot prevail over hunger like Kacha. Would Kacha be able to escort the victory horse through Aryavarta? His body is lustrous by virtue of his penance and beautiful because of his youth. But, for his life he would not have been able to sling a bow and arrow.

When the principal part of the sacrifice was over without a hitch there was a three day celebration. Kacha participated actively like a child. He had an ear for music and could swim as if he had been a fish in an earlier birth. Once while a lyric was being sung, a child started to cry. Even his mother was unable to soothe him. Kacha picked him up and went outside to pick some berries strewn on the ground. He ate a couple of them and put his tongue, now tinged a rich purple from the berries, out to the child. The child was amused and smiled. It was as well that I knew that this childish Kacha and that other who chanted the religious hymns with sonorous clarity were the same. Otherwise I would probably never have believed in two such divergent personalities.

Did I say two personalities? No. Kacha was a many-sided personality. I was baffled by every new appearance of him. Once a lovely sweet fruit had a worm in it. He turned to me and said, 'Prince, life is such. It is sweet and beautiful but no one knows how

41

and when it will be infected.' He paused in deep thought and recited a verse which said, 'In life, it is the sweet fruit that is most likely to be infested.'

That night, I saw Kacha as a poet. Now and again when anything struck him, he used to compose poetry effortlessly. I should have jotted them down as they came. But it is only when a thing is lost that we value it. We were together for a long time. But I cannot recall a single line of any of his compositions — only a few words of one line — 'Oh, leaf of the tree of life.'

The occasion for that verse is distinctly before my eyes. It was a moonlit night. Suddenly there was a gust of wind and a leaf dropped in Kacha's hair. He was anxious that it should not fall off and get trampled over, but he could not catch it. He picked it up from the ground and gazing at it in a trance came out with, 'Oh, leaf of the tree of life.' I do not recall the other lines of that verse but they were to this effect; 'Oh little leaf, why should you grieve over this sudden death? You have in your own way contributed to the beauty of this tree. You have done your part in giving your little shade to us. Your life is fulfilled and your place in Heaven is secure.'

Once a tiny little affectionate girl dragged us to her house. She wanted to show us the first bloom on a tree she had planted. But suddenly she seemed steeped in deep thought. There were two guests and only one flower. She was puzzled whom to give it to. She gazed at the flower in deep thought. Kacha saw her dilemma and said, 'Child, you should give that flower to the Prince.' I said, 'No, you should give it to this great ascetic.'

She was about to pluck the half open flower when Kacha took her hand and said, 'Child, I am grateful for your lovely gift, but let it remain on the plant. Let it blossom there. I shall come and talk to it every morning. Would you not like that?'

The girl was happy at these words, but I was restless. I brought it up that evening. I said, 'That flower will be in full bloom in a couple of days and wither in three or four. Then it will drop. What is the pleasure in seeing all this? Are flowers only to be admired from a distance? On the other hand, there is greater pleasure in plucking them for their fragrance ... for making garlands and braids, for beautifying the hair and for spreading them on the bed.' Kacha smiled with the words, 'There is joy in it. But it is transient and derived from indulgence.'

'Is indulgence a sin?'

'No, not if it does not violate ethics. But life has other joys to offer, which are greater than those from indulgence.'

'For instance?'

'The joy of selfless sacrifice.'

I asked again, 'Is renunciation the only way to happiness?'

Kacha was grave and emphatically said, 'No, not at all. Your duty is to look after your subjects justly and to strive for their happiness. Kingly duty is as great as asceticism.'

I asked, 'Is it possible to live like an ascetic while yet a king?'

He said with deliberation, 'Prince, man's most natural instinct is for family life. It follows that in doing so he indulges his senses in different ways. If God had meant that man should not so indulge, he would certainly not have endowed him with a body. But mere indulgence is not the object of life.

'With the body God has also given man a soul; all bodily desire must be regimented by the soul. It is, therefore, necessary that the soul should at all times be alert. A driver under the influence of drink, loses his control over the reins and the horses run away with the chariot, which crashes into an abyss and is smashed killing the brave archer inside for nothing.'

He paused, then gazing up at the starry sky said. 'Prince forgive me. I forget myself talking in this vein. Certainly, but do not forget one thing. Like you I am also an inexperienced youth.'

Not only now, but he often talked thus. I would not agree with his views. Skirmishes between gods and demons had been going on for years. With Maharishi Shukra's power to revive the dead, their differences were obviously going to flare up into a major conflict. It was just to avoid such a calamity that Maharishi Angiras was performing the sacrifice for peace. While Indra and the gods were preparing for war, this son of the Preceptor of Gods was here contributing to the sacrifice for peace. He often said, 'Gods are addicted to the pleasures and the demons are blindly worshipping power. Neither can bring happiness to the world. Nothing can come out of a war between them.'

He had a curious mind. I was so near him but yet unable to fathom his mind.

Yet one fact remains. I was restless at the thought of the imminent separation from him. The time for it however came unexpectedly. Father was very ill, almost on his deathbed, and I had to return immediately. I did not know what to do and went to Maharishi Angiras for advice. Like a father he stroked my back and said, 'Prince, you must return at once. You need not worry about the sacrifice, the principal part of which has been possible owing to your presence. You owe a duty to your father as much as to religion.'

I bowed to Maharishi Angiras in devotion. With paternal solicitude he said, 'Prince, I will not bless you to be happy. I am not yet clear, even after my long penance, whether happiness is the shadow of misery or misery follows happiness like a shadow. Do not waste your time thinking of it. You have a kingdom to look after. Religion, wealth and desire are the three principal prongs of your duty on earth. Of these, wealth and desire are very sharp weapons. As the beauty of a woman is enhanced with modesty, so are wealth and desire when allied to dharma. The conviction that one must do unto others as one expects others to do unto one is to my mind, the essence of religion. Let such religion be your guiding star.'

I was distressed by the news of father's illness. What was the curse on father? Is father's illness due to that curse? If so, what was the remedy?

I could not contain myself and said to Maharishi Angiras, 'I want to ask you something. Does father carry a curse?'

He was sad and silent. Then he said in a heavy voice, 'Yes, but every man is born with a curse.'

'Every man?' I asked. The tremor in my voice frightened me.

He smiled and said, 'I, Kacha, your father, we all in one way carry a curse. Our lives are circumscribed by chains of circumstances. Some are limited by actions of previous lives, some by the actions of our parents.'

'Is life then by itself a curse?'

'No ... no, life is a glorious blessing bestowed by God in His mercy. Only the blessing is tainted with some curses.'

'What then is the purpose of human life?'

'Man must strive to free himself of the curse. The perception of the rest of the animate world does not extend beyond bodily pleasure and pain. Such perception is given only to human beings. It is by virtue of such perception that man has risen above the animal kingdom and is mounting the steep ascent of civilised culture. He will one day reach the peak, and he will be free from his curse. Never forget that bodily pleasure is not the principal aim of life. Its principal aim is the satisfaction of the soul.'

He stopped there and said, 'May you have a good journey and God bless you.'

Upto the time I entered Hastinapur, my mind was lulled by the philosophy propounded by Kacha and Angiras. But the lull vanished as soon as I entered the town. I was constantly troubled by the thought that I might not have the good fortune to see my father alive.

I sat by father's bed. I called to him. He murmured something, but did not respond to my call as if he was not of this world.

The Prime Minister came to me and, placing his thin hand affectionately on my shoulder, led me out. With a lump in his throat he said, 'My Prince, you are young and unfamiliar with the ways of the world. This world is mortal. You will not be able to bear the agonies of your father. A couple of miles from here is Ashokavan ... a beautiful haven of comfort. It is quiet and restful like a cave in the Himalayas and there is an underground passage from here to Ashokavan. It is very near that way. You should live there for sometime and visit your father twice a day.'

The Prime Minister had provided well for my comfort in the Ashokavan, but I was bored. There was very little I could do. Among the maids provided was one Mukulika, evidently new. She was about twenty-five, very clever and pretty. To ensure quiet and peace for me, she used to send the other servants away as much as she could, and remain in silent attendance on me.

I was striving night and day to keep the shadow of death off my mind but my effort came to nought everytime I went to see father. Death is supreme and sovereign in this world; the mind was distressed and helpless at the thought that none can defy it. I realised that I would also be lying on the deathbed some day like father. The childish thought kept recurring that I should run away and hide myself in a cave where the cold hands of Death could not reach me.

Death must be even more horrible as was evident from father's condition in that illness.

Occasionally, his delirium would abate. Once when father did not know that I was also there, he beckoned to mother. She leaned forward. With difficulty he lifted his right hand and caressed her. In a low voice he said, 'I must go leaving all this splendour and beauty behind.'

Mother was confused. She did not know how to bring my presence there to his notice. Father was sobbing like a little child. 'I have not had my fill of this honey but... .'

46

Mother sent me away but that pitiful crying of father's kept ringing in my ears and rankled in my mind. It was uncanny. They were the tears of a hero whose prowess was acknowledged with reverence even in heaven. They were the tears of the Supreme Lord of Hastinapur. Those tears were unintelligible to me and I was baffled by the thought that some deep mystery of life lay behind them.

Yet the experience which burnt in my heart was quite another. Mother was tired from keeping awake all night. I sent her away to rest and sat by my father. He was unconscious for a long time; the physician administered medicine from time to time.

The daylight was fading and it was getting dim and gloomy outside. When father once opened his eyes he must have recognised me. Grasping my hand, he screeched like a terrified lamb, 'Yayati, hold me fast! I want to live! No, I will not go. Yayu, look, there are the messengers of death. You are so mighty ... then how did they get here? How did you let them come here?'

His hand was trembling. He screamed again. 'You are all ungrateful. Even if you give me one day each of your life ... Yayu, Yayu, hold me fast!'

He relapsed into coma. His hand told me what he could not put into words. How tightly that hand clasped! That clasp contained all the fear of a stag mortally hit by an arrow.

If death is the inescapable end of life, why is man born at all? I tried to recall to my mind the philosophy enunciated by Kacha and Angiras. But it did not provide a satisfactory answer. The darkness of the new moon night is not dispelled by a few glowing fireflies.

I went to the Ashokavan in a dazed condition. Darkness was gathering outside. Mukulika came in quietly and lit the golden oil lamp. The place brightened up. In that glow, her bent figure by the lamp with her back to me, looked very beautiful.

She was slowly moving towards my bed. Her steps were graceful like those of a dancer. She said softly, 'Are you not feeling well, Prince?'

'I am baffled, Mukulika, seeing father's condition... .'

'They say, now there is no cause for anxiety. Only today, the royal astrologer was saying that all evil stars of the King will soon... .'

'Bring me some wine. Stars, illness, death ... I want to forget everything.'

She did not move. I shouted in annoyance, 'I must have some wine.'

She hung her head and said, 'Prince, the Queen has directed that wine may not be kept here.'

Is a woman naturally intuitive? Or is it that she is very conscious of the power of her beauty?

Her eyes were cast down. How then did she know that I was devouring her with greedy eyes? For a moment she looked up. It felt like lightning in a clear sky. The enchanting smile and the dimple on her cheeks — I saw for an instant all this in the intoxicating golden glow.

I looked again. Mukulika was looking down. She was very near my bed. I had not taken wine but intoxication was coursing through my body. The next moment father's words. 'Yayu, hold me. I want to live,' were humming in my ears. I said, 'Has mother directed that wine is not to be kept here?'

'This is a peaceful retreat far from the town. All the visiting rishis and ascetics are lodged here. There should not be on the premises things which are impure to them.'

Those piteous cries of father were humming in my ears again. I was trembling all over. I was frightened of being alone. I wanted support. I turned on my side and held Mukulika's hand.

That night!

Again and again I say to myself — I should be reticent about that night! Nothing at all should be said.

But I am going to bare my heart. It would be wrong if some parts of it remained in darkness when laying it bare. Coyness is the ornament of beauty, not of truth. Truth is naked like a new born babe. It must always be so.

That night I lay in Mukulika's arms — No!

Mukulika lay in mine. No!

Even the God of Love himself would not be able to tell who was in whose arms that night.

I had only to take her hand in mine! That was enough to snap the bonds of the world! I was no longer prince nor she a maid. We were just two lovers. Two birds, two stars —

As soon as I put my lips to Mukulika's my fear of death vanished.

That night, how often must we have kissed each other! Can one count the number of stars in the sky?

I had read poems of the beauty of women and I had been vaguely attracted by it for some years. The mad excitement of union with a beautiful young maiden and the spray of heavenly bliss which emanated from every part of her being, I experienced for the first time that night. I was wildly intoxicated with it.

I was woken up from the reverie by the twittering of birds. I looked out of the window. The chariot of the Sun was fast rolling up the Eastern Gateway. The golden dust raised by its wheels was very enchanting.

I sat up in bed. In utter dejection had I come to this bed last night. It was the same room, the same walls, the same bed and the same trees outside the window — but in that one night they had apparently been reborn. Now everything added to the happy mood gushing out of my limbs. The trees looked more green, the song of the birds sounded sweeter, even the walls of the room seemed to be winking at each other pleased that they had been witness to the greatest mystery on earth.

Mukulika came in to see if I had got up. She came near and said, 'Did you sleep well?'

49

What a superb actress Mukulika was! Last night she had played the role of a lover to perfection. And now she was acting a maid just as well.

Unconsciously, I called Mukulika. She stopped and looked back. Then she quickly came to the bed saying, 'Did you call for me, Prince?'

I had called to her, but why? I myself do not know. I kept quiet.

On this, she folded her hands and said softly. 'Have I done anything wrong?'

'You have done nothing wrong ... I have.' I wanted to say some such thing but that was only in my mind. In fact, I said nothing. Just then one of her assistants entered in a hurry. The maid handed a letter sent by the Prime Minister and went out.

It was a letter from Kacha. It said:

Prince,

I am also having to leave here after you. We saw the sacrifice for peace through. War between the gods and demons has flared up. You may recall that we had already heard of Maharishi Shukra having attained the power of Sanjeevani*. On the strength of that power, he is bringing back to life all their men killed in action.

War to my mind, whether between two individuals, two communities or two powers, has always been something to be deprecated and outlawed.

How vast and rich in resources is this beautiful world brought into being by the Creator! Cannot all of us live happily in it? I do not know if this foolish dream of mine will ever come true! At least today such a thought is more than indulging in moonshine!

---

* Sanjeevani was a hymn which, when recited, had the power to bring the dead back to life.

50

It is evident that the gods will be defeated in this war. But it is hard to witness with open eyes the defeat of one's community. I feel it my duty to do something to avoid it. I restlessly paced about all night in the courtyard before the hut. The stars were out in the sky. But my disturbed mind was in darkness. How much did I think of you! In the end, towards the morning I thought of ... no, an inspiration came to me. I became aware of how a poem comes to a poet!

It is only if the gods acquire the power of Sanjeevani that their defeat can be avoided. And that secret is known only to Maharishi Shukra, the Lord Preceptor of the Demons. Someone must therefore go to him as a disciple and acquire that power. It seems unlikely that anyone from among the gods will venture forth, so I have decided to go to Vrishaparva's (the Demon King's) kingdom and become a disciple of Maharishi Shukra for acquiring that power. The future is uncertain. Maybe I shall succeed in my object. Maybe I will have to lay down my life.

Maharishi Angiras ... did I tell you before that he comes from our family? ... has blessed the venture. He casually said in his blessing, 'You are a Brahmin by birth. It is true you are going to acquire a kind of knowledge, but the venture is more appropriately that of a Kshatriya than a Brahmin.'

I replied, 'If Prince Yayati had been here, I would have ventured into the Kingdom of Demons only with him; the daring part of the venture would have been his and only the acquisition of knowledge mine.'

What harm can there be in every class imbibing the qualities of another? In our worship, do we not mix the waters of many rivers for bathing the image?

Prince, we came together during the sacrifice for peace. I shall always remember you with affection. If I return safely with the power of Sanjeevani, we shall certainly meet sometime.

Some stars get together at short intervals ... some at long intervals. It is difficult to say when we shall meet but it is certain that we will. And that time, I fondly imagine, I shall meet my friend in a deep embrace as the meritorious King, the upholder of religion and of all that is holy in this world.

There is little else to write about. Even *Vedas,* the essence of learning, fall short in the expression of feelings!

Maharishi Angiras sends you his blessing and we pray to Lord Shiva for the speedy recovery of King Nahusha.

Oh, I forgot one thing ... that sweet little girl next door is crying her heart out because I am leaving the hermitage. Her creeper is laden with flowers. She is worried as to who will admire them. So I have told her that the Prince will soon visit her cottage to admire not only their beauty but their fragrance also.

This letter of Kacha's was very disturbing. Kacha had set out to lay his life for his side. And I? I even forgot last night that my father was on his deathbed. I was scouring round for happiness.

Did I sin? Last night was I guilty of sin? The thought of sin agitated me. That the beehive should come alive while one is tasting honey and bees should sting spitefully all over the body —

There was no improvement at all in father's condition. Mother was sitting before the golden awning of a miniature temple set up in the room. I sat near her and she stroked my back. The touch of her hand was like love incarnate.

My dejection grew at the sight of my grief-stricken mother and the idols before her. I could not dare to look at her.

Seeing that I was reluctant to look at her, she said, 'You must have been restless all night, even in the Ashokavan anxiously thinking of your father and me. If the little ones are to waste themselves in anxiety, what are the elders for? See if you cannot find entertainment in song, dance, music and drama?'

Just then the Prime Minister came in and mother said to him, 'It looks as if the arrangements in Ashokavan... .'

The Prime Minister intervened, 'There is a girl Mukulika by name ... She is new but she is very clever. She has been enjoined to cater to all the comforts of the Prince.'

Mother said, 'Your arrangements there maybe very good, but Yayu must find pleasure and entertain himself with them.'

'Madhav, the second son of our Poet Laureate, is a great connoisseur of the Arts and a good conversationalist. I shall ask him to keep the Prince company.'

I tried to smile and said, 'You must ask him to first take me to a philosopher. At the moment, I am baffled by abstruse questions concerning life and death.'

Madhav took me to the house of a great scholar. On the way he related a number of tales commonly in circulation about the scholar.

The scholar attended court only for the more important ceremonies. If a song or dance were in progress, he would lower his eyes and mutter verses to himself. You could never be certain what he would ask of a visitor.

Once a hairy ascetic came to him for a discussion on the character of the God Almighty. The discussion was getting deeply interesting when suddenly the scholar asked him when he was going to shave. The ascetic was flustered, being unable to trace any connection between the question and God Almighty. He stared blankly at the scholar when the latter droned, 'Ascetic, it is very difficult for sunlight to penetrate a deep forest. I am afraid the same is happening to you. Nothing seems to penetrate your head for this mass of tangled hair.'

Another time, a scholar from West Aryavarta who came to this learned man asked him how many children he had. Prompt came the reply, 'I do not know. You had better ask my wife. I have no time to bother with such trifles.'

53

Madhav was gifted with a fluent tongue. He related these stories so delectably that it was impossible to stop laughing. The learned are queer in many ways. As their intelligence is uncommon, so is their behaviour out of the ordinary. It is because of this that we vie with each other in relating such coloured stories about them.

I was amused by Madhav's colourful narration of them. The scholar welcomed us in the library itself. His first few sentences convinced me that the scholar's whole world was centred in this room. He was in ecstasy when reading to me from a rare archaic volume. His learning naturally evoked respect. Even in meeting one of my simple questions, he quoted profusely from memory and took out numerous references in support of his view.

But he did not have enough erudition to answer to my satisfaction the questions which were worrying me. My saying that I was greatly troubled by the thought of death, he countered with the words: 'Who has escaped death, Prince? We discard our clothes when they get old. In the same way the soul discards the body.

'Prince, remember one thing, that life is essentially an illusion. There is only one eternal truth in this world, Brahma, the all pervading power at the root of all creation. Everything else is an illusion.'

My fear of death — unreal! The bliss which I had experienced in Mukulika's arms was unreal and so was the prick of the conscience at the thought that it was sin. Gods and demons, both illusions! Then why did Maharishi Angiras take so much pains over the sacrifice for peace? Why has Kacha set out on his venture of acquiring the power of Sanjeevani?

If the animate and inanimate world before our eyes and all the experiences, pleasurable and painful, are mere illusions and transient appearances, why do I grieve so much at the inert form of King Nahusha? The body maybe perishable but it cannot be an illusion. The intense experiences of pleasure and pain may fade with time but they cannot be untrue. Hunger is not unreal and neither are its pangs. Tasty food cannot be unreal nor the pleasure it gives.

Madhav requested me to spend the afternoon at his house. His elder brother was a poet. Madhav said that on his wife's death, his brother had got tired of life and had gone on a pilgrimage. That the philosophy of our erudite scholar was at material variance with the facts of life was no longer in doubt.

On our way to his house, Madhav recalled the story of how his brother came to be a renowned poet. Once in the capital, there was a poetic competition. Poets from far and near had assembled to participate in it. The composition was to be extempore and the subject for the competition was *The Spots on the Moon*. His brother did not join in at first.

A bee in the lotus, the black of a rock on the Himalayas, and many such similes were used in the poems composed. In the end, a poet from the Land of the Five Rivers spoke of the moon as the white breast of a beautiful young maiden and the spot as its nipple. That wayward and sensuous flight of imagination had enraptured and carried away the audience. Everyone felt that the prize must go to its poet. It was the triumph of the theme of Love.

The judges now called others, if any, wishing to take part. His brother got up. He put forward, in beautiful words, the idea that the speck on the moon was a fingermark deliberately put on the moon, her child, by mother Creation to ward off from her beautiful offspring the evil eye. His composition appealed even more to the audience. He got the prize. It was a triumph of motherly love over passion.

Madhav's orphan niece was waiting for him on the doorstep. She made a charming picture. Her unruly hair, sparkling eyes, small lips, delicate mouth and her defiant stance! She looked like a charming butterfly, momentarily sitting quietly on a flower. On seeing Madhav's chariot, the butterfly rose and ran to him. She put her arms round Madhav, looked gravely at me and asked, 'Who is this, uncle?'

'Taraka, you must first bow to him.'

'He is no God that I should bow to him,' she said.

'He is the Prince.'

'What is a prince?'

Madhav had to find words of explanation which would be intelligible to her. He explained. 'This chariot, the horses and all this belongs to him. That is why he is called Prince.'

Looking steadily at me, she folded her hands and said, *'Namaste,* Prince.'

If I was a painter, I would have drawn her with that graceful figure of hers and the sweet innocent childish expression on her face.

'Namaste,' I said.

She said, 'Prince, will you give me one of your horses? A marriage is to be celebrated.'

'Whose? Yours?'

'Oh no, my doll is to be married!'

'When?'

'Day after tomorrow.'

'Who is the bridegroom?'

'Bridegroom!' she exclaimed and with her hands made it clear that she did not know. That waving of her hands in uncertainty was very fascinating. It was like a sweet little fledgling moving its tiny wings to shake off a drop of water.

Taraka's doll was to be married day after tomorrow but a bridegroom had yet to be found. I teased her with the words, 'I shall give you my horse for the wedding but where would you find a bridegroom?'

'Yes, indeed, where to find a bridegroom?' said she and was engrossed in deep thought with her small chin cupped in her palm.

Madhav was inside. Taraka talked freely, smiling and playful. How enchanting was that little form absorbed in deep thought! I wanted to pick her up. But I was reluctant to interrupt her reverie.

In a little while she looked up gravely and said, 'Prince, will you be the bridegroom?'

Just then Madhav returned. He had overheard that strange question. Another time he would have chastised the innocent little child for it. But in my presence he could do nothing and was fretting. How unrestrained is a child's imagination! I pictured to myself the ceremony in progress. On one side, a tiny doll and on the other a tall hefty Yayati, with one of Madhav's old overclothes for a wedding screen!

After lunch, I proposed to rest and asked the charioteer to return after sunset so that I could spend the night in the palace.

In the afternoon, Madhav gave me a copy of his brother's poems. I opened the book casually and glanced through it. One poem dealt with the mood of the ocean. This was a fascinating description of the waves on the ocean at high tide.

Reading his poetry brought back even more vividly the enchanting figure of Mukulika. I felt sorry that I had been abrupt with her in the morning. How was she to blame for what had happened?

I bade goodbye to Madhav and left in a trance steeped in poetry. The chariot was headed for the palace but I stopped the driver. It was then that I remembered my resolve of that afternoon. The poor fellow was not to blame and I said gently, 'Take me to Ashokavan. I am not feeling well.'

When I stepped inside the room I found that it shone with flowers and decoration just like yesterday. Mukulika followed me into the room with a beautiful jar of wine. She poured some in a glass and gave it to me. I sipped it and asked her, 'I had told you that I would not return and yet... .'

'To tell the truth, Prince,' she said biting her finger mischievously, 'we women do not heed a man's word but rather his eyes.'

~

I was leading a life of sheer self deception. The first moment of temptation is the first step down the ravine of sin. I have taken that first step. However beautiful it maybe, it is the first step in decadence and fall. Where is it going to take me? Into a frightful chasm or ravine? Or maybe to Hell! Sometimes the clash in my mind assumed terrible proportions, though it was rare.

One evening Madhav and I were returning from a dance, when I got a message from the Prime Minister saying that father was now conscious and was asking for me. I hastened my way to him. He was very pale, like the sun at eclipse. I was taken aback.

Father tried to lift his right hand to draw me beside him. It cost him a great effort doing so and tears came to my eyes. It was that hand that had given courage to me in my first illness. That hand was my shield — and now, that hand —

By his bedside, there was also a small jar of wine. He pointed to it with difficulty and asked for a little.

I poured a little. He stared at it and asked for the cup to be filled up.

'I have a lot to say to you and I must have the strength. Give me plenty, not just a few drops.'

I filled the cup and put it to his lips. He sipped it and closed his eyes for a while. When he opened them again he was looking refreshed.

He took my hand and said, 'Yayu, my son, I long to live yet. If anyone could give me more life, I would be prepared to give him even my kingdom. But... .'

He had the reputation of being a lion of a man. But his eyes — now they were the eyes of a mortally wounded stag. He said in slow measured words, 'Yayu, my son, I am leaving behind for you a very prosperous kingdom.'

'Father, I am well aware of your competence and prowess. To be born to a father like you is a matter of great good fortune. Of that I... .'

Father intervened with the words, 'And misfortune too.'

I was shaken and did not know what to say. The curse father was smarting under! Does he perhaps mean that?

Father spun out each word slowly. 'Yayu, my son, your father once defeated God Indra. He was then the King of the Heavens, but as to why I had to leave that throne... .'

'I was never told about it.'

'Umm ... what was I saying? Oh yes ... I changed at the prospect of taking Indra's throne. Yayu ... never forget one thing. Pride of one's prowess and arrogance are two different things. In my arrogance I thought I could take Indra's wife as a concubine. She accepted me on one condition ... that I should go to her in a unique conveyance. My palanquin, bedecked with heavenly jewels was carried by some of the great rishis. I was impatient and in order that the bearers might go a little faster, I kicked one of them on the head. That happened to be Rishi Agastya and he pronounced a curse.'

With the last words, father was gasping. Those words were indistinct and blurred.

He could speak no more. He pointed to the jar of wine and as I could not bear the agony in his face, I poured a little more wine in the cup and put it to his mouth.

The wine cheered him up. His lips moved in an effort to speak when I said, 'Father, you should rest now. We can talk tomorrow.'

'Tomorrow?' he said, with all the pathos in the world.

He was introspective for a minute. He then said quietly, 'Yayu, I, Nahusha and my children will never be happy! That was the curse! Both the good and the sins of the parents are visited on the children. That is a universal maxim. Yayu, your father is in the wrong, forgive him! Remember always, never transgress the decencies of life. I did and...'

Father closed his eyes and his face was haggard. He was muttering to himself. I bent low to hear him — I heard the words — curse — Yati, death. I could not contain myself and said, 'Father, Yati is alive.'

His hoarse voice said, 'Where?'

'I met him when I was escorting the victory horse.' He was trembling all over. He said, 'And you kept it from me so long? You feared he would succeed to the throne after me and you... .'

He could not speak anymore and he looked so queer that I screamed, 'Mother!'

Mother rushed in, followed by the physician, the minister and the maids. The physician put a few drops of syrup into his mouth, which seemed to revive him.

He whispered to the minister, 'My life is now uncertain. Show me once the signet of my victory over Indra. Let me die looking at it. One should die in the halo of victory!'

Mother was upset at his words and was wiping her eyes. I did not know how to console her. The Prime Minister brought the signet.

Father said, 'Give it to me.' He turned it over and round and round and asked, 'Where is the symbol of my prowess on this ... the bow and the arrow ... my bow ... my arrow... ?'

Father stared at it, and called to me. He asked, 'Yayu, is there any engraving on it?'

'Yes.'

'What does it say?'

'Victory, Victory be to King Nahusha!'

'Why can't I alone see the engraving? Has it also conspired against me?'

Tears were streaming down his eyes and he sobbed, 'No, I cannot see! Victory to Nahusha! No, all that is not true. He has been defeated today. Death has vanquished him. Death? I cannot see anything ... I ... I!'

He fell back lifeless.

Mother tried to control herself, but broke down! The physician with the help of a maid was putting drops of syrup into his mouth.

Stealthily death had entered. None saw it but its oppressive shadow was evident in all faces.

I could stand it no longer and came out, covering the face with my hands. I wanted to cry but could not.

A little later, the physician and the Prince Minister came out. The physician put his hand on my shoulder and said, 'Prince, at the moment he is feeling a little better and there is no cause for anxiety. But there is no certainty now and we must depend on God. You should go and rest in Ashokavan for a little while. If there is a change for the worse, the Prime Minister will immediately send word.'

I was going down the main road. Crowds were everywhere — some cheerful, others humming tunes to themselves and yet others sauntering as on a picnic in cool moonlight. Their gaiety only added to my misery.

Mukulika was standing at the door all dressed up when I returned to Ashokavan. I went in without a word to her. She came forward to help me to change. I stopped her with a sign. She was afraid and looked away.

With hesitation Mukulika asked, when I would like dinner. She had got something made specially for me. I said brusquely, 'Not now. Tomorrow morning please go away to the palace. Remember, you may not come here, unless I ask for you.'

I was annoyed. I was angry with myself, the world, death and Mukulika. I did not realise what I was saying.

I lay on the bed without taking my clothes off. Suddenly, I was reminded of father. The signet and his longing to see the inscription on it. A little while ago, he had lost his sight — now perhaps his other movements have also stopped. Father had a worldwide reputation for having brought Indra to his knees. Now, he could not even move his hand without an effort. In a while his body will be lifeless like a piece of wood.

The uncanny fear of death was haunting me again. I lay still with my eyes closed like a frightened child. By and by, I fell asleep. I do not know how long I slept, but I woke up with a frightening dream. In it, Yayati was lying on his deathbed instead of his father.

I had heard for a long time that body and soul are two distinct entities, but without the body, what worldly pleasures can the soul enjoy?

I was sorry that I had been cross with Mukulika earlier and called to her. I wonder if she was listening in at the door. She opened it, closed it behind her and slowly came forward. When she was near the bed, she stood with her head hung low.

I said, 'Why are you standing like this? Is it because as I said earlier that I did not want to see you again?'

She looked up and gave me a delightful smile. She must have been crying outside. That is why like the earth after a shower she looked even more beautiful.

I was about to get up and put my hand on her shoulder, when I heard someone calling, 'Prince.'

I asked her if she had called me but she said no. Yet she must have also heard it. She quickly moved away from the bed and was looking at the door, frightened.

Again the same call: 'Prince... .'

Someone was calling across the wall. I was reminded of the tunnel leading from the palace to the Ashokavan. I scanned the wall carefully. It sounded hollow in the middle and near the middle, barely perceptible, was a catch. On pressing it, a doorway slid open. At the top of the stairs of the tunnel, Mandar, the trusted servant of the Prime Minister was standing. He said in a broken voice, 'Prince, please hurry. We do not know if the King... .'

Without even turning to Mukulika, I descended into the underground passage, closed the secret door and followed Mandar like a puppy.

◡

In the eyes of the world Yayati was now King, the lord of a great kingdom. But in fact Yayati had become an orphan, with no one to look up to.

Sometimes the memory of father used to make me sad. The royal preceptor would then console me with the words, 'Your Majesty, the soul of King Nahusha is now free from bondage.'

Poor preceptor! I would listen to his verses from the *Rigveda* and in irritation would say to myself, where does this soul of man reside? What does it look like? What does it do? What is that something different that a body has not? The preceptor says, father's soul will now merge in the happiness of self.

When the funeral pyre was lit for the last rites, the priests chanted:

Oh, God of fire! Bring back to life for the service of the forefathers the dead who has been offered to you in sacrifice. Let him again take a body and come to life. May he get a body!

What is the significance of that prayer? I toyed with this central theme of the prayer. It became an obsession with me. What body will father take in the next birth?

Would he be glad to be born as Yayati's son? Is it possible? Perhaps rebirth is only a poetic fantasy! Why did I grow up into a youth? Why did I become King? Where is the Yayati who was equally attracted to the blooming flowers in the garden and the sparks flying from the sacrificial fire? Where is that confident, fearless, innocent child?

I shall not today go near a fire to catch the sparks. I now know that fire burns. I shall not confide my secret to any bud. I am conscious that it will open and perish the day after!

Is knowledge a curse or a blessing bestowed on man? Is youth which comes to all living beings a blessing or a curse? Youth is the first step towards old age. And death is the last step. How can it be youth if it lures old age? It is a terrible curse!

63

When the word 'curse' thus somehow came to mind, I remembered father's last words, 'Nahusha and his children will never be happy.' I felt that someone was ever writing these words in the interstellar space in burning letters.

That curse had partly come true. Father was not happy. In his last struggle, he was even unable to see the memento of his unique victory.

Father had in arrogance kicked Rishi Agastya. He in turn had quite rightly pronounced a curse. But what had we children done to offend him? I was not even born then. And even so, is the curse going to haunt me like a ghost all my life?

What has destiny in store for me? Is it possible that I will not be happy even after my enthronement?

I had reached a strangely inert state of mind. I was not inclined to talk to anyone, eat or drink but just lay down quietly. Mother had noticed it and one day asked if I was ailing. She said, 'Your maid Mukulika came from Ashokavan yesterday. She is very sweet and clever. I would like to bring her to the palace. She was saying, "The Prince is very uncommunicative. He will not openly ask for anything that he wants." Shall I send for her today to attend on you?'

'Mukulika is silly and perhaps you are even more so. Truly, mother, I have lost interest in everything. I feel like renouncing all this grandeur and... .'

Mother looked petrified. She held me by the hand and said, 'Yayu, do you remember your promise to me?'

To humour her I said, 'As a child I made promises to you everyday. So many of them are now crowding my mind that I do not clearly remember any of them.'

'You have all along been wily. When you are cornered... .'

For a moment, I wished to tell her of Yati and press her to go to him and prevail upon him with her love to come back, adding, 'He is the elder brother. Let him be king. I am dejected. I do not want the throne ... in fact nothing.'

Even if she went in search of him he was unlikely to return, inspite of her tears. It is easy to tame a lion or a tiger but not an obstinate ascetic like Yati — I wonder how his life is going to end. Will his path lead him to the pinnacle — realisation of God in person? If he gets to his goal, the whole world will be all admiration for him. He will be acclaimed as a great ascetic. But what if his foot slips while on that difficult ascent up the snowbound hills of renunciation. If the snow suddenly thaws he will be drowned in the avalanche.

Mother said, 'You are very obstinate. You can hardly help it. It runs in your family. Now of course, added to your obstinacy as a child, is the obstinacy of a King. I can also exercise my rights as the King's mother. Yayu, shall I tell you why you are dejected?'

After all, a mother's heart bleeds even at the simple prick of a thorn in her child's foot and it brings tears to her eyes. It was no wonder then, that my mother was concerned about my strange behaviour.

In order to change the topic, I said, 'Mother, I know you are loving but your penetrating vision... .'

'This is knowledge which comes with experience and age, son! I was also your age once and haven't forgotten what it felt like then.' She obviously felt I needed to marry a princess of my choice to regain my good cheer.

Mother left to fix a date for the coronation. She was smiling. Her last words should have struck a happy note in my mind. I was King of Hastinapur, but I kept thinking of mother. I had often been greatly troubled by the thought that father's death would be too much of a shock to her and that she would soon follow him.

What in fact happened was quite different. She grieved for a few days but soon thereafter took her place as the Queen Mother, looking after the household and the affairs of the state. She was active and seemed to take interest in her new life. That her happiness hung solely by my father was a mistaken idea.

In this world everybody obviously lives for himself. As the roots of the trees and creepers turn to moisture nearby, so do men and women look for support to near relations for their happiness. This is what the world calls love, affection or friendship. In fact, it is only the love of self. If the moisture on one side dries up, the trees and the creepers do not dry up, but their roots look for it elsewhere, be it far or near. They find it, draw it in and so remain fresh.

Mother's fresh zest for life must have come thus. She paraded as the Queen upto a few days ago, but did not her greatness depend on keeping the King in hand on the strength of her beauty?

The reason why she did not nurse me as a child must have been the difficult role of being the wife of a great man. She had greater need to preserve her beauty than be a mother. For her the husband was all in all. And yet she had no authority over him, but she also had nothing else to turn to.

She was now the Queen Mother. Her influence as a mother over her son was evident in every act of hers.

When Madhav come to see me today he was not alone, Taraka, his niece, accompanied him. I was pleased to see that naughty girl. I called her to me and asked, 'Well, lady Taraka, did you in the end find a husband for your doll?'

Taraka nodded.

I asked her, 'Is the husband good?' She shook her head.

'Why do you say he is not a good husband?' She sniffed and said, 'He has a snub nose and lisps,' she said. Madhav said, 'She says she heard him lisp in her dream.'

I laughed heartily. Madhav pointed out, 'She has specially come to the King today.'

'What do you want then?'

She looked up at me shyly with her head hung and said, 'You are now King, and are going to mount the lion? Is it not?'

I said with a laugh, 'A king has to mount the throne ... a seat made of lions or else who would call him King?'

'Do the lions bite?'

I said gravely, 'No.'

'Then will you make me your Queen?'

So, Taraka had come to be my Queen. This was rather an unusual kind of *swayamvara**, which amused me.

I said, 'You are very small yet. I shall make you Queen when you grow up.' I sent her away loaded with sweets.

That evening two disciples of Angiras brought his letter. Reading it, I was shaken out of Taraka's innocent world into a very different one.

The sage had written:

I am writing to you sometime after the demise of King Nahusha.

Soon after you left, Kacha went to Vrishaparva's kingdom to acquire the power of Sanjeevani. Our prayers had fallen short of being able to prevent a war between gods and demons. It is not part of a man's duty to sit back with folded hands in the presence of evil occurrences! I therefore left the hermitage resolved to go to the Shivtirth and do penance in solitude. I heard about the demise of King Nahusha, on my way back after the penance. I returned today and am writing to you now.

Yayati, death is as inevitable as it is distasteful to all living beings. That is a part of the routine of all creation, as dramatic and mysterious as birth. As the delicate fresh reddish foliage appearing on the trees in spring is the play of the power of creation, equally so, is it seen in the faded yellow leaves falling off in autumn. That is just how one must view Death. Sunrise

---

* A festival at which a lady, normally a princess, chooses a husband from the assembled suitors.

and sunset, summer and winter, light and shade, day and night, woman and man, pleasure and pain, body and soul and life and death are all inseparable pairs. Life manifests itself in such quality. It is with such web and woof, that the Prime Power weaves the fabric of the life and growth of creation.

King Nahusha was a great warrior. May his prowess inspire you. A king is blessed with his subjects which are like the Kamdhenu to him. May you serve them well! I shall ever pray to the Prime Power to this end.

I was going to stop but that bad news never comes singly is unfortunately true.

A young ascetic returning from the borderland of the demons' kingdom says, Kacha entered their land and preceptor Shukra accepted him as a disciple. Kacha had hoped to be able to please his preceptor with his devotion and service and acquire the Sanjeevani. The demons naturally turned inimical to Kacha. They mercilessly murdered him while he was out as usual tending his preceptor's cattle, and fed his meat to the wolves.

That is all the ascetic knows. A number of brave young ascetics living on the border are engaged in getting information, at the peril of their life.

There is, however, no purpose in it. Now that Kacha has thus been put an end to ... Yayati, some words in the last four lines have got dimmed. Unconsciously, tears came to my eyes and dropped on the writing. I tried my utmost to control my tears but even an ascetic who has renounced everything is only a man.

I am distressed by the memory of Kacha. His positive tendencies were so pronounced ... I had hoped that he would succeed in the great task of stopping the war but...

It is given to man to hope, whether it succeeds...

I understand your mother's grief. I pray to God that He may give her the strength to bear it.

68

You are now King and maybe I should have addressed your more formally, but that would not have shown my affection for you.

Only one part of Angiras' letter was truly touching. That was the tears which came to his eyes while writing about Kacha's death and words that were disfigured thereby. Tears and the disfigured words! All the rest was preaching, just dry philosophy. But does man live by philosophy? No, he lives in hope, dreams, affection, glory and heroism. But merely by philosophy? How is it possible? These bearded ascetics are always very fond of sermonising.

Kacha's heroism, evident from that letter, went to my heart. How brave he was, though unarmed. His face must have held the glow of lightning when he was killed. Playing with his *rudrakshamala**, he must have said to the demons, 'You can cut my body to pieces, but what about my soul? You cannot even touch it. It is immortal.'

I was spending idle days in the palace instead of undertaking a venture like him.

Even after father's death, there was no rising anytime, anywhere. The affairs of the state were running smoothly and I was like a bird in a gilded cage. Kacha was soaring high in the blue sky like an eagle. I wished to be similarly engaged in some unique venture somewhere. With this thought I spent a restless night and in the morning I had a dream. Yati was saying in the dream: 'You selfish wicked wretch, what right have you to the throne? Get up and vacate the throne or I will destroy you with a curse.'

I got up and called to mother and told her of my meeting with Yati and my dream. At first she was confused. Then she looked deep into my eyes and asked, 'Yayu, I trust you are telling the truth?'

'I swear by father.....'

---

* Rosary made of the seeds of the *(L.) Elaeocarpus Ganitrus* tree, having special religious significance for the Hindus.

She said disparagingly, 'Swear by anything else. Your father was a warrior, but he never kept any of the promises he made to me.' Mother put her hand on my shoulder and said, 'My son, he alone that is hurt suffers. I was not the great Queen, I was the great maid. I danced to his tune all my life. I refuse to do so any longer.'

She had spoken the harsh truth. That was why I could not bear to hear it. To console her, I said, 'Mother, I shall never do anything to hurt you.' In the excitement of the moment I got up and touched her feet. She calmed down then.

She reluctantly consented to my going to East Aryavarta in search of Yati. She agreed that it should be kept quiet and that my retinue should be as small as possible. She insisted, however, that if I failed to meet Yati or his whereabouts could not be ascertained, I must return straight to Hastinapur. I agreed.

She was now preparing for the journey instead of the coronation with equal zest. Mandar was the Prime Minister's most trusted servant and was to go as my bodyguard. So that there maybe no inconvenience, she detailed servants and even one or two maids for odd jobs. I asked for Kalika but was told that she had gone to visit Alaka, who was now married.

Mother decided to select two princesses by the time of my return — one for me and one for Yati. I do not know if Taraka who wished to be my queen or mother who was contemplating marriage for Yati was more childish. Is a mother's heart no different from that of a child?

I looked at mother and wondered if anyone ever understood another person fully. She was my mother but as to knowing her! It would be easier to fathom the sky than to peep in a heart!

∼

Although the hermitage of Angiras was a little off the way but I paid him a visit. He greeted me from the bottom of his heart.

I was very glad to see him but before I could say a word, a young ascetic entered. In great misery he announced, 'The demons are celebrating, with great eclat, the "Wine-day". They rejoice because wine has helped their cause ... they killed and cremated Kacha and mixed his ashes in the Maharishi's wine! As you know, Maharishi Shukra has a great weakness for wine and the demons have succeeded in making it impossible for Kacha to come to life again.'

The hermitage was plunged in gloom.

It was with a heavy heart that I left Angiras. On the way, I was attracted by the high mountains, deep ravines, magnificent rainbows, tiny butterflies, the tall swaying palms and the waterside willows and reeds. All the way I was witness to towns and villages, the strong well-knit bodies of men and women, their varied costumes and various jewellery and the rich variety of their songs, dances and festivals. The cavalcade was a balm to my misery.

What does a Kacha, Yati or Yayati matter in this vast expanse of life on earth? How insignificant man is in the vast background of this world? Why talk of his pleasure or pain? Is anyone bothered about the feelings of a blade of grass floating on the waves of the sea?

We were hurrying to get to East Aryavarta quickly, yet the entire retinue was equally concerned about my comfort.

Yati had left his cave. I made careful enquiries in the surrounding villages and talked at length to many people young and old. All that came out was that Yati was now a little more tolerant of society, unlike his earlier aversion to anyone staying near his cave. Society was now an experimental laboratory for him. He could work miracles. To that end he had undergone terrible penance. It was in this unbalanced state of mind that he had heard of Maharishi Shukra's Sanjeevani which could revive the dead. He was convinced that only a preceptor like Shukra could show him the one way to his objective — the power to convert all women into men — and had therefore gone to the kingdom of the demons.

All this was merely hearsay collected from the rustics inhabiting the small villages in the sparsely populated area about the cave. It is

71

difficult to say how much of it was true and how much was coloured. But one thing was clear. Yati had abandoned the cave for good and had probably gone to Shukracharya.

We set out to return. We made for short cuts and travelled fast for three or four days at a stretch. On the fourth or fifth day we reached a nice little place, a little off the main route.

Hill, dale, river and forest together contributed to the beauty of the spot. Each added to its charm. The hill was not high and but for the deep pool in the middle, the river flowed placidly. Except for the central part the forest was like a neatly laid out garden. The first sight of it brought the thought to my mind that God must have made this pleasure garden for the play of Creation in her childhood.

There was no habitation for a mile but one did not experience at all the strange lurking fear usual in such regions. The twittering birds appeared to be talking to one another. The rippling stream, humming a tune to itself like a young maiden in a reverie. The dale was like an inviting bed and the hill like a sacrificial place. The oppressive effect of great grandeur or the frightening effect of the grotesque — none of these marred the spectacle. It was sheer beauty, just sheer unbounded feast for the eyes.

I was conscious that I must return to Hastinapur as early as possible. My mother would be waiting. But I was enchanted with that beautiful spot. I enjoyed it for hours on end and was still not satisfied. It was difficult to tear myself away from it and I lingered there despite the journey ahead. Suddenly I would be reminded of Yati. He must have come across many such spots. Why did he not feel like spending his time delighting in such beauty? Why had he set out on the trying path of meditation and mystic achievement? He had gone to Maharishi Shukra to serve him and to attain the power to make the world exclusively male; why had he turned a woman-hater? If he had seen this beauty spot, he would probably have set out to turn it into a desert. Is the purpose of man's life to love the natural and the beautiful; to adore it and to enjoy it so as to make his own life fuller or is it —

Two days went by and the third passed, but I could not leave the place on my homeward journey.

I wondered when I would return to that beautiful spot. Perhaps never. The scroll of life is written by a wayward destiny in a sprawling hand. Is it possible that she will let me visit this spot again? The only time to reap happiness is while one is happy.

I was prolonging my stay with this thought uppermost. At last on the fifth day, Mandar said we must leave the next morning.

I did not like the compulsion in his tone. In the end, towards the evening, I set out with a heavy heart to take leave of the place. I was like a man in misery, faced with long separation from his dear one. The long shadows of the evening gradually spread to the hill crest, the tops of tree and bush and rolled leisurely on the placid water of the pool.

I watched all this, perched on the tree. I was uneasy that I would have to leave in a few hours, when suddenly on the opposite bank, I saw a deer gracefully poised. She must have come for a drink but stood there without bending to the water as if some sculptor was modelling her figure. Instinctively my right hand searched for the bow and arrow on my shoulder. The hunter in me was roused. Looking on that graceful figure, my hand was stayed. Unlike my earlier conviction that killing was part of my Kshatriya dharma, now I felt a sense of guilt at wanting to hunt that beautiful creature.

The deer stood its ground. Casually I turned to the near bank. I was surprised. There also a deer — No — it was a young maiden! Her back was turned to me. Why had she come to this wilderness?

She looked at the sky, folded her hands and the next moment, flung herself into the pool.

When I dived in to save her it was purely from compassion. I pulled her out of the pool and put her head in my lap to revive her.

My compassion gave place to fear, then surprise and finally joy for she was Alaka!

She had not taken in much water and soon opened her eyes. And on seeing me, with a faint smile, she closed them again. In a low voice she said, 'Mother, when did Prince come?'

She was obviously not conscious of her surroundings yet.

'I am no longer prince, Alaka! I am now king,' I said smiling.

She opened her eyes, and fixing them on me said, 'I beg your pardon, Your Majesty! I erred,' with such an enchanting smile that the charming Alaka of many years ago, reappeared before my eyes. The sweetness of that first kiss that night seared through my veins. She still doubted whether what she saw was reality or a dream! I was tempted to kiss her and bent to put my lips gently on hers. She realised this, shivered a little and said, 'No!'

Her voice was a little hoarse but its firmness did not escape me. I drew away. Slowly she said, 'Your Majesty, I am now someone else's!'

Her hand was trembling and anxiety showed in her face. Inspite of my protests to the contrary, stammering and pausing at intervals she started telling me of the intervening years. She was not conscious even of her wet clothes clinging to the body or of her wet hair!

Her aunt had arranged her marriage with a young, handsome and well-to-do farmer, but he was given to gambling. Once he took Alaka out on the plea of going to a fair. His dear friend who practised black magic was with them. There her husband gambled heavily and lost and all three had to run away. He lived on in the hope that with the help of his friend's magic he would one day win back his money and be rich again. His friend was all absorbed in his evil pursuits, hoping that one day he would be able to turn a man into a donkey! He also boasted that he could turn a man into a dog or sheep. They wandered together far away from their home. She was helpless. Her husband would growl at her if she dared attempt to admonish him and he would ask his friend to change her into a bitch or sheep. The friend would proceed to light a fire, put some salt and condiment in it and

74

recite a few hymns. Alaka was terrified to death at the prospect and would beg of them to stop.

She had not, however, come to the end of her misfortune. A few days earlier, the husband had staked his wife and lost. The winner smirked at her with greedy anticipation. Somehow, she bolted from there. In darkness, for days on end she sneaked from place to place, eating when she could and drinking when water was to be found. Life became unbearable and she decided to commit suicide.

She was distressed to relate all this. Listening to her, I could not help feeling that destiny was cruel and took delight in playing with man's life.

The sun was going down in the west. But it was necessary to say something to kindle a ray of hope in her. I tenderly stroked her hair and said, 'There is no need to worry, Alaka. You are my... .'

She jerked herself away from my lap and protested vehemently, 'I, I am not yours, I belong to someone else.'

I patted her head with the words, 'Alaka, you are my sister! I have fed at your mother's breast, you remember?'

How powerful is a word of comfort and a touch of loving tenderness! Alaka smiled in gratitude. It was as if a dying flame had been revived with fresh oil!

Evening was fast descending on earth. It was undesirable to continue any longer in that wilderness. I helped Alaka to sit up and we walked back.

The setting sun streaked on her hair while she was bent over the water. A few hair sparkled. I had not noticed earlier the lovely golden brown tinge in her hair. It was clearly visible now and I said, 'You have golden hair.'

'Yes, a little.'

In the middle of the night I felt that somebody was touching my feet. The lamp was low but I recognised that the figure standing near my bed was Alaka's. I got up and asked her, 'What is the matter?'

75

She could not speak but was trembling. I took her hand in mine. It was wet with perspiration. I made her sit on my bed and for courage, I stroked her back gently. I suddenly seemed to see a shadow flitting across my tent. I looked around but there was nobody.

Alaka had been unable to sleep a wink. She was terrified by dreams of her husband pushing her off a mountain top. In the end, she had taken courage to come to me.

Just then an insect put out the light and there was a footstep outside. It must have been the sentry.

I sent her away reassured but it was clear that she was scared of her gambling husband and his friend, the black magician. No amount of reassurance could dispel her fear completely.

I had thought she would not come to me during our halt the next night. But as on the previous night she did, trembling all over. All her subconscious fears were tormenting her like ghosts in the darkness.

That night, Alaka complained of something else; she had seen a ghost which looked like Mandar. Thinking that she was asleep, the ghost tried to kiss her but disappeared as soon as she moved.

On the third night, I asked for her bed to be made in my tent. The front flap was always left open and the sentry did his rounds in front. I could therefore see nothing wrong with the arrangement. Who could doubt anything in the circumstances?

Maybe because of implicit confidence in me or because her fears gradually lessened with the passage of time, Alaka now slept well. She was thus disturbed only four or five times during the journey! If she was trembling with fright, I would seat her on my bed and pat her on the back and reassured she would return to her bed.

I am carefully recalling all those incidents but at no time, not even when she was sitting on my bed in the dead of night, did I ever entertain any sinful thought in respect of her. More than her beauty, I valued her implicit confidence in me. The thought that she could lie down without a care, with her head in my lap, gave me pleasure of a different kind than the pleasure of kissing her.

Those days of travelling, how quickly they went by! But their lingering memory is still with me. I have no idea of what the Creator put together in creating women, but in Alaka's presence I often felt as if a poem dripping with feeling and set to a harmonious tune was moving about in me. That poem was not a love theme but it was a beautiful blend of smiles, affection and pathos.

Those days filled with innocent happiness, selfless love passed in no time. When Hastinapur was only twenty miles away, Mandar asked for permission to go ahead so as to prepare for my welcome.

I gave him the permission but felt that a welcome other than love in mother's eyes and the burning lamps of affection in Alaka's eyes was quite unnecessary.

We reached Hastinapur late in the night. I explained to mother how I had met Alaka.

I retired to bed after dinner. I thought mother would bring up the subject of Yati in the morning but she said nothing. She must have been very sorry that I had returned alone. In life there is no pain greater than disappointment.

The whole of the next day was busy. The Prime Minister and others called and talked about the coronation. Madhav called with his niece Taraka. I rang for Alaka to give her sweets but she did not come. I was busy all day yet called for Alaka three or four times.

At dinner I asked mother, 'How is it Alaka is nowhere to be seen?'

Mother almost ignored the question and said, 'Yayu, you are now King of Hastinapur. Kings think of princesses and not of maids!'

Mother spoke without a trace of feeling. I kept quiet but all the tasty dishes in front of me turned sour and I got up from the table.

Mother beckoned me to her room and I quickly followed her. She said, 'Alaka is counting the last few moments of her life.'

I did not know if I was awake or dreaming and said with a heavy heart, 'What?'

'There is only one way to be born into this world but death comes in many different ways. There is no knowing how it comes.'

'But the royal physician... .'

'In this there is no need for the physician. It is a question of the prestige of the royal household. That you misbehaved on your travels... .' Mother turned fiercely on me, adding, 'To cure you of your dangerous illness I turned Mukulika out of the Ashokavan and warned her that she stood in danger of her life if she returned to the town. If she were here today, all the symptoms of your illness... .'

I hung my head in shame. I did realise that I had behaved wantonly with Mukulika.

'While your father was lying on his deathbed you had taken a wretched maid servant to your bed in Ashokavan... .'

That day when the Prime Minister had sent Mandar through the underground passage, at that time Mukulika was standing by my bed and I had not had the presence of mind to send her away before opening the secret door.

My head was spinning. Is Mandar so wicked? What had he gained by telling mother?

I wished to tell mother of all that had happened at Ashokavan without concealing a thing, but shame kept me back. However passionately I might reiterate the truth, it was unlikely that in her present mood, mother would believe it.

As ruthlessly as one cuts through dry wood, she tore at me with reprehensive words, 'You are not at fault. It is my fate which is to blame. It is in your blood. As a wife I suffered a lot. I was hoping that suffering would not be my lot at least as a mother. But... .'

Her words suddenly stopped. She beckoned to me and I followed. I thought there was another underground passage here. I descended behind her but I did not dare to ask where we were going. It was not far to go. At the far end, there was a cellar. There was a tall, fierce-looking sentry at the door who saluted us.

Mother turned to me. 'Go in but you can stay there for only ten minutes. It is said that one should fulfil the last wish of a dying person. Therefore I have shown Alaka this mercy...' She stopped for a while and said, 'Listen, Prince. You will be king soon. If he so wills a king can command a new beauty everyday... .'

She turned away. The sentry opened the door. I stepped inside dumbfounded. There was a low light in that small narrow room and I could not discern anything there for a few moments. I then saw Alaka squatting on the floor with her head between her knees. I went near with a heavy heart. She could not have heard me coming! I was very close to her and put my hand on her shoulder. It was only then that she slowly looked up. She simply stared at me with watery eyes. Her face had gone black. She peered at me again and again and asked, 'Who is it?'

She could neither hear nor see. Terror struck at my heart. I shook her violently by the shoulders and screamed, 'Alaka!'

She recognised my voice, a smile slowly spread over her face and with a heavy but caressing voice, she said, 'Who? Prince?'

I sat close to her and putting her head on my shoulder, said, 'What is the matter, Alaka?'

Nearby was an empty wine glass. With great difficulty she pointed to it and said, 'Ask that cup. That ... that ... cup contained love, I ... I ... drank it.'

She could speak no more. Once she said with a heartache '... That ... that ... Mandar ... him ... him ... I... .'

She was getting convulsions. Suddenly in a low voice from somewhere deep down: 'D ... d ... do ... do not forget me. M ... m ... my one ... golden hair ... keep ... Oh! Oh!'

I gently plucked a golden hair. She was now in her last few moments and all because of me! Should I not have given her as a memento, something imperishable to keep up her courage on that journey?

79

But in the presence of death, even a king turns a beggar. There was nothing I could give her.

Unconsciously I bent down and put my lips to her. She was probably a little conscious and struggled to turn her head away. She muttered, 'N ... no ... p ... poison!'

But she had not the strength to draw away. I was madly kissing her.

That first kiss and this last kiss tonight! What a tragic episode life is! In trying to draw away from me, she toppled to the ground. I tried to shake her into wakefulness. The bird had flown away.

Her lifeless body was in front of me. Her soul — I wondered where her soul was —

Mother shouted for me and I returned to my room. The Prime Minister was waiting for me. He explained that he had come at that hour of the night with good tidings.

He said, 'The war between the gods and demons has ceased. Kacha acquired the power of Sanjeevani and could revive the dead on the side of the gods. So the demons ceased fire. It is a great relief, because if the demons had won, they would have transgressed into our territory.'

Kacha had acquired Sanjeevani! The war had stopped! To me all this was utterly insignificant. I was crying out desperately to myself, 'My Alaka, where is she? Where is the only sister of the brother hankering for affection?'

DEVAYANI

Outside, it is spring. There is a gentle breeze scented with fragrance, but I am perspiring in my bed. Outside, the moon of the fourteenth night looks like a huge white lotus in full bloom. A cuckoo is singing in sweet wild notes. But in my heart, I can only hear the stifled notes of the broken reed. My heart is blighted like the withered delicate *parijat** flower.

Can it be true that what lingers in the mind comes back in dreams? Perhaps, perhaps not.

What a terrible dream it was! I was trembling all over when I woke up with fright.

Maybe I am angry with Kacha. Why the doubt? I am angry. I am very angry. When he rejected my love and sought to go away I pronounced the curse: 'The power which you have acquired you will never be able to use.' But is that any reason why in the dream I should —

For many days after Kacha had left, I was still greatly distressed and often cried bitterly and left eating. I urged father over and over again, 'It does not matter if the power of Sanjeevani is now available to someone else also. You should do penance again to please Lord Shiva and get another blessing. And bring back to me that heartless, wily and ungrateful Kacha!'

---

* a night-flowering jasmine.

81

I wished to punish Kacha so that he would remember it all his life. Even today I want to! He went away, disregarding my love and breaking my heart. He pronounced a cruel curse on me that no Brahmin's son would accept my hand in marriage!

How vividly I remember every detail of the dream:

Kacha was standing shackled in the court. His eyes flashed like lightning. King Vrishaparva, the demon king, said to me, 'The Lord Preceptor Maharishi Shukra, your father, is undergoing penance for our uplift. Before he started on it, he ordered me to see that you are always happy. We all know that Kacha has hurt you deeply. Therefore, we have brought him here from the kingdom of the gods. He is your prisoner. You pronounce the punishment and it will be instantly carried out.'

What punishment can a true lover award her love, even if he has deceived her? At most, to make him captive in her arms for all time. I did not even order that. I pleaded with the heartless one, 'Kiss me once ... only once!' and added, 'You will be free from bondage if you kiss me.'

Even in the face of death, he was arrogant. He said, 'Devayani, they cremated me and put my powdered bones into Maharishi Shukra's wine. He drank it and I thereby got access to his heart. It was there that I learnt the Sanjeevani hymn which none else knows. But it was also because of that I am now your brother. You and I are the same flesh and blood.'

I lost my temper. I said, 'You seem to think that Devayani is a silly woman. It needs no great intelligence to know that children grow on the flesh and blood of the mother, not of the father. I am no sister to you and you are no brother to me. I am your lover. I beg nothing more of you. Kiss me only once and I shall issue orders to release you thereon.'

King Vrishaparva said, 'Devayani, what shall be the punishment?'

82

Kacha whose ashes father had swallowed with his wine and for whose revival, even at the price of losing Sanjeevani, I had begged father with folded hands — such a Kacha to be punished! But how could I —?

I said to King Vrishaparva, 'Behead Kacha and bring his head on a salver to the court. I am going to show you all what an adept danseuse I am!'

Kacha was led out of the court and beheaded. The guard brought his bloody head in. I put the salver down and danced the love theme round it. Love smiles like a blooming flower and sometimes flares like a fire. Sometimes it twinkles like a star or it strikes like lightning. It may take the form of a tame deer or a vicious cobra! It may rejuvenate or slay. I depicted all this in my dance.

I do not know how long I danced thus. I was intoxicated and could see nothing except Kacha's head. Blood was oozing from it and I imagined it to be my lover's head anointed with the auspicious red *tilak**. I forgot that the head was lifeless. I danced up to it, knelt down and kissed it with the words: 'Kacha dear, you did not want to kiss me, but there you are, I have you in the end.'

I am still in love with Kacha. How then could I be so cruel? Where do dreams come from? Do they not stem from the mind? Ah! I know now. A dream is like an intricate weave. How did this dream come to my mind —

Kacha used to say that a disciple must observe the vow of purity. He would gather wild flowers for me with unfailing regard but he never put them in my hair. My slightest touch was to him heavenly bliss and he used to come alive for an instant, even with a passing one. But he was constantly on the alert to avoid it.

---

* Sacred mark of sandal or *kumkum*, etc., on the forehead.

Or is it that my foolish heart is still in love with him? And the conscious mind hates him? Love and hate. Fire and water.

When will this conflict of the conscious and subconscious end? How foolish, soft and blind is a woman's heart! Kacha has never even enquired of me since he left. He had achieved Sanjeevani on the plea of my love for him and returned to the realm of the gods. He was hailed there as a great ascetic and hero! The mortal danger to the gods had receded because of him.

Now he can claim any celestial beauty of his choice. Why then should he remember Devayani? Men are so ungrateful! Wily, hard and heartless! Like the birds in a fable, they fly away with the net with ease. As for the women, their hearts are entangled in the invisible web of love and they sit and weep helplessly.

No, I will not sit and fret like other women. I am made of sterner stuff. God has given me beauty and father has given me intelligence and education.

All of father's earlier penance has now come to nought. He is going to undertake another to acquire a different power. I am the daughter of Maharishi Shukracharya, who has risen above the world. I am going to forget Kacha.

No, I am going to banish him from my mind. He has left me with a curse. But how can a true lover curse his beloved? What does it matter if a Brahmin's son will not marry me? Has the Creator given me all this unique beauty so that I may only bedeck myself with flowers? Is it for nothing that a beauty like Princess Sharmishtha, the King's daughter, is always envious of me? She must be racking her head as to the clothes she must wear to look prettier than Devayani. On the first day of the spring festivities tomorrow morning, the princess and her friends are going for a picnic in the forest and then go bathing. I am also going for father's sake, in that beautiful sari which Kacha brought for me from heaven, when all eyes will be dazzled. I had put it away for a long time specially for these festivities. Sharmishtha probably does not even know. When she sees Devayani clad in that beautiful red sari...

84

But that was given to me by Kacha. It was a present he brought when he came to stay with us. Then he was in love with me! I had also fallen in love with him. It would have been becoming if I had worn the red sari then. But to wear it now when we are no longer in love? No, if I wear it now, the dying embers of that love will flare up again in my mind. He would climb impossible hill slopes in order to collect the flowers which I fancied; he would sway like a cobra to the tune of my autumn dance; he would recite his hymns in a low voice in a bower in the far corner of the garden lest it might wake me up in the early morning. Very rarely but in such sweet words he would say, 'You are prettier than the most beautiful damsel in heaven.' If I countered with, 'You are a flatterer,' he would retort with a smile, 'The world only worships the beautiful.'

Enough of those memories.

I have resolved to forget my love for Kacha. The sari that he presented maybe it is very pretty. But why should I wear it now? However beautiful, it should be torn to shreds. It should be used for a mop. That would be an appropriate punishment for the ungrateful wretch!

I fetched it from the pile of clothes set apart for the spring festivities. I wished to tear it up. But my hands would not move. Perhaps a man could have torn it. Almost certainly Kacha would have cut it up to bits, but I am a woman. The worship of the beautiful is our creed. Women can never destroy anything beautiful.

When I wear this tomorrow after the spring festivities, I shall look very enchanting.

Sharmishtha puffs with pride that her father is a king. Every now and then she boasts about it. I must put her to shame at the festivities tomorrow —

I shall not tear this beautiful sari. But the other things which remind me of him. I turned to the bower in the garden. This was his favourite spot. The bower must be ripped up.

It is fancied by father also. What if he asked me in the morning about it? It will be possible to explain it away. The young calf in the cow shelter runs amuck these days. She must have broken loose at night and trampled on and ruined the bower! Some much explanation —

I headed towards the bower when I heard someone calling me, 'Devi.'

I was pleased with the word. It was good father had mended his habits. Upto yesterday, always even before strangers, he would without a thought call me, 'Deva.' As if I was a boy! When he called me thus before Kacha, I used to blush red. All great men have some queer trait. I insisted that he must never again call me Deva. He said, 'Calling you Deva does not make you one ... you are only a Devi.' What could you do with him? That a young maiden's heart is like a sensitive plant and that, even little things caused embarrassment, was something which ascetics cannot realise. These men live in a world of their own all the time.

On hearing father's call I turned round. He slowly came forward, raised my chin, looked deep into my eyes and said, 'You are still awake, my girl?'

'I could not sleep, father, so I thought, a turn in the garden...'

He caressed my back and said, 'I know you girl. There is nothing worse than a broken heart... .'

It was distasteful to me to dwell on Kacha anymore. In an effort to change the subject, I said, 'Father, did my movements wake you up?'

He said no and with a gulp added, 'My defeat is a thorn in my side, my girl. All the time I am thinking that I should again undertake long penance and acquire another unique power which will dazzle the world.'

'Why don't you begin then? I was small during your penance for Sanjeevani and hardly realised what a great man my father was. Now, I shall attend on you and your penance, see that the hardship... .'

86

He smiled derisively. 'That is not possible.'

I had lost my mother in my childhood and father brought me up like a delicate plant. Even so, why should he form such an unkind opinion of me? Why should he think that I am pleasure-loving and therefore cannot be of any service during a penance?

I was worried that father might notice the sari but he was absorbed in his own thoughts.

He seemed to look at the glowing moonlight spread all over and said, 'Deva... .'

'No, Devi... .'

'Oh yes, I forget,' he smiled back. 'I could renounce wine instantly, but the tongue has got used to your childhood name...' Later in great agony, he added, 'When I had the Sanjeevani, the entire world trembled before me. But today, I am only one of the thousands of ascetics roaming the world. No, I cannot bear the thought. My girl why should the lion live after he has lost his teeth and claws?'

What a terrible blow Kacha had struck at my father by carrying away the power of Sanjeevani. Even after so long, the wound was bleeding. I consoled him, 'You could acquire another equally potent power by penance, father.'

'I will, undoubtedly! Not one but many, but it will need grave penance. Last time, you were small. Now you have come of age and must be married. I do not know for how many years the penance will last considering that Lord Shiva is a difficult, moody deity.'

'But, father... .'

'You were too small even to crawl about. Since then I have been both father and mother to you. I found the satisfaction of both knowledge and wine in your childish behaviour and I know of no pleasure greater than these three. While I had the power of Sanjeevani with me, any rishi, king or god would have made a bid for your hand. In my zeal to see the demons win, I neglected all this. Today, my girl, the lord of the rishis, your father is a penniless beggar. I may have to fall at their feet begging that one of them accept your hand in marriage!'

I was furious with father. It is true the power of Sanjeevani was lost. That maybe! But Devayani still had her beauty. On the strength of that alone she...

~

All of us girls arrived at the huge lake in the forest. The blue sky itself seemed to have descended into the lake for us to sport in the water. The trees were fanning it a little. Further away the girls were squirting water at each other. But none of them dared into deeper waters.

I said to Sharmishtha with a smile, 'Water sport is not wetting oneself from a water vessel. Let us swim out so that these girls, frightened of water, will feel reassured. Look there. Those two swans playing with the lotus. They look like two white clouds floating in the sky. We will swim out as far as there and come back. Let us see who wins.'

Sharmishtha only smiled back and we two set out. I was rapidly gaining distance and swam like a fish. When I looked back, there she was crawling like a tortoise. I was elated that today she would be put to shame. She was bound to lose in this competition. When with a small face she returns to the bank beaten to it, she will be even more furious to see me in the red sari.

I reached the lotus, leaving her way behind. But I was feeling tired. I rested for a while but when I looked back, Sharmishtha had closed in on me. I turned back quickly and made for the bank with all speed. I was swimming well but the speed had slackened considerably. I was tired. There was a gale blowing. The trees and creepers were being violently tossed about and dust filled the air, making it murky.

I was frightened and shouted to Sharmishtha as she overtook me and was swimming away. She did not respond.

88

She was on the bank before me. She was surrounded by half a dozen friends. With them, she went to the maid and suddenly disappeared behind a tree.

On getting to the bank I walked with my head hung low to the maid, who gave me my clothes. I lost my temper. Those clothes were not mine. She had given to Sharmishtha the beautiful sari presented to me by Kacha, which I had intended to put on. She had put on my beautiful sari, the one I had carefully put away for the spring festivities! I was beside myself with fury and tugged at the sari she was wearing. Sharmishtha was afraid the sari might come off.

Sharmishtha flared at me, 'What do you mean, Devayani? Why are you annoyed with me for having lost the race? If one is lame... .'

I retorted fiercely, 'Whether I am lame or crippled, we will think of later. You should first remedy your blindness. Whose clothes are you wearing?'

'My own, of course.'

'Have you lost your sight? This sari is mine.'

'No, it is mine. Mother told me last night that she would give me the sari which was presented to her by Indrani on the cessation of war.'

'You had better return my sari.'

'I will not. What can you do?'

I tugged at it and said, 'What am I going to do? Do you know who I am?'

'Oh, yes. I know very well that your father is dependant on King Vrishaparva!'

I was dumb with fury.

With my silence, she was even more aggressive. She said, 'You wretch! After all I am a princess and you are only the daughter of a dependant of my father. Never again forget the difference.'

I was trembling with anger. I thought I was going to faint —

89

Our friends came on the scene. They must have noticed that I was trembling and burst into laughter. The humiliation stung me. I wanted to return to the town, relate everything that had happened to father and say that I was not prepared to stay in that place a minute longer —

In fact I started running. I heard Sharmishtha calling after me, 'Devayani, please stop, Devayani stop for a second.'

I did not even look back.

Sharmishtha ran after me. Evidently her friends were also following. In a little while, I slowed down. I realised that she would now catch up on me.

I looked back. She was very near me and it was no use running. I looked around. A little further there was a large open well covered over with shrub and grass. There was no knowing how much water it had! I stood by its mouth. Sharmishtha came near me.

'Devayani ... I ... I... .'

The tigress in me showed up in place of the gentle deer. 'Take off the sari! Give it back to me... .'

She was muttering something like, 'But ... dear.'

I tugged at it the harder screaming, 'Take it off. Will you not take it off?'

I have no recollection of what happened in the next few moments, of what I or Sharmishtha said or did. What I remember is a sudden shriek, 'Help, help.' Was it Sharmishtha's? Had I pushed her into the well? No — I was shrieking. She had wickedly pushed me into the well. I do not remember how much later it was. I had fallen into the well —

I shouted out aloud, 'Help ... help me out of the well.' I shouted once, twice, thrice! I shouted again after a while. Devayani had fallen into a well. Devayani, daughter of Maharishi Shukra had fallen into the well.

I was burning inside but the water was cold and I shivered. On the one hand I was burning for revenge and on the other stark fear had come over me. I could see myself shivering, then dropping in a faint and getting drowned. And I started sobbing like a child.

Someone standing at the mouth of the well was clearing the growth and bent over, asking who it was.

It was a man's voice. I could not make out whose and asked, 'Who is it?'

'Yayati.'

Was I in a trance? I eagerly asked, 'You mean King Yayati of Hastinapur?'

'Yes, I am King Yayati of Hastinapur. Absorbed in hunting, we came deep into this forest. We were very thirsty and were looking for water. My charioteer has gone another way and I thought I saw a well here and came this way. But let that be. Who may you be fair lady?'

'Please don't be so formal.'

'What do you mean?'

'I shall tell you later. But first would Your Majesty take me out? I am shivering! But ... how will you get in?'

I first heard laughter and then sweet came the words, 'Yayati has learnt archery in his younger days and some of its tricks too.'

I heard something like a hymn being chanted. This was a feat of archery something like the power of Sanjeevani. I noticed that the arrows had been arranged like a lotus to make a cradle on which I was being lifted up.

The lotus of arrows rose to the mouth of the well and stopped. Apart from Kacha, I had never seen so handsome a man. I blushed under the gaze of the King. I hung my head. My wet clothes clung to my body.

I was still looking down. The King smiled at me and said, 'May I have the favour of knowing the name of this angel?'

'I am not an angel.'

'Is it possible that there is so much beauty on earth?'

My beauty had captivated the King, but I had to load that beauty with a little more. I looked up with a coy glance and looking down again, said, 'I am Devayani, daughter of Maharishi Shukra.'

'Maharishi Shukra, the Lord Preceptor of the Demons?'

'Yes. I would prefer you to be less formal.'

The King smiled and said. 'If I have been of some service to Maharishi Shukra today all the weariness of the hunt will have vanished from me.'

I put out my right hand. He took it in his right and helped me out. He tried to disengage his hand when I said, 'No, you can't. You have taken my hand in marriage.'

He was taken aback. 'How is it possible? You are a Brahmin and I am a Kshatriya king! Such a marriage... .'

'There have been many such marriages in the past, Your Majesty. There is the precedent of Lopamudra... .'

'No, no.'

With a smile I said, 'Fate apparently wills Your Majesty, that I should be your queen. Why otherwise would you have come to this forest today? It could only happen from something done in our earlier birth.'

'But fair one... .'

'There can be no hesitation, Your Majesty. I gave you my heart the moment I saw you. You are free to accept it or refuse me. If you do not make me yours, I shall retire to a cave in the Himalayas and tell the rosary in your name for the rest of my life. A virgin like me, who has never even thought of a man before, would not otherwise hold someone's hand even for a moment.'

'But Devayani, your father is revered as a rishi in all the three worlds! If he does not approve of this alliance... .'

'You need have no care... Oh, but how foolish of me to forget that you are thirsty.'

'At the mere sight of you, I have forgotten hunger and thirst. I had set out to capture a comely deer. I myself have been captured by her.'

I smiled and hung my head blushing. I said to myself, 'Rishis like father are only fit for penance. Only last night father was so worried about getting me married. Now, when I bow to him for a blessing not as Devayani but as the Queen of Hastinapur how surprised he will be!'

I wished that wily Kacha had also been here to witness the revenge I have taken. Truly, how pleasing even revenge can be.

The King suggested that we should go to the town in the chariot and apprise father of all this, but I did not want to go anywhere where Sharmishtha still paraded as a princess.

That was not necessary. Just then a chariot arrived post haste raising a cloud of dust and stopped short of us.

King Vrishaparva and father got down. Father took me into his arms. I was overcome with pride and joy and closed my eyes. Tears were streaming down father's eyes. The great ascetic, Maharishi Shukra was shedding tears of joy.

He suppressed a sob with great difficulty and said. 'Dev... .'

I said, 'Father, Devi is no longer yours.'

He was surprised. I glanced bashfully and meaningfully at King Yayati and lowered my eyes.

King Yayati came forward and bowed to father. With his help I related everything. Father was delighted and gave us a hearty blessing, then turned to King Vrishaparva with the words, 'Good fortune sometimes comes by way of calamity. King, make arrangements to celebrate her nuptials. Bedeck the whole town. This is a day of great rejoicing for the demon world. Once I have said farewell to her and sent her on the way to her new house, I shall be free to undertake another penance. Fate, which had turned perverse, seems to be changing. Come King Yayati ... Let us go to the town in this chariot. Devi ... you go ahead... .'

I did not move or open my mouth. King Vrishaparva came forward and said, 'Forget the past... .'

I was up in arms and said, 'It is easy for the aggressor to forget. But the nasty things which she said about father ... words which pierced the heart...'

Father's tone had hardened, 'What did Sharmishtha say?'

I said, 'How can I tell you, father? She derided me with the words, "I am a princess and you are but the daughter of a dependant".'

Vrishaparva said with humility, 'My girl, Sharmishtha also is young like you. She told me just now that you had quarrelled over a sari. The young are immature and lose their balance. One word provokes another... .'

'Is she not to blame even for pushing me into the well?'

'Who would say that? But rage is blind. I beg of you to forgive her.'

'Begging is the creed of dependants like father ... not of kings like you! If father wishes to, he can go into the town. But I do not wish even to go where father and I have been grossly insulted. My father who is famed as an ascetic in the three worlds has been denigrated as a beggar.'

Father had kept silent so long. He joined in, 'And, King, neither will I! That I should be insulted and an attempt should be made on my daughter's life... .'

Vrishaparva intervened, 'Lord Preceptor, Devayani has somehow misunderstood... .'

Father thundered, 'I am leaving. I have no time to waste on the right and wrong of it.'

Vrishaparva fell at father's feet. 'If the Lord Preceptor himself thus turned his back on us, what will be our fate except being annihilated? I shall immediately send for Sharmishtha and direct her to fall in obeisance at your feet and Devayani's a hundred times and beg for your forgiveness. If you think this too mild, I shall banish her from the kingdom this instant.'

'She has deeply offended Devayani, I shall return to the town only if she is willing to suffer, without demur, the punishment given by Devayani.'

Vrishaparva turned to me, 'Devayani, my girl, whatever punishment you pronounce... .'

I intervened with a warning. 'King, one should not pledge the word one cannot keep. What if I award a punishment which is distasteful and unacceptable to you?'

'After all, you are a friend of Shama's. You grew up together as children. You will not be unreasonable in dealing with her. I swear by the feet of the Lord Preceptor that I shall willingly abide by whatever punishment you pronounce... .'

I thoughtlessly said, 'Sharmishtha must be my maid.'

'Maid... ?' Interjected King Vrishaparva in agony, with a wry expression, suddenly aged.

I had won. I said in a shrill voice. 'Yes, Sharmishtha must be maid to the Queen of Hastinapur. She must go with me to Hastinapur, to wait on me all her life.'

SHARMISHTHA

The hour has struck. One out of the two hours has gone by! In the hour — in that short time — I must make a life's decision. To be Devayani's maid or...

Father's note is lying there. His first and only letter to his dear daughter! His Shama had so far never gone away from him! Where, then, was the occasion to write a letter? It is here today — an unpredictable occurrence, an enemy from an earlier life come for revenge.

Today — on the first day of the spring festivities — the sun rose as on everyday in my childhood, sprinkling his red glow through the window all over me. All of a sudden I blushed. The reddish dawn seemed like the sacrificial fire at a wedding.

Then I remembered mother's words while sending me to bed. Caressing me she had said, 'Shama, it is very well that the war has ceased. Now we can look for one of the good kings for you ... I believe the King of Hastinapur is very brave and good. While yet a youth he went out with the victory horse to conquer the world. I am told that he is very handsome too. He would be just the right man for this delicate flower of mine.'

It is true that on hearing this I feigned to be angry and pulled the coverlet over my face. But the whole night I did float on sweet dreams. One of those dreams had taken me to Hastinapur where I had been made the Queen of King Yayati!

Even when I woke up at dawn, the sweet dreams were still with me. But how terrible life is. How full of contradictions! How bitter in contrast to a dream! Before the morning sun has turned westward, fate has called me to Hastinapur! Not as queen but as the queen's maid.

~

During spring festivities in the morning, I said many things to hurt Devayani which I should not have done. But how could I help it? I had lost control over myself, my tongue and in fact everything. Was it my fault that she was born to a sage and not a king? But time and again, at every step she has obstinately striven to establish that I am no match for her.

We may have been three or four years old. The nurses had taken us out boating. Devayani bent over the side and clapped with joy, saying, 'Shama, see this pretty girl calling me to play with her.' I bent over the side and saw another girl resembling me, also calling me with a smile. I said, 'Look a pretty girl is calling me also!' She sniffed and squealed, 'No. Your girl is ugly, mine is pretty.'

We were eight or ten years when in one of the plays at the spring festivities, the school teacher gave us both a part. She was to be the queen of flowers and I the forest queen. Devayani was pretty and good at dancing; so she was chosen to be the queen of flowers. She had been given three dances; first portraying the bud, then the half blown flower and then the flower in full bloom. The forest queen had no dance. But because the queen of flowers was lower in rank than the forest queen, Devayani insisted on being the forest queen. I had no aptitude for dancing and had to dance. By her obstinacy the show was ruined.

We grew to fifteen or sixteen years of age. In that year's festivities, there were many competitions organised for the teenagers of the well-to-do. Competitions to cover dance, song and drama. Devayani stood first in all — dance, song, beauty ... but my poem was rated better than hers.

'I am the daughter of Maharishi Shukra who is a renowned poet in the three worlds and my poem must be the best,' she argued. 'It is because Sharmishtha is a princess that the judges have unjustly rated her poem higher.' The judges had to divide the prize between us. That time my only first prize was in sketching. And that because Devayani just could not draw.

Her father had secured the power of Sanjeevani. The demons were to score a victory over the gods from that power. Father accordingly aimed at not offending Devayani and I had to follow suit.

Many instances of her vanity lingered deep in my mind. That morning when she tried to snatch the sari which I was wearing, it all exploded. How can I explain it?

Some nasty offensive words escaped from my mouth. But they are about to ruin my whole life. For that one mistake, a princess is to be reduced to be a maid.

Sharmishtha — a maid? I, to be maid to that heartless stone image in love with herself? No, that cannot be!

No, I was not merely guilty of offending words. Mother has told me that the sari is Devayani's. That Kacha had presented it to her. I should not have worn it. Why did mother not show me the clothes properly last night? How was I to know that the sari was not mine? No, it was altogether a mistake that I was born a princess. It is because of that, that I have grown to depend on the maids for everything. To what end? Devayani's insistence that Sharmishtha must be her maid all her life.

She maintains I pushed her into the well. I ran after her to hold her back. She was near the well already. In the scuffle, she lost her balance and fell in. I still think so.

There are only two witnesses in this world to good and bad, to truth and falsehood and to right and wrong, Kacha used to say. One is conscience and the other is omniscient God.

If I thought He might come, I would have asked God for an answer to the terrible dilemma before me. Devayani has imposed slavery on me for life. Shall I or shall I not accept it?

Father's letter says:

> My dear daughter, if you ask me as your father whether you should agree to be a maid, I shall never consent.

> But man has several roles to play at the same time. We have been utterly defeated with Kacha's acquisition of Sanjeevani.

> It is in such adverse circumstances that the demons must again rise. The patronage of Maharishi Shukra is vital to us. He has unbounded love for Devayani. If the conditions set by her are not met, he will never again set foot in our town and in his absence, our kingdom will be razed to the ground. We who aspire to conquer the inter-stellar space will be reduced to crawling on earth.

> Shama, I shall not be angry if you refuse. I could not make up my mind what to do. That is why I wrote this letter.

> Shama. My beloved Shama! May Lord Shiva guide you to choose what will ever after make you happy.

From childhood I had often heard the words at weddings, 'The moment has come.' Recently I had come to realise its significance. Those sweet words, indicating that the auspicious moment binding two hearts together was imminent, those words thrilled me to the core.

But at that moment, they seemed to be terribly ominous to me. I did not wish to hear them. I kept feeling that the moment should never come. Because when that moment arrives, mother will come in and stand before me with tears in her eyes. I shall have to give a firm answer to father.

Oh God! What shall I say? Shall I gladly accept being a maid? How is it possible? Be a stranger to everything including love, affection, the company of a mate, the joy of motherhood?

No, I shall tell father that rather than be a maid to Devayani, I shall turn a mendicant! If she wishes to avenge herself, send for her and in her presence, behead me yourself. But remember, please, even the lifeless head must not fall at her feet. I shall not on my life accept being a maid. Not even in a dream. Shall I consent to be Devayani's maid?

I was deep in thought. Think, think, think. My head was ready to split.

And all because of what? I had by mistake worn this sari. This sari which was Kacha's present to Devayani. This sari — I swear by my father — I only wore it by mistake.

Does destiny have a hand in this abnormal occurrence? Kacha came here for Sanjeevani. He was our enemy. But at heart I worshipped him for his learning, his devotion and sacrifice and his manner. I often wished I had him for my elder brother.

Devayani never let me talk to him freely or be natural with him. She was jealous. But even his presence cheered me up. I was happy with even a smile from him. I recalled for days together an occasional word uttered by him.

The demons mercilessly tortured him to death three times. But everytime he said, 'Some things, which are terrifying from a distance, are not in fact quite so frightful. Death is the same. Princess, these are words drawn from my experience.' And with that he would smile genially.

What do those words mean? Could Kacha foresee the future? Being a maid; what else is it but death? The death of one's individuality.

And do individual qualities and defects hang by a caste? Both Kacha and Devayani are Brahmins. But does she share even one of his qualities? No. In life nothing whatever follows birth or caste.

For a Brahmin, what great courage did Kacha show in coming to our kingdom for Sanjeevani. He put all Kshatriyas to shame. He stayed his ground fearlessly until he had acquired Sanjeevani.

This sari — it is an unwitting gift from Kacha to me! I must keep it all my life. I remembered him only because of the difficulty before me...

Who has escaped danger and difficulty? On the contrary, there are more difficulties to the lot of the good ones on earth. Kacha was so good, so selfless, so affectionate and so learned. Even so, did he have any less of misery? The pain of shattered love and the curse of the beloved. But there was not a flicker of unhappiness on his face.

I said, 'I would have been happy to bid you goodbye if you were returning to heaven with your bride. But... .'

He calmly replied, 'Princess, life is ever incomplete, all its beauty lies in its being so.'

This is a good philosophy. But I had read in the epics how enormous is the pain of shattered love. I had cried profusely reading of it. I said, 'Would it not have been better if one did not fall in love in the first instance?'

He said, 'No. Love bestows the quality of being able to look beyond oneself. When it is altruistic, dispassionate and humble it becomes the first step to progress.'

That day Kacha was in a hurry to go away but he nonetheless came to see me and said, 'Sharmishtha, do not be distressed that our love has come to nought. Even if I have failed in love, I experienced love. That memory will ever be with me. Your friend Devayani is short tempered and an egoist. I am conscious of these faults! True love has the power to accept the beloved despite the faults. Such was my love for Devayani. But I had to disappoint her for the good of my fellow beings.

'What could I do? Love is a lofty sentiment in life but duty is even higher. Duty is very exacting but it is the basis of all religion. If Devayani ever opens her heart to you, tell her only this, "Kacha's heart is wedded to duty. But a corner of that heart is forever hers." '

I failed to see how for so long I had overlooked that last meeting of Kacha and his words. I was groping in the dark. I could not see a ray of light, but Kacha had shown it. I ran to the door as the hour tolled. Mother opened the door as I was about to. I ran into her arms, smiled and said, 'Tell father to make arrangements for my going to Hastinapur. Sharmishtha is ready to be Devayani's maid.'

~

I was a little shaken while entering the palace at Hastinapur, I will not deny it. But I soon recovered and took my place as a maid.

Devayani called on the Queen Mother and I followed her. The Queen Mother said, 'Devayani, my daughter, your friend is as pretty as you are.'

Devayani was arrogant. 'Mother, she is Princess Sharmishtha. But I did not bring her as my companion. She is no longer a princess. She is a maid ... my maid.'

'What do you mean?'

'His Majesty will tell you what a great sage my father is... .'

'Your father-in-law King Nahusha was also a great warrior. That a Kshatriya princess should be a maid in this his palace is not what I consider proper.'

'That is for me to decide!' retorted Devayani and she walked out. I had been the cause of this first clash between mother-in-law and daughter-in-law. But clashes would continue.

Devayani had been a spoilt child. The Queen Mother also was perhaps cast in the same mould. It was like two streaks of lightning crashing in the sky. Fate had similarly brought these two together.

The clashes sometimes brought me unexpected happiness! Occasionally I was reminded of my mother's loving hand. The memory made me very uneasy. But after a clash between the two, the Queen Mother would draw close her, maybe to taunt Devayani or because I was a Kshatriya princess and pat me on the back. That relieved the agonising memory of mother. It may have been only a show but even such illusions help make life bearable.

Once the Queen Mother's love showed up in a strange way. A renowned palmist had come to the town. Devayani sent for him and showed him her hand. He predicted that a son would be born to her in a year's time. We were all happy. I happened to be there. The Queen Mother took my hand, made me sit down and asked him to read my hand. Devayani scowled at this! But I was helpless before the Queen Mother.

He looked at my hand for a long time and said, 'This girl is unfortunate.'

Devayani said, '*Panditji,* she is only a maid, not a princess!'

He was surprised and looked up. He scanned the hand again and said, 'She has much to go through but her son... .' Devayani laughed and pointed out that since I was her maid, who was going to marry me and from where would a son come?

The palmist was annoyed that his knowledge of the science was being scoffed at. He turned to Devayani, 'Forgive me, Your Majesty. I know my science. I know nothing else. I am telling you of what I can read in this palm! Her son will be heir to a throne.'

Devayani was grave when she said, 'By throne do you mean the skin of a dead lion? Will you look at her hand again?'

My heart bled with the taunt! I quickly withdrew my hand and rushed out of the room lest tears should come to my eyes.

That night I cried into a wet pillow. Which young maiden does not dream of a husband and their children? Where is the girl who does not toss restless in her bed, contemplating the shape and form in which those dreams would come true in her case?

I was just such a one. But I had come to Hastinapur with all such dreams turned to ashes. I was a maid to Devayani. She had full authority over me. Perhaps she will never let me marry anybody anytime. Where the prospect of marriage was doubtful the hope of a son and his being heir to a throne — how could a maid like me entertain it? But the palmist today...

As the delicate red shoot of a leaf sticks out from a grave covered with black stone, the prediction stood out in my mind! Sharmishtha, who had not shed a single tear even at parting from her parents, was now shedding copious tears in the frightening solitude of the palace.

With the memory of father in my mind, I woke up. I remembered clearly every moment of bidding farewell to him.

I was about to leave the palace where I had grown up from birth. Father stood still and erect like a mountain. There was not even a flutter in my eyes. I went up to him and bent before him with a bow, saying, 'Goodbye, father.' I waited an instant for his blessing. He said nothing but put his head on my feet! I was confused, drew back and somehow, quickly raised him up. As he was getting up, he said, 'My girl, I am not fit to receive your obeisance. You are not a daughter but a mother. Mother, we your children crave your blessing.'

I melted and asked, 'Father, how would you have felt if I was your son and you had to send me to war?'

'I would have been proud!'

'You should feel the same pride at this moment. Father, your Shama is going into battle and seeks your blessing.'

I had nothing to do unless Devayani gave me some work. Every vacant hour was a bore. In the end, I found an excellent means to occupy myself. I was earlier fond of drawing. Thereafter I spent every spare moment in painting.

Having some hobby is an unfailing palliative for misery. I do not know how good my paintings were! But in painting them, my mind had an occupation. How many sketches I made of a wee little rabbit alone!

And it is not only the wee little rabbit. The deer, the peacock, the swan and for that matter, all animal life.

What a variety of flowers there is on earth with their variegated colour and odour. What numerous genii of trees and creepers. The sunrise and the sunset are different everyday. Moonlight in the spring, a river in the rainy season, the green crops of autumn and the leafless trees of winter — everything is a fit subject for painting.

I thought of life in this vein. Variety is the essence of life, contradiction is its soul. The essence, joy, attraction, indeed the soul of it, lies in variety and conflict.

I did not come much in contact with King Yayati. The extreme care which Devayani took to ensure that this did not happen was evident from the very first day.

One thing everyone would have noticed was that he was very reluctant to order me about as a maid. If I took anything to him and Devayani was not about, he would whisper, 'Why did you bring it? You should have told a maid.'

I would smile back and say, 'I am also a maid.'

He would retort, 'You are Devayani's maid, not mine.'

His Majesty was very fond of chewing betel leaf. Devayani used to make it for him. One day he was apparently not satisfied with the one she had given him.

Devayani was lying on a bed. I was fanning her. She asked me to make another one for His Majesty which he liked. He then stood before the mirror and called out to Devayani, 'Look at my mouth.'

'What kind of a jest is this? I do not like such levity.'

'This is no joke.' He opened his mouth. Just like a child he was. It was flaming red. The betel leaf had coloured it really well. He said, 'It is believed that the betel leaf made by the person who loves more colours the better... .'

'I see. So Sharmishtha loves you more. Then you should have married her.'

His Majesty should not have indulged in such a joke. Devayani raised Cain in the palace that day. The news soon spread and the maids were whispering! I was dying of shame. Never again did I make any betel leaf for him! But if Devayani was not around, he would ask me if I had any! I had to say no a dozen times. Thereafter I always secretly carried one on my person and I would give it to him quietly when no one was near.

Sometimes he would say to Devayani, significantly meaning me, 'Your betel leaf coloured very well indeed.'

~

What do memories resemble? The straying butterfly? Girls playing hide and seek? The colour gradually merging into the background and heightening the beauty of the picture? The lightning flitting unrestrained in the monsoon sky? Who knows!

The one memory which should have been related first, still lingers in the mind.

The wedding of Yayati and Devayani was celebrated with great eclat at Hastinapur. The first night of the honeymoon came to shower happiness on the couple. I had resolved not to look miserable. Fate which had taken her to the throne, had dragged me down from one. There is no truck with Destiny. Why then should Sharmishtha alone rebel against bowing before it?

But man's real enemy is not Destiny, but himself. Devayani was annoyed at my calm. On her way to his apartment she cooed, 'Sharmishtha, His Majesty is very fond of your betel leaves. Keep a dozen ready and wait. His Majesty and I will be talking far into the night and His Majesty will need betel leaf now and again. I shall send you away when His Majesty is fast asleep. I do not want any other maid here today.'

Could not Devayani have taken the salver into the apartment? But...

Devayani went in. I got the betel leaves ready quickly and stood far away with the salver. In a little while His Majesty came along and I offered him one. He did not touch it. He did not heed me. All he may have been conscious of was that there was a maid standing there. That was natural! One whom even an Apsara would have envied for her beauty was waiting for him inside. He had no eyes for anyone except her.

The door was closed and I stood there solitary like a ghost with the salver in my hand. The mind was now straying wildly. I had pangs of regret that if only I had not quarrelled with Devayani that day, I would not have been subjected to this degradation; but it was not regret alone. It was tinged with curiosity about love and the fulfilment of love.

Suddenly, angry words vaguely came to my ears. It was Devayani.

The first night of the honeymoon? It should have been steeped in love. Then why such words of anger?

I had heard of the heavenly bliss that crowns the union of lovers. An empty pot reverberates while being filled; but the sound ceases when it is full to the brim. The hearts of lovers are the same; I recalled one poet describing this blessed state with the words — when the hearts are filled with love, there is no room for words.

But angry words could be heard from inside the royal bedroom. It was Devayani talking; by comparison, His Majesty's tone was lower.

Suddenly, out came Devayani flinging open the door. She was rushing to her apartment. I stepped forward a little, holding out the salver. She blazed at me, flung the salver away from my hand and went away trampling on some of the betel leaves.

YAYATI

The first night of our honeymoon. In the life of a husband and wife, the first night is so intoxicating, so poetic and so full of mysterious intimacy, that it is something they have never experienced before. The confluence of two rivers, the kiss of the sky and earth — no. Even a great poet could not adequately portray in words, the eager expectancy contained in the union.

It was evening. Crowds of people lined the royal highway to see the festival of lights. I stood on the terrace of the palace looking at the sight for a long time.

I looked up. Very slowly one star after another came out twinkling, like buds which show up from behind the leaves.

I must have stayed there a long time but it was not quite dark yet. Like one pours wine into a glass drop by drop, the sky seemed to pour darkness into the night by stages. Its tardiness was quite unbearable.

Devayani was so near me. And yet so far. Visions of her, many and varied, haunted me; like her wet figure when she stepped out of the well blushing, Devayani bedecked with jewels and sitting next to me by the sacrificial fire.

Even after drinking in her beauty at will, my eyes were still thirsty. I desired for the Devayani hidden behind the many visible forms.

I went into the apartment. I closed the door and looked round. There was Devayani on the bed, half sitting up, her eyes full of meaning. I impatiently went forward and sat on the bed. She was standing now. I smiled and said, 'One has to offer one's hand to help a lady out of the well but is it necessary to offer it for sitting down?'

I thought she would blush and say something lively. But she stood silent. There was a crease on her forehead — I could not make out whether her anger was real or feigned.

To propitiate her I said, 'My father once defeated Indra. I am going to do it again.'

I thought she would quickly come forward and blushingly say, 'We have more pleasant and intimate things to talk about than war just now.' Or perhaps, 'I shall be your charioteer in the campaign.' So I thought.

'I shall conquer Indra with your help, I shall ask him if there is a beauty to match you in heaven,' was something like what I was going to say. But she never gave me the opportunity. I thought she maybe ruffled due to some disagreement with mother. However, I decided to stay out of it.

An angry woman makes a pretty picture. Looking at her, I forgot myself and pulled her to me on the bed. I lifted up her face and was bending over to kiss her.

She pushed me away and like an infuriated cobra turned on me and stood in a far corner. I was unable to understand her strange behaviour. Her obstinate and short tempered manner had been apparent in her insistence on making Sharmishtha her maid. I had seen it myself. But that to me — her husband — she should behave like this.

I controlled my rising temper and said, 'Devayani I do not understand... .'

'There is nothing to understand. It is terrible. Today, here on this auspicious occasion ... at the happiest moment of my life, that you should be drunk ... the smell of your mouth... .'

I said, 'I have not been drinking liquor. Only a little wine.' I added sarcastically, 'I am fortunate that I am not a Brahmin and am permitted liquor.' I was furious with her that she should have ruined the exquisite joy of a happy occasion on a slight pretext.

She retorted, 'You may not be a Brahmin but I am the daughter of Maharishi Shukra. I cannot bear the smell of liquor even at a distance.'

'As you are a daughter, you are also a wife. I am a Kshatriya and drink is not prohibited to a Kshatriya.'

'But father has given it up. And "he" abhors liquor.'

He? Who was this he? Angry that I was, I was now suspicious.

I shouted, 'Who is he?'

She was biting her lips in exasperation when she replied, 'I am not afraid of anyone to name him. Kacha also was averse to liquor.'

A tinge of jealousy sparked in me. I said harshly, 'This is the palace of Hastinapur. This is neither the hermitage of Maharishi Shukra nor the cottage of Kacha. I am nobody's slave. I am the King of Hastinapur ... Yayati. I am Lord and Master here. Kacha has no place here. And Maharishi Shukra has no business to interfere here. You are my wife and it is your duty to tend to my happiness...'

'You can tend to your happiness yourself ...' said Devayani fiercely, her eyes sparking with barbs of fire. She banged the door open and walked out.

I collapsed on the bed. That terrible curse on father. 'The children of King Nahusha will never be happy.'

This was to have been the night of the consummation of our love. I did not even dream that the curse would prove itself in this strange way on this our first night of love. The craving body and the agitated mind tore at me all night.

I had come to the apartment with great expectation. I desired Devayani. I desired all of her. I was now very eager to experience a love much nobler and more intense than the vulgar momentary pleasure such as that which I had shared with Mukulika. But...

This brought back to my mind Alaka's death, which was soon followed by the coronation. Mother gave me her hearty blessings. She had her fill of Yayati's appearance in regal clothes and royal splendour. But at the same time, Kalika was wiping her tears away in a corner at the memory of her daughter.

Mother saw those tears and she chastised her with harsh words! 'Leave the palace this instant and go to your sister's. Don't cry here in ill omen.' My hair stood on end at mother's words.

I was very angry with mother. I resolved in the instant that somehow or other Alaka's death must be avenged.

As a first step in that revenge I stopped talking to mother. I indulged myself at will in wine and hunting. Deliberately, I rejected individually everyone of the pretty princesses enthusiastically chosen by mother. This satisfied my thirst for revenge a little, in respect of Alaka, but I was dissatisfied with life and thirsty for something undefined.

It was in this state of mind that I reached the foot of the Himalayas while hunting. While in chase of deer I entered the demon kingdom and returned with Devayani as my bride to Hastinapur.

That day I accepted Devayani instantly. What a strangely mysterious occurrence! I looked upon it as very romantic.

That I was taken with her because of her sheer beauty is true. But I also thought I would wreak sweet vengeance on mother by marrying her. Mother was keen on a Kshatriya princess for a daughter-in-law! My marrying the daughter of a Brahmin sage would be a permanent thorn in her side. She would learn that fate avenges the murder of an innocent girl.

That I accepted Devayani's hand in marriage was not for these two reasons only. The shadow of a deadly curse from a great sage hung on our family. It would need the blessing of an equally great sage to ward off that curse. He would undertake grave penance to counter the curse.

Without a thought for the past or future and without consulting anyone, Devayani was eager to be my bride; I was equally eager to take her hand in marriage.

However, my personal experience of Devayani's father, Maharishi Shukra, proved quite different. He was very fond of his daughter. But he did not seem to value much the fact that she was the wife of a great king. Maharishi Shukra had no thought for the fact that it was necessary to identify himself with my well being and to earn my goodwill.

Sharmishtha readily agreed to be Devayani's maid! She had willingly sacrificed herself to the burning anger of Devayani, so that Maharishi Shukra might not leave them in a huff, so that she might not imperil the safety of her people. That was great of her; but as an ascetic, an elderly wise man or at least as the friend and preceptor of King Vrishaparva, should he not have consoled Sharmishtha?

I was in the demon kingdom for only a short while. But even in that space of time, it was borne in on me that father and daughter lived in a world of their own.

When sending the daughter away to her new house, tears rise in every father's eyes. Maharishi Shukra was no exception. But he immediately took me aside and said, 'King, Devayani is my only daughter. Remember, her happiness is my happiness. Remember always, that my blessing is in itself a great power on earth. You have yourself witnessed how King Vrishaparva has had to give in, how Sharmishtha has had to humiliate herself by having to be Devayani's maid. So beware, never do anything at anytime to hurt Devayani. Do not forget that her unhappiness is my unhappiness.'

I had thought that he would also address a few words of advice to Devayani. I had heard that on such an occasion, it was usual to counsel a young bride married to a king, how she should tend to the comfort of the household, how it is her duty as a wife to conduct herself to contribute to her husband's happiness, how she should live in amity even with her co-wives. But after all Shukra is a great sage. It never occurred to him to offer any such advice on mundane

112

matters! In the end, I took my leave thinking that the great are in a world apart.

It was well past midnight. I had heard the hour toll a long time ago. All these memories were crowding my mind and I was tossing in bed and turning over from side to side. I could not sleep.

One moment I thought the whole palace must be astir with the scene which Devayani had created today. No one could have seen elsewhere, a maiden arrogantly running out of the bedroom on the marriage night. The stringency of social obligations increases with the status. But what should never happen even in a hovel had taken place in the palace.

How much better it would have been if man did not have imagination enough to build castles in the air.

Devayani will come now sometime and with her coming we shall forget everything. I shall say, 'You have been brought up in very different surroundings. I should have known that. Forgive me for this once. You will not see Yayati with a drink inside him in your bedroom. If that is not enough, I swear by you, never to touch a drop again. Never again will my lips touch any liquor anywhere.'

She will put her hands round me and say, 'Like me you have also grown up in a very different environment. You are a Kshatriya warrior king, you have to rule and go into battle. The stimulus of liquor is necessary to you. It is not right for me to stand in the way of such trivial indulgences. But what can I do? I just cannot bear the smell of alcohol. All I beg of you is that, hereafter you should not take a drink before coming to me.'

Another hour tolled. I was still tossing about in bed! Without rhyme or reason I was listening for Devayani's footstep. But none came.

I got up from bed with a tormented mind. The pricking of disgrace and a craving body are indeed strange. Like the poison of a snake, outwardly insignificant but mortally effective within.

113

I was looking out into the darkness from the window. I had taken Devayani's hand in marriage to gain a love nobler and greater than what Mukulika or Alaka had given me. But the bed of roses which I had chosen for the bridal night was infested with the young of reptiles.

The man in me woke up! The king in me was roused. I kept repeating to myself that I could find the pleasure I was seeking anywhere at anytime on earth. I am an uncommon man, a warrior and a great king, and if I so will, I can have a new beauty in my bed everyday.

Next morning also, I was still very angry. I thought of going hunting to a far off place, when Sharmishtha came in hurriedly and with folded hands said, 'Her Majesty is not well since last night. The royal physician was called a little while ago. There is no cause for anxiety. But if Your Majesty would be pleased to call on her, Her Majesty is likely to benefit more than by any medicine.'

While talking, Sharmishtha had a fascinating smile on her face. It seemed like the golden streak of lightning in a cloudless sky. I suddenly remembered — last night there was a maid standing outside with something in a salver. I tried to recall. I did not remember clearly. I asked her, 'You ... were you standing outside yesterday?'

She hung her head as much as to say yes! How was it I did not notice Sharmishtha last night? Had I been pressed into drinking too much wine?

Seeing that I was thoughtful she said, 'Your Majesty, I have been Her Majesty's friend from childhood. She has always been a bit short tempered. Your Majesty must not take it to heart.'

She paused a little and then said, 'A maid may not indulge in poetry, it is true, but all poets agree that love is tame without strife.'

My heart unconsciously melted looking at her. She was pleading for Devayani who had last night made her stand outside the bedroom and thus trampled on and tried to crush all her tender feelings.

I said in jest, 'Sharmishtha, who taught you such love?'

114

Idly looking at her nails, she queried. 'Must one have a teacher for everything?'

'Who has attained knowledge in this world except through the words of a preceptor? And love is the greatest knowledge of all. Even greater than Sanjeevani.'

'In that case, I will give you the name of my tutor!' She said 'It is Kacha!'

'Kacha?' I interjected in surprise.

Sharmishtha urged, 'Is not Your Majesty coming to the Queen's apartment?'

I went to Devayani's rooms with Sharmishtha following me. My agitated mind had calmed down talking to her. Anger had given place to forgiveness.

Was Devayani really ill? I do not know. But I thought her wan face resembled the gloomy paleness of the moon, showing behind grey clouds. I took her hand in mine. Our hands conveyed what we could not say in words or express in our eyes.

I bent down to kiss the tears away. Suddenly she clasped my hands and said in an endearing tone — not unlike the drawl of a person half awake — 'You will not take it again?'

I realised she was talking about liquor. My pride was hurt. But Devayani was ill. My Devayani was ill! It was necessary that nothing should be done to upset her.

She rubbed her palm — delicate as a flower — on mine and said, 'You won't take it? For my sake... .'

'Promise me,' she said, smiling.

Outwardly smiling I said, 'To retain this tender hand in mine for all time, I could make a hundred promises!'

'Oh no. It is not that easy. You have to swear by the feet of my father.'

It was very difficult for me to hold myself in this time. But I did somehow and took the oath.

115

Devayani was smiling now. It was not the smile of a lover only, it was obviously tinged with pride. It was the smile of a pretty woman, who in her arrogance thought she could reduce a man to utter subjection.

I had suffered sheer defeat in this first battle of love. I religiously kept my word about liquor. Our life was now normal.

I still recall those days. The days hardly count. I mention them as days because the sun used to rise in between and separate us for twelve hours or so. Otherwise, if it were night, Yayati would be swimming in an ocean of pleasure, all the time.

At dawn, I would be annoyed at the twittering of birds in the garden. To me they appeared unromantic. Hearing their twitter, Devayani used to get impatient to return to her apartment. Then I would say, 'The night is still young. You need not go away yet!'

She hardly ever believed me and I would protest: 'No, I just cannot bear this long separation. How can I pass the time? Leave me something for a token.'

Then I would start kissing her all over — once, twice, thrice — but I was still hungry.

She would gently disengage herself and say in a tantalising tone, 'Enough. Too much is bad for one.'

I would not stop and ask for only one more...

'But your one becomes a hundred... .'

'You have grown up in a hermitage. You will not understand the arithmetic of love. In this arithmetic, one may even mean a hundred, a thousand or a million; it depends on the occasion.'

She would smile and turn away. I would be left looking avidly at her retreating figure.

Other memories fade with time, but the colourful memory of love seems to shine brightly forever. I do not know why it should be but it is so.

116

For the first few months each night danced into my rooms, with tinkling bells made of stars, bringing with it innumerable jugs of honey. I drank them down and was yet thirsty. Those lights were beautiful lakes. Multi-coloured with the lotuses of love blossoming...

But what is the use of narrating all this? It is not considered decent to talk freely of bodily pleasures. But if one can talk of the soul which brings eternal happiness why should it be taboo to talk openly of love which brings to men and women as great a pleasure? What is there in it that one need conceal or be ashamed of?

The fragrance of those sweet memories of love has evaporated and its petals have fallen; all that remain are the thorns! That is why...

I strove for sometime to build an unusually beautiful world of our own round Devayani and myself. A world in which I was not the son of King Nahusha with the curse and she was not the daughter of Maharishi Shukra; a world in which if death called Yayati, Devayani would answer the call and if eternal Time asked for Devayani, Yayati would meet the challenge; a world in which Devayani would turn her back on heaven and gladly face hell if Yayati was condemned to it, and no matter how bad Devayani was, Yayati would lay down his life for her — such a world was my dream. But —

Saris of every colour suited her. Like the sky made pretty by clouds of every hue, she would stand out in any clothes. If she wore jewels, it was the jewels which borrowed her splendour. What varied and beautiful coiffure she could make. At times she sat making herself up before the mirror for hours. I liked her doing this. But my one thought was that even — yes, even by day — Devayani so made up should be somewhere near me.

I cannot tell you how far my thoughts were tinged with desire. But there certainly was at least a particle of sentiment — plain, straightforward, clean love.

She had beauty in full measure. She was a devotee to beauty, she was an adept at make-up, but none of it was for me. Devayani lived for herself and only for herself.

117

Sharmishtha once mentioned that she was a great danseuse. I was eager to see her dance. But she put me off with, 'There are many dancing girls at court.' When she was the daughter of a sage, she delighted in dancing — now, she was queen. If she danced even for her husband, what a great blow it would be to her dignity!

She often talked about herself.

The betel leaf which Sharmishtha made coloured the mouth better than any she could make; so in jest I had lightly remarked, 'The betel leaf of hers who loves more colours the better.' That was enough to rouse her temper — how she raved. And with what diligence she has kept Sharmishtha from me since then.

The golden hair of Alaka was kept away carefully as a memento in a gold casket. Accidentally it came to her hand once. She insisted on looking inside. She asked, 'Where is this love of yours now?'

She wanted to throw the hair away. I alone know what considerable difficulty I had retrieving it.

I am unable to state coherently what I want to say — this thought persists. Is a man incapable of laying bare his heart fully? How many outlets are there to the heart? Shame, decorum — setting all considerations aside, our first year together is narrated here.

No. It is very difficult. But one thing is certain. My imperfection was hurting and tormenting me. I wanted fullness of life. The hankering had reference both to the body and the mind.

Devayani did give me some bodily pleasure. But even in its giving, she never overflowed with life. Quite often she pretended to be asleep in bed. I would tip-toe up to her and place my lips on hers. But the kiss chilled me. During my sojourn with the victory horse, I had kissed the stone image of the goddess of love. I was unconsciously reminded of it. The kiss did not make my blood surge like lightning. My loneliness, my imperfection, my incompleteness remained to torment me. If we were near each other in body, we were poles apart in mind.

I had learnt from Mukulika that love was a natural escape from all fear and unhappiness. The love she gave me was like a forest path, and strewn with thorns untrodden. But Devayani's love was quite unlike it. It was not stolen, it was not sinful in the least. It was pure, it was blessed and authorised by divine canons. It was the royal road laid over with carpets of flowers and ornamented with designs in coloured pigment. And even so, I was the solitary traveller on it.

I wanted love fragrant as a flower, imperceptible but gently pervading all round. I never had such love from Devayani.

Were we even at least of one mind? No. If she had given me a place in her heart, then perhaps Yayati's life would have taken a very different turn.

If and then — all such speculations are mere flowers of fancy. That I was unsatisfied even with a beautiful wife like Devayani is the truth — nothing but the truth.

Hunger of love — what else is it but hunger? Hunger at midday, deep sleep at midnight and thirst in summer are all a strange phenomenon. It is as subtle as it is irresistible!

The physical part of the hunger of love is easily described. Every youth experiences it. But the mental counterpart of love is different. I also cannot clearly define it. But even when Devayani was in my bed, the consciousness of being lonely was often unbearable.

I had to spend my days in such loneliness. I was hankering for a mate all the time. I was looking for one to talk to, to joke with, to confide in, to share my unhappiness. I was looking for a companion, who would not move even if stung by a scorpion, lest I, who was sleeping peacefully in her lap, be disturbed. I was looking for a friend to whom I could relate my golden dreams and confess to my lapses. I was looking for partner who could create confidence in me that even if we did not get anything to eat on this uninhabited island, we would live on the honey and nectar in our lips — and if death came to take away one, insist that he take the other one also.

Devayani was never able to satisfy this hunger of mine.

Once I casually said to Devayani, 'There is something I very much wish for; but I do not think it will be granted in this life.'

She said smiling, 'What is there in this world that the King of Hastinapur cannot get?'

I replied, 'Poverty.'

'You want to be poor?'

'Sometimes I wish that a powerful enemy would invade our kingdom, that I should be defeated, that then we two would sneak away into a forest in disguise and live among the open mountains where I would hunt for food, which you would cook into delicious recipes, that you should cling to me from fear when a serpent wriggles past, that a firefly should light up our faces when lying in each other's arms we would be passionately kissing, and you would blush because the goddess of the forest had with the aid of this tiny light been witness to our amour.'

I might indefinitely have carried on in this strain when she interrupted with, 'It was by a mistake that you were born to King Nahusha! In some poet's house... .'

But she had married me only because I was the son of King Nahusha. She loved the royal splendour, she loved to be Queen! She did not love Yayati. Yayati was only an instrument of fulfilling her wishes.

This realisation often made me restless. And yet, I did everything possible to make her happy. I was not prepared to forego the pleasure, which I could take. Unbeknown she had ensnared me with the wile of her beauty. But I could never openly share my unhappiness with her.

One whose only thought is for himself, one who is absorbed in oneself, one who looks at the world through one's eyes alone, indeed one who does not see the world as anything beyond oneself is never able to realise the sensibilities of another; but engaged in self worship, unconsciously turns blind in his/her mind and deaf in his/her heart.

120

Devayani would always find in everything only that which suited her own inclination.

This is what happened at the first town celebrations after our marriage. It was celebrated with great eclat. Everyone was all admiration for the new Queen. Every night there were staged varied items of entertainment. We were both present to see them.

On the first day, a play based on the life of my great grandfather Pururava was staged.

Urvashi was staying with Pururava on certain conditions. Unknowingly, he breaks the conditions. She, therefore, leaves him. The king is distraught at her separation and roves the world in search of her. In the end he comes to a lake. There he finds his beloved. The king entreats her with all he can to return with him. But she will not give in. In the end, he is bent on suicide. Urvashi replies thus, 'Do not throw yourself down the precipice. King, remember one thing, it is not possible to remain friends with women for all time, because their hearts are like those of wolves.' With these words she vanishes into the air. The king embraces the stone where she was standing and faints away.

At this last scene, the audience sighed and were touched. Devayani was the only one in the audience who clapped in applause. Devayani was smiling at me, victoriously, perhaps implying that she was the Urvashi and I the Pururava of this generation. That stung — but no — let me forget it.

Next day was scheduled a scene based on the dialogues of Agastya and Lopamudra from the *Rigveda*. Agastya was a Brahmin sage and Lopamudra a Kshatriya princess. When I helped Devayani out of the well, she had mentioned Lopamudra. So, I said in jest, 'In this scene, I should have acted Agastya and you Lopamudra.'

Even after marriage, Agastya was a celibate for a long time. He was saying to her, 'Every dawn rises to bring a new day on earth. But everyday is slowly taking us nearer old age. In old age, the limbs of men and women weaken into senility. Their beauty fades. Dear

121

Lopamudra, with this bitter truth openly staring us in the face, why should we stay away from each other any longer?'

Lopamudra doubts what he says. To resolve her doubts, he says, 'There is nothing improper in a husband and wife coming together. If the pleasure of their union was undesirable as to be prohibited why should the Prime Creator have indulged in making man and woman two different beings?'

Even then Lopamudra does not go to him. In the end Lopamudra puts her head on his shoulder and only says, 'Men talk about it; women don't. But they are both longing for the same pleasure.'

This scene was appreciated by the audience with great understanding — even gaiety. But Devayani was displeased. She said, 'Lopamudra is a great fool. She should have replied to this bearded sage in some such vein as Urvashi's yesterday.'

She was however deeply interested in the show on the third day. The story depicted a king posing as a danseuse. The part was acted by a dancing girl herself. But Devayani said, 'How well the king acts the part. I am wondering for sometime now what part would suit you most.' After a little thought, she said, 'You will make a perfect sage. With a beard and long hair, a *rudrakshamala,* wooden sandals, a water carafe in the hand and a deerskin under the arm would do it. Even I could be deceived.' And she burst out laughing.

Retorting in jest I said, 'I have taken an oath before mother in my childhood.'

'All right. We shall see... .'

~

Messengers came from the north with the news that the Dasyus, tribals, were making a nuisance of themselves. Earlier, thanks to father's bravery, all tribals had stopped their raids into our kingdom and were peaceful. I knew that unless our authority was restored, trouble would not cease. I resolved to lead an army there myself.

An auspicious time was set for the departure. The day was drawing nearer. I had imagined that Devayani would be in distress. But even on the previous night, she had been calm. I had said, 'I will find it hard to go away from you!' She had retorted sarcastically, 'Did you really escort the victory horse?'

It was dawn. I bowed before mother and took her blessing. It only remained for Devayani to bid farewell in the traditional way. Sharmishtha brought the salver containing the lamp and other articles of worship. Devayani was about to take it in hand, when a maid came in hurriedly and announced the arrival of a messenger outside.

Devayani started out. The priests muttered something like, 'Your Majesty ... the auspicious time!'

The priests were troubled lest the auspicious time might pass by. In the end, Sharmishtha was asked by mother to perform the traditional ritual. She put the red *tilak* on my forehead.

That first touch of Sharmishtha — does the nature of man reveal itself even in a touch? Devayani was undoubtedly prettier than Sharmishtha — but her touch always felt like that of a statue in stone. On the other hand Sharmishtha's was like that of a delicate flowering creeper.

After taking the light round my face and sprinkling rice on my head, she said in a soft low tone, 'Pray do take care of yourself.'

Those words were enough to calm down my agitation. I looked at Sharmishtha, tears had welled in her eyes. Sharmishtha was giving me what Devayani had failed to.

Devayani pranced back with her father's letter like a child. She suddenly turned to mother and said, 'Mother, His Majesty will certainly return victorious. Father has sent him his blessings just in time.'

She gave me the letter to read. It said:

I am very lonely in the hermitage since you left. There is nothing wanting, yet I have the persistent feeling that something is lacking! I do not know if every father, sending his daughter away, has the same experience.

Things being thus, I think it would be better to undertake the penance. I was unable to keep Sanjeevani as I should have. And Lord Shiva must be angry with me for it. I shall probably have to undertake an even more difficult penance. But have no care, my girl. Your father will not rest until he has acquired some unique power like Sanjeevani.

You might feel that I need not subject my body to such hardships, but Devayani this is a world of power politics. I had acquired a unique power. I lost it from being an addict to wine. But it is one thing to live honourably as the Lord and Master of the world, with such power in one's armoury and quite another to exist as a weakling who is helpless and therefore reduced to an insignificant life. The first can be called life, the second living death!

You will now understand why I am anxious to sit in penance. If you start immediately after getting this letter, you will still be in time to see me before I enter the cave.

I am eagerly looking forward to your visit. If your husband can spare the time from his royal obligations, bring him along. God bless him.

I looked up from the letter. Sharmishtha had perhaps hoped that Maharishi Shukra might have mentioned her in the letter or at least remembered her enough to send his blessings. She was sure that if there was a reference, I would tell her.

With some such thoughts I heaved a sigh at which Devayani said, 'Your Majesty need not take it to heart. I shall return soon after seeing father. I shall certainly not stay long! We women leave our hearts behind us in our homes, even on our visits to our parental home.'

The priests were grumbling because the auspicious time for leaving the palace had lapsed. She ignored them and said, 'I have in mind to perform a sacrifice to wish father well on my return. By then, Your Majesty will also have returned.'

'I may not return in time.'

'That will not do. You must specially return for the sacrifice and then go back.'

I was about to oppose her when mother came to her rescue. She was glad that great sages and ascetics would be among us for the sacrifice. I quietly agreed to Devayani's proposal. She said, 'I shall not leave until after the arrangements for the sacrifice are on the way. At least fifty ascetics should be here. Kacha should also be called... .'

'Kacha?' I said in confusion. Why has she so much regard for Kacha? He stayed a long time in Maharishi Shukra's hermitage. Is it possible that they fell in love? Or were their relations any different?

Devayani had once talked in her sleep somewhat incoherently. It was quite clear in a moment. While in the hermitage, Kacha probably gathered flowers for her; she desired that he should braid them in hair...

That plainly points to love. It was not mere friendship.

No, there would be no point in calling Kacha for the sacrifice.

I looked at Sharmishtha. Her gloom had disappeared at the mention of Kacha. She had told me, 'Kacha taught me to love.' What did that mean? Whatever it be! If he came and met Sharmishtha, the unfortunate girl, leading the life of a slave, will get some respite.

I said, 'Consult the Prime Minister in issuing invitations to the principal sages. But do include Maharishi Angiras in them.'

It maybe this sudden remembrance of Maharishi Angiras or the sight of the glorious Himalayan peak visible from the northern border ... one could not take one's eyes off that trident shaped peak among them. In this campaign I was reminded of Yati over and over again. I had practically forgotten about him in the last year. I had

125

omitted to make even casual enquiry if Yati, in search of his objective, had come to Maharishi Shukra and if so, what had happened to him? One unconsciously centres on oneself. If it were otherwise, I should at sometime have given a thought to Yati. The remembrance came now, and I even thought for a moment that I should go as far as the foothills of the Himalayas. Learning that King Yayati was himself leading the army, the guerilla Dasyus scattered into the forest and there was no cause for actual battle.

In a way, I was free to search for Yati. But I was restless with thoughts of Devayani. I knew that my love for her was largely physical. But the body ached for her. I renewed the arrangements for protection against the Dasyus and returned to the capital.

Devayani had returned from her visit to Maharishi Shukra before me. Arrangements for the sacrifice were in full swing in the capital. But although everything was going according to her plans, she did not seem pleased to welcome me back.

The cause was the letter from Maharishi Angiras. He wrote:

I cannot come. Unless I am satisfied that the penance of Maharishi Shukra stems from benign motives and that the power achieved will be used only towards the good of the world, I am unable to participate in a sacrifice directed to wish him well.

When, on purpose, I told her that Angiras had been preceptor to Kacha, she was stunned for a moment. Knowing that Sharmishtha would be disappointed if Kacha did not come, I said, 'I wish Kacha could come. He is a friend of my childhood.' I had not seen Sharmishtha since my return. I asked Devayani about her when she said, 'I have sent her to Ashokavan.'

She added, 'What was her right to perform the ritual for you and put the red mark on your forehead on the day you set out for the campaign?'

'But mother asked her to do... .'

'As a Kshatriya princess, she is very near to her … almost a blood relation. She must be planning to make her your queen!'

I laughed, 'Mother may have her plans, but you are hardly likely to let her succeed.'

'Umm. What is so difficult about it? Do you know that your worthy mother poisoned one of the maids of the palace? I can tell you all about everything that goes on.'

The conversation had taken on unpleasant turn. I kept quiet so as to stem it.

But a night equally filled with happy dreams had rarely come my way. That night Devayani told me of her secret. The very intimate sweet secret. The mystery of woman's life. She was expecting.

I was thrilled. Devayani — to have a baby. I was going to be a father. Will it be a boy or girl? If a boy, what would he look like? They say that children with the face of their mothers are happy. Whether a boy or girl, we must both pray everyday that it has the mother's features.

Devayani was to be a mother. Her little one was going to prattle ma-ma! That night every moment was enlivened with a sweet dream. I was floating like a swan on the waves of dreams.

The sacrifice was performed with due eclat. Some prominent sages like Agastya and Angiras were unable to come. Barring that blemish, the ceremony went well. Devayani kept hoping that some day Kacha would come.

Court was held in honour of the assembled guests. Even mother was present behind a curtain in rear of the throne.

A pregnant woman carries a peculiar glow, not unlike the earth with the bloom of crops. I realised this when I saw the eyes of the ladies in the gathering glued to Devayani in admiration. I was greatly flattered.

I was filled with joyful pride when doing obeisance with her, before the saints and sages, and later mounting the throne with her.

127

Devayani had particularly sent for Sharmishtha from the Ashokavan. Her intentions became apparent at court. She wanted Sharmishtha to be near to fan her.

The sages took grains of rice in their hands to bestow their blessing. Just then the Prime Minister whispered in my ear and said, 'Kacha is outside.'

Devayani overheard and said, 'Escort him in with deference and take him to his place of honour among the gathering.'

'He does not seem to want to come in.'

Devayani was angry. 'Why? Like Angiras ... has he also gone queer? Does he wish to insult us after coming to the capital? In that case... .'

The Prime Minister folded his hands, 'No. Your Majesty there is no such thing. He is accompanied by an ascetic who appears to be beside his mind. So Kachadeva prefers... .'

Devayani said, 'No matter... bring him in with the mendicant. And look, I am a sister to him. Bring him straight to the throne. I shall bow and take his blessing and then you can lead him to his place.'

The Prime Minister hastened out. In a little while Kacha and his companion came in. The whole gathering turned to them. A faint murmur from the sages, welcoming Kacha, rolled up.

I scanned the mendicant accompanying him, when Kacha came forward. I could not believe my eyes. I did not know if I was dreaming or had gone off my mind.

He was Yati.

The three of them stood before the throne. Devayani got up to bow to Kacha. It would have been contrary to decorum if I had continued sitting. I also got up smiling.

Just as Devayani was about to bow, he noticed Sharmishtha standing there with a fan. He was astounded. He suddenly exclaimed, 'Princess? You... here?'

Devayani quickly raised herself up a little and said, 'Sage Kacha, she is no longer a princess.'

So far Yati was casting wild glances around. Pointing to Sharmishtha, he said to Devayani 'Will you give me this maid of yours?'

She asked Yati, 'Why do you want her sire? For a wife?'

Kacha was warning Yati off with his eyes. But Yati's eyes were fixed on Sharmishtha.

On seeing Yati in this condition I was reminded of the curse 'The children of King Nahusha will never be happy.'

Yati laughed grotesquely, 'Wife? No, I am going to change her into a man.'

The gathering burst into laughter, which immediately subsided and was followed by a pall of fright.

From behind the curtain mother shouted, 'Prime Minister, take the lunatic away. If he talks such nonsense again, have him flogged!'

The Prime Minister made a sign. The guards came forward to take Yati away.

I did not take in what was happening before me. My mind was whirling with the curse. I could not bear to see Yati's humiliation. I ordered, 'Don't touch him. He is the rightful heir to this throne.'

Devayani wondered wide-eyed if I had lost my senses. I calmly said to the court in words which were distinctly audible: 'He is my elder brother. His name is Yati.'

From behind the curtain came the wail, 'Yati' and immediately mother rushed out, in defiance of all decorum. She had only to look at Yati. She could not bear to see that terrible apparition. She closed her eyes and collapsed to the ground, with her arms outstretched saying: 'Yati? My Yati?'

129

DEVAYANI

Is Kacha an enemy from my earlier birth? The whole ceremony had gone off well. Kacha had parted from me pronouncing a curse. On the pretext of the sacrifice, I sent him an invitation to make him realise that I was not the least bit worse off for his curse. Now Devayani was a ruling queen.

I felt that he might not relish facing his beloved as queen but I also knew how deeply he had loved Devayani at one time. Man may spurn love but can he ever forget it? Kacha was not there at the start and he had not come till the finish. The queen in me was pleased. But the Devayani in me grieved.

The Prime Minister brought the news of his arrival in the court. My joy knew no bounds. I sat on the throne, thousands of eyes centred on me in admiration of my beauty with Princess Sharmishtha fanning me as a maid. The great sages chanted auspicious hymns, in blessing us. Kacha would see and realise how grievously he had erred in rejecting me.

Kacha denied me fulfilment of my love. I thought I would have the pleasure of wreaking vengeance, but my weapon boomeranged. The satisfaction of revenge was there, but for Kacha.

~

Mother is invariably taciturn. Her mind is deep as a well. Nobody can fathom from her appearance what is going on inside. But throwing

130

decorum to the winds, forgetting her place as Queen Mother, she had come forward screaming, 'Yati! My Yati!' and collapsed on the ground before the gathering. What a shame! How derogatory to a Queen Mother's dignity!

There was chaos in the courtroom. The wretch had brought great ill omen to father's penance! After all, Yati was off his head. But why could His Majesty not keep his? Nobody at court except he knew that Yati was his brother. Even Kacha who brought him in was unaware of his identity.

Somewhere along the way, villagers were stoning the looney! Kacha saw it and his compassion was roused. He brought him along.

Or is it that this house is cursed with insanity? What a figure that Yati is. His Majesty's behaviour also — I cannot foresee what calamity might not befall us if the wretch continues to stay here. Mother might even insist that a regency should rule in his name. Her filial love has awakened, and in passing, she could humiliate me. After all, he is the elder brother. His Majesty had himself said in open court, 'He is the rightful heir to the throne.'

Oh no. His Majesty had acted irrationally at the court.

This house is not cursed with insanity only. There is weakness for women also. Truly hereditary. They say my father-in law defeated Lord Indra! He may have but he was also smitten by Indrani's beauty. Mother had hidden it from me but the old maid told me everything.

Yati, with a beard and long hair, wearing his saffron coloured gown of renunciation had only to look at Sharmishtha and he asked for her in the presence of the whole gathering.

Why laugh at him? He, poor wretch, ran away as a child and took to the jungle.

But look at King Yayati renowned for his heroism. He won laurels when out with the victory horse. Now anointed king, did he also not melt at the sight of a beautiful maiden stepping out of a well? How readily a woman sees through a man. She can read his good and bad points clearly in his eyes. When I stepped out of the well, how avidly His Majesty was looking at me.

A woman can instinctively read passion in the eyes of a man. She is certain from his avid eyes that he would be an easy prey.

If it was Kacha, I would not have dared even to say, 'Give me your hand!' Even if I had, he would not have given it.

I was attracted to Kacha by such traits in his character. I would not have given him a second thought, if from the moment he came into the hermitage he had hovered round me, seeming eager to be near me, or if I found him looking avidly at me. But I never saw desire in his eyes. There was no passion in his bearing. Women like just such men. They turn their backs on men who chase them and they chase men who turn their backs on them. How strange but true!

Kacha used to gather my favourite wild flowers at some risk to his life. Those flowers often told me how deeply he was in love with me. In the dead of night they would whisper into my ear. But Kacha never mentioned it.

Once, a thorn pricked me in the garden. In jest, I told him that I had been bitten by a snake. The tears that came to his eyes then plainly reflected his feelings.

He used to say his prayers to the Almighty in a bower in the corner of the garden before going to bed. It included the words, 'May Devayani be happy.' These words reassured me over and over again of his deep love.

I wanted such love.

I did not intend to stay a miserable frustrated lover, telling the rosary of her frustration.

Kacha had inflicted a deep wound on my heart, I wanted to forget the pain of that wound. I therefore locked up the lover in me in a dark corner of my heart. For good. I was determined to spend my life in the intoxication of being the mistress of myself.

The Devayani who fell in and the Devayani who came out of the well were different persons. With the realisation that the man standing on the edge of the well was the King of Hastinapur... In that instant I was determined to be his favourite queen. To forget the pangs of unrequited love, I needed the intoxication of splendour, the arrogance of power and a husband who would dance to my tune... . A lusting husband would stay in my control.

All this I gained in a moment. But that wretch of an ascetic accompanying Kacha...

It does not matter whether this mad man stays here or goes away. I am the queen and propose to stay queen.

I insisted that he should not be kept in the palace so that his influence and following might not grow. It is just as well that they have all gone to the Ashokavan. Who knows what foolish things that idiot would have done here?

So that I maybe kept informed of what goes on at Ashokavan I have deputed the old maid, among others, ostensibly to wait on the Queen Mother. She narrates funny stories. He has not yet recognised his mother.

In his pilgrimage, God bestowed a good gift on Kacha. What a jewel he has found! And with great regard he brought him here.

Evil seems to follow Yati everywhere. On that day of the farewell ceremony, we drove to court in a chariot in perfect sunshine. There was not a speck of cloud anywhere in the sky. It looked more like spring than the rainy season. But Yati had only to enter the courtroom and there was chaos here, there and everywhere.

When we returned that evening, the sky was overcast with thick black clouds. It was dark like an underground passage. Soon lightning flashed! Lightning? It looked like snakes in an underground passage.

Then came pouring rain. For four days it simply rained! River Yamuna was in flood. Life in the capital had become disorganised. The Prime Minister was troubled that the Yamuna would rise further, devastating villages on its banks.

133

It was the midnight of the fourth day! It was still raining, now a downpour and then a drizzle. When the rain stopped, you could hear big drops of water dripping from the higher branches to the ones below. After a while, it poured again. His Majesty was asleep, but I was awake. My thoughts toyed with the idea of the coming baby, wondering what it would look like. Seeing it, will it remind people of me? Whose eyes and nose will it have? Would it have thick hair? Will it have a small, tiny mouth? Will it run to me stumbling on the way calling me ma, before turning to His Majesty saying da, da?

Suddenly I heard the sound of hooves on the cobblestones outside. Was I dreaming?

I opened the door and hastened out. I had indeed heard horse's hooves. Mother had sent a messenger.

Agitated, the messenger asked me, 'Has the ascetic come here?'

I knew that Kacha was in the habit of wandering far away into a quiet place to sit in meditation there. As it was past midnight, mother must have sent the messenger to find out if he had come here.

I replied, 'No. Kacha has not been here.'

He stuttered, 'Kacha is there, but that other ascetic ... revered Yati.'

'What has happened to him? Who knows where he has run away? When?'

'He was in Ashokavan till three hours after nightfall. The Queen Mother awoke a little later and found that Prince Yati was not in his bed.'

I awoke His Majesty, who promptly rode to Ashokavan. Despite a diligent search, Yati was not to be found.

Next day, there was a strange rumour in the capital. They said, someone had seen Yati walking across the flooded Yamuna!

Where Yati had hidden himself in the darkness, how he got away inspite of the vigil for him, where he went to in pouring rain, whether

134

he walked on the waters of the Yamuna or was drowned in it, no one knew for certain.

I said to myself, 'It is good riddance.'

I went to Ashokavan to enquire about mother. I pressed her to return to the palace. She preferred to stay where she was.

I met Kacha there. We talked for a while, but it was very casual. He never visited the palace. His Majesty used to visit Ashokavan everyday to see his mother. Everytime on coming back he said, 'It was very nice to meet an old friend like Kacha. Time flies in his company.' Kacha had time to talk to everybody and to undertake insignificant little tasks for all and sundry but not to see Devayani.

I had asked him once when I was there, 'When will you visit the palace?' He only said, 'We shall see.' His egoism remained. Even now he does not understand Devayani!

Something within me assured me, however, that one day he would come to see me. Every morning the cheerful dawn would whisper, 'Kacha will come today. He wishes to surprise you by coming without warning.' I would then merrily set about preparing for his welcome. A seat which from a distance appeared like a throne, delicious fruit artfully laid out in a golden salver, small delicately made garlands of his favourite flowers, everything was kept ready in my apartment. After all, he was an eccentric sage. Who could tell when he would appear?

One, two, three, full seven days passed by. Kacha had time to sit chatting with His Majesty for hours. But he had no time to come and see me. I was so angry with him. He came to Hastinapur on an invitation. And that too from me. But he did not have the ordinary courtesy to call at the palace.

Nonetheless, I did want all the time that he should come to see me, that we should talk together freely, that he should enquire about me, that we should recall the happy days we had spent together, that

135

their memory should distress me and tears come to my eyes, for no particular reason, and with them wash away the Devayani who was Queen.

When Kacha had left me with a curse, I had resolved never again to shed tears. At parting from father I bowed and bid him farewell. He put his hand on my head with a blessing. How he was trembling. I was greatly moved but not a tear came to my eyes. Devayani was never, never again, going to cry.

I did feel, however, that when Kacha came, sweet old memories should come up and I should give way to tears so that I would feel easier in mind. Is there comfort in tears? No, tears are the sign of a weak mind. Queen Devayani cry? And that for some musty old memories? No, that is not possible.

I was now almost certain Kacha was going to leave without seeing me. On the eighth day, I did not prepare for his welcome.

And by chance on that very day he came. What a time I had looking after him. The servants brought in a stately chair but he squatted on his deerskin.

I urged, 'Kacha, you must sit here.'

He looked at the chair and said, 'Not that this beautiful chair will hurt me. But I have made a rule. Why needlessly break it?'

'And what is the rule?'

'It is really nothing much. If one can sleep on a deerskin, why take the trouble of making a feather bed? If one must eat wild roots and herbs, why should one occasionally indulge in a banquet and pamper the tongue? Devayani, man's tongue is his worst enemy. I do not mean that only in the sense that it indulges in words which hurt. But if it tastes a crisp delicacy one day, it prompts one to taste it again.'

Tauntingly I retorted, 'I suppose it is wrong for me, even as a queen, to wear these expensive clothes!'

He smiled and said, 'Oh no, your case is different. You are a householder. Family life is your creed. I am an ascetic. Renunciation

136

is my creed. Indulgence of various kinds has an acknowledged place in your life. In renunciation, it is unforgivable.'

Looking lingeringly at some flowers in a golden vase on a table nearby, he said, 'So you still remember what I like. That you have time for such small things, inspite of your great responsibilities as a queen, is... .'

'It was because I thought of you, that I particularly sent you an invitation.'

'You remembered me inspite of my curse and sent me an invitation. It is great good fortune to have such a generous sister. It was unworthy of a young ascetic and even more so of a brother.'

With these words, he folded his hands. How grave he looked. He asked, 'Am I forgiven?'

I hung my head saying, yes. Next moment I wondered if it was not all playacting! If Devayani was so dear to him and he wanted to beg her forgiveness, why had he kept away for so long?

I said with a smile, 'It is many days since you came to Hastinapur. You never came to see me. So I wondered if the brother had forgotten his sister?'

'A rich brother might neglect a poor sister but how can a poor brother forget his rich sister?'

He added, 'I was looking for the way to the heart of the mistress of the palace.' I was unable to understand him.

He calmly said, 'I am going to ask something of you!'

I stammered, 'What is it?'

'You should release Sharmishtha from bondage!'

Angry, I asked him, 'What shall I do with her on releasing her? Exchange places with her? Make her the Queen or my rival?'

He kept calm and said, 'I can understand that in a fit of anger you insisted on her being your maid. But man's greatness lies in mastering the passions with the help of thought.' Seeing that I was quiet, he

137

added, 'Devayani, imagine yourself for a moment in her place. If you had to spend your life as her maid... .'

I said disparagingly, 'I? A maid?'

Calmly he said, 'Devayani, destiny can be very wayward and heartless. When it will beggar the queen into a maid and make a queen of a maid... .'

I said deprecatingly, 'I understand these subtle words, Kacha!'

'Forgive me if I have said anything to offend you. There is only one way to understand the unhappy plight of another; that is to imagine oneself in his place. So far Kacha has not had to ask Devayani for anything. He thought maybe she will give these alms to her brother.'

I realised it was no use getting into an argument with him. I turned blind, deaf and mute. His eyes were neither hard nor pathetic. They were blank. But the essence of all mystic power and magic was concentrated in them. Kacha's looks were no different.

I was gathering my strength to fight him.

By bringing Yati to court he had brought ill omen to father's penance. Father was his preceptor. Father had brought him back to life. But he had no word of respect for or devotion to him. He has seen my dazzling palace but has no praise for me. And yet, he had the audacity to offer me gratuitous advice to release Sharmishtha from bondage. He did not hesitate a second when breaking my heart! I will not give him any alms!

I got up to leave without looking at him.

Kacha also got up. He said calmly, 'Your Majesty, I am leaving for Bhrigu Mountain tomorrow. I propose to engage myself in prayer and meditation in solitude.'

I bowed to him while he was still talking. Blessing me, he said, 'When and in what circumstances we shall meet again, the Almighty alone knows. I only pray that He may give the Queen guidance and you, Devayani, happiness forever.'

Next morning, mother sent word that she had decided to accompany Kacha into the mountains. His Majesty was upset at it. The thought that mother was renouncing life and going into the jungle made a child of him. I also pressed mother to stay, so that people should not say that she left because of me. But she was determined.

She left directly from Ashokavan. Before leaving she drew me aside and said, 'My girl, there is nothing that I now wish for. But for no reason, I am anxious about Yayu. He is like a child. Remember a word of wisdom from my experience. It is not enough for a young woman to be her husband's wife. She has to be companion, sister, daughter and indeed, on occasion, even a mother to him.'

I was convinced, from what the old maid told me about a conversation between mother and son, that her advice was mere pretension, in fact, sheer playacting.

Mother had advised His Majesty to look after himself and added, 'Do let me know when my grandson arrives. I shall be flattered if you give him your father's name. Do you mind coming into the garden with me? I would like to show you a herb.'

'What is it a specific for?'

'The ailment is... it has no specific name. But sometimes man is tired of life... his own or someone else's. I hope you will have no occasion for it. But Yayu if you had a wife like Sharmishtha, I would have gone away without a care.'

Kacha was of a piece with mother. A fraud, an actor and treacherous. At parting he had left a note with Sharmishtha for His Majesty.

In the end I plucked courage to ask His Majesty, 'Anything special in that letter?'

He handed me the letter, adding, 'Not really! But I keep thinking it would have been far better if, like Kacha, I had been born an ascetic.'

Kacha's letter ran:

We have met after a long time. Meeting a dear friend or acquaintance and talking freely together is not a mere formality. It has an element of communion of souls. On such occasions, the captive soul, even if momentarily, experiences the joy of being free. Sages and ascetics undergo arduous penance to perpetuate that joy. I had it in a measure in your company. I shall always remember those happy moments.

I pray that both of you will forgive me with generosity for one thing. Until coming here, I did not know of Yati's existence. I took pity on him as an unknown ascetic who had lost his wits. I should not have brought him to court in these circumstances. But the Prime Minister conveyed to me the urgent bidding of the Queen. I thought Yati would be interested in the company of the other sages here and keep quiet.

But what transpired was quite different. And strange. The anticlimax to the celebrations was my doing. I have heard that friendship forgives. I beg for forgiveness.

I heard about Yati from you for the first time. His condition today is very pitiable.

I have tried to reason why such a lot has befallen him. His loss of reason must be attributed to an extremely one-sided and faulty line of thought. Body and soul, man and woman are the dual entities on which life is based. Yati revolted against this basic fundamental conception. How could it succeed?

Life is full of numerous conflicting duals. An ascetic does achieve and experience eternal happiness in a condition where duals cease to exist. To realise it he adopts a rigid code of conduct. But this code rests essentially on his acceptance of the fact that conflicting duals do exist. It is only when the soul reveals its existence through the body that it can see the world. If the woman does not bear the child for nine months, how can man be born? How elementary these facts are! The

140

ordinary man accepts them as a part of his life. Being a natural part of creation, he accepts its suzerainty.

Yati not only did not acknowledge the suzerainty of creation but denied even its existence. Half of man... his body... is regulated by numerous laws of Nature. It is only through the body that the soul can soar. And it is only then that man rises above Nature. He can dictate to Nature. This he can do, not by turning away from Nature or spurning it, but by bowing to its existence.

Man is the supreme link between Nature and God. God transcends all conflict and Nature has no conception of conflicting duals. Man alone has it. The river that provides water for the thirsty person also drowns him when he ventures into deep water.

Nature does not differentiate between right and wrong; man alone can do it. If a mother's only child is being drowned the river does not feel anything in the matter. But if another man is there on the bank... provided it is a man who has progressed from the bare instinct to live to higher values... he will do everything possible to save that life, even at the risk to his own.

No, even after writing at such length I have not succeeded in making myself clear. My knowledge and meditation are so little. I am a traveller in quest of truth, but I have a long way to go yet.

In our talks I frequently referred to the soul. You asked me once or twice with a smile, 'Where is this soul?' I was unable to offer a satisfactory explanation. But I pray that you will constantly keep before you the following allegorical sketch drawn by an ancient sage. The allegory runs thus:

In human life, the soul is the passenger, the body the chariot, conscience the charioteer and mind the reins. The different senses are the horses, all the items of enjoyment are the roads, and the soul with senses and the mind attached to it has to use them.

If there is no chariot, where will the soul sit? How will he get to the battlefield of life quickly? How will he fight the enemy? Therefore, one must not underrate the importance of the chariot i.e., the body.

Yati made that unpardonable mistake.

The senses are the horses of this chariot. Because without them, he cannot move at all. If the horses are just harnessed to the chariot, there is no knowing when they will run amuck and the chariot be thrown into a deep chasm and be smashed to smithereens. Therefore, the horses in the form of senses must be controlled by the reins, i.e. the mind. But even these reins must always be in the hands of the charioteer. Otherwise they might as well not be there. Therefore, the mind must be under the control of the conscience. The mind and the conscience working together can regulate the chariot with caution.

The 'I', an infinitesimal part of God, which wakes up in all of us and which pervades all beings... which transcends conscience and mind and can also see beyond life and death... the soul itself is the passenger in the chariot.

I have written at length. I forgot that although this puzzle is of absorbing interest to a man like me, following the path of asceticism, it can be very boring and abstruse to others.

I am not being modest when I say that I often feel that the path of asceticism is much easier than life as a householder. This struggle of the soul for salvation manifests itself in many forms. The cult of asceticism is one exacting form of it.

On the other hand, love of man and woman is another attractive form of the same struggle. But this love must not merely be physical infatuation. That can only lead to a union of bodies. True love is a communication of minds. After sometime, it grows into a communion of souls.

This delightful path of the union of souls is perhaps even more difficult than the arduous path of asceticism, for the

142

attainment of God. Being a householder is noble and pure sacrifice. But if this sacrifice is to bear fruit, the first thing that the husband and wife have to offer in sacrifice is their ego.

Devayani will soon attain motherhood. May the Almighty ever bless you and the Queen.

I was so bored reading the letter. His Majesty asked me for the letter. He wanted to read it again. I asked him in jest if the letter was more delightful than myself?

He looked steadily at me and said, 'The Creator must be troubled these days because he cannot make anything more beautiful than you.'

'You are a born flatterer,' I said blushing. He lifted my chin and looking deep into my eyes said, 'Truly Devayani, you now look even prettier then before.'

'But do you know why?'

'No, I don't !'

I buried my face in his side and, 'Men are so dense. You see, I am going to be a mother, that is why!'

It was only now that he saw it. He paused and added, 'You will now be craving for things, will you not?'

'Not will be. I am already.'

'Whatever it is, tell me and see if it is not fulfilled in the instant.'

'I will tell you. My first wish... Don't read this letter of your friend again.'

'But...'

'I will not have it. Like that hair of the girl friend of your childhood which you have kept ... in the same box if you like, put this away too. In our dotage, we shall read it together over and over again. But today? No, not this foolish dissertation on the soul, at a time when my body and mind are blossoming to new heights of pleasure

143

at the prospect of motherhood, when all the worldly pleasures are at our command.'

'As you wish.'

The next month or six weeks were of great happiness. I wished to witness over again the plays staged during the town celebrations. During their performance, I was reminded of our earlier conversation. I had then said, 'You would look well as an ascetic.' While reading Kacha's letter, he had also said himself, 'It would have been much better if I had been an ascetic like him.'

The very idea was tantalising. But how to make it come true? I thought of a plan. I said, 'I feel like spending two or three hours quietly by moonlight on the banks of the Yamuna, in the company of an ascetic.'

He said laughing, 'We can go to the bank of the Yamuna in moonlight anytime, but your desire to go there in the company of an ascetic is rather... ?'

'But where do we find a sage whom you know? It will be enough if you go with me as an ascetic!'

'What nonsense... .'

'You don't really love me,' said I fretting. Thereafter for a couple of days, I did not even talk to him. I kept away from him.

What a powerful weapon feigned anger can be in the hands of a woman! If hesitatingly, His Majesty agreed to pose as a sage. In the evening of a moonlit night, the King accompanied the Queen into the green room. On the way out, it was a grand, lustrous sage carrying a stick and a water carafe who accompanied her.

I asked the charioteer to drive down to the Yamuna. I had already taken him into my confidence. At the moonlit river bank I told His Majesty, 'I had once said, "You would look well as a sage!" to which you said, "I will never be one!" But today... who wins?'

We both enjoyed the joke for a long time. Ashokavan was not very far from there. Sharmishtha would never recognise His Majesty in this garb. I saw no harm in such a practical joke. We turned towards Ashokavan.

I said to the servants, 'I have brought a great sage here so that Sharmishtha can also see him. In a little while I shall come back for him again.'

His Majesty could say or do nothing. He quietly went in. Inwardly, I could not help laughing at Sharmishtha's plight. In all reverence she would attend on the sage. How abashed she will be when reminded of it. There will be no end to her embarrassment!

After spending another two hours on the banks of the Yamuna, I took His Majesty back to the town.

On the way back he looked unusually cheerful. I could not make out what could have caused it. But looking at him, I was reminded of the glorious west, which in the evening glows in the same colours as the east in the morning.

'What did you say in your blessing?'

'The same as to every unmarried girl ... that she may find a worthy husband!'

I burst out laughing at the blessing pronounced by His Majesty.

It was three months since father started on his meditation. I wanted to see him. His Majesty felt that I would be unable to stand the long journey, but I would not be reassured unless I saw him with my own eyes.

I did go there. I was very happy to see him looking fit, but the journey was so arduous that I myself was taken ill. I had to stay away from His Majesty longer than I had expected.

In time I was a mother. I had a boy. Not only the capital but the entire kingdom was festive.

145

The name to be given to the baby was debated. His Majesty suggested first his father's name and then his grandfather's. But I did not want to borrow a stale name. I found a new one — Yadu!

Sharmishtha came to the palace for the naming ceremony. There was now a kind of halo on her face. I had imagined that she would get so bored in the solitude of Ashokavan that she would abjectly fall at my feet and beg of me, 'Please release me from my bondage!' But what I saw was quite different. She looked happy and contented.

Although that was the impression I gathered from her face, I suspected something else from her manner and bearing. I asked my old maid to keep an eye on her for a while. The old maid soon came back and whispered something in my ear. She, a princess! Would she go astray? And that with a mere servant?

That she has had a love affair was quite clear. Such sin can never be concealed. I sent the other maids away and called Sharmishtha in. She came in and hung her head.

I asked harshly, 'Is it true that you are expecting a baby?' Her lips moved but no sound come. In the end, she nodded assent.

'This illicit affair... .'

'This has been nothing illicit; it was by the grace of a great sage... .'

'By the grace of a sage? Who was the sage? Who conferred this boon on you? Was it Kacha?'

She said nothing. She did not smile nor was she frightened. She just stood there like a statue.

SHARMISHTHA

I was stunned at Devayani's question: 'Are you expecting a baby?' No, I was not only stunned, I was frightened. I was both abashed and terrified. I was trembling.

We were childhood friends. When such friends meet later in life they exchange their sweet secrets — what great joy there is in such a situation. But cruel fate had not ordained it for me.

On hearing the word illicit from her, my blood boiled. I could have silenced her with one word — just one. That one word would have raised hell at the palace. If I had told her the name of the father of the child I was bearing, she would have been crestfallen.

In doing so, I would have had the momentary pleasure of revenge; but that one word would have ruined the naming ceremony of her child Yadu. Gloom would immediately have descended on the palace. Devayani would have mauled His Majesty with bitter invective. There would have been permanent estrangement. God knows that more would have happened.

I do not know how, in the nick of time, I thought of saying, 'I am not a wanton. It was by the grace of a sage... !' But those words gave me great courage. They enabled me to keep my face. They were both true and false.

'Who conferred this boon on you? Was it Kacha?' How poignant, how poisonous the words were in casting such an aspersion on the noble figure of Kacha.

Will anyone throw mud on the image which I worshipped with white lotus flowers? But the queen of beauty Devayani had dared do it.

I had only said, 'By the Grace of a sage!' If she wanted to indulge in cruel jest, she could even have named Yati; that would not have hurt me so much.

In any case, at court that day Devayani had humiliated me not a little. It is as well that Yati was mad and the runaway brother of His Majesty, otherwise I would have had it. He asked for me and Devayani asked whether he wanted me for wife. Yati, however, was truly insane. I never understood the cause of his insanity. One night I was fast asleep. I woke up with a start. I felt a cold hand at my throat. In fact, someone was trying to strangle me with both hands. I was choking and terrified.

Trembling all over, I opened my eyes. Yati was sitting beside me. He was smiling to himself. What a grotesque smile it was! I screamed for fear of life. He quickly got up, bolted for the window, jumped out and disappeared. God knows where he went.

I would not have minded if Devayani had said that my coming baby came from a madman. That would have been insulting to me only; but the malicious words she uttered about Kacha...

Can one forget yesterday's love? Yes, it is possible. How otherwise could Devayani have said such strange poisonous things about Kacha?

Devayani might have forgotten her love of yesterday, but Sharmishtha is not thus forgetful. She will not only not forget her love of yesterday, and tomorrow, for all time, she will not betray her love.

What would Kacha say if he heard Devayani's malicious words? No. He will say nothing. He will only smile. When he along with the Queen Mother, came to bid farewell at leaving Ashokavan, I asked, 'Kacha, when shall we meet again?'

He smiled saying, 'Who knows? Fate is very wilful. It may bring me back here tomorrow. On the other hand, I may not come even in the next ten or twenty years.'

Kacha stayed so little at Ashokavan. Even in that short time, he was a pillar of strength. How much heart he put into me. It was as if my soul was reborn.

I asked him, 'Where are you going for so long?'

'To the Bhrigu Mountain for meditation.'

'What is the penance for?'

'If by my penance I could influence Devayani's behaviour, I would undertake grave penance indefinitely for that alone.'

I had never envied Devayani even in my dreams, not even when she became Queen of Hastinapur. But hearing Kacha I thought to myself how fortunate Devayani was. What more does one need in this world if a sage like Kacha is prepared to stake all his penance for one? What is worth more than such selfless, great love in this world?

Kacha had said all this with a smile on his lips. But that very smile revealed to me his heartache. He was distressed at Devayani's behaviour — at her maliciousness. But even so, his concern for her was no whit less. There is no greater unhappiness than bleeding of a lovelorn heart. But who and how can anyone else alleviate the pangs of such hidden sorrow?

Seeing me quiet he said, 'Maharishi Shukra is sitting in grave penance again. He will thereby achieve some mysterious power like Sanjeevani. That will again set off a war between gods and demons! Gods, demons, human beings and Dasyus ... all inhabit the world. But seeing this beautiful world forever torn with strife gives me sleepless nights. I wonder if this must continue from generation to generation. Does Lord Shiva truly wish that war, misery, strife and conflict should prevail in this world? I would like to do long penance to please Him, and then fall at His feet insisting that, "I want no other boon, but bless me with the power to establish peace and goodwill on earth!" It is because of this ardent wish that I said I may not return for ten or twenty years!'

As soon as the chariot bearing Kacha and the Queen Mother left for the Bhrigu Mountain, Ashokavan became lonely.

How promptly after arrival at Ashokavan he came from the guest rooms to my room at the far end of the building to enquire after me. I got up on seeing him. He insisted again and again that I sit down. In the end I said, 'Kacha, Sharmishtha is no longer a princess who can sit in your presence; she is now a maid.'

He looked at me very affectionately and said, 'Sharmishtha, the musk deer does not know that it secretes fragrant musk. You are the same. You maybe doing the menial duties of a maid but your soul is not slave to anybody or anything. It is only he whose soul is free that has the power to see God. The salvation which great sages fail to achieve after years of penance... .'

Blushing I hung my head. I said, 'Kacha, I am one of Devayani's least liked maids. Things like the soul are foreign to me.'

'You are not a maid! You are a sister to me. Kacha has two sisters ... one is Devayani and the other Sharmishtha.'

Kacha added, 'You are not only my sister but my preceptor. I thought that I had made great sacrifice for my kind when setting out to acquire Sanjeevani; but you have a made a much bigger sacrifice. This humble disciple of yours begs you not to brood on your being a maid.

If in the eyes of the world you are a maid, to me you are a gracious queen. The slave is Devayani. She is slave to her splendour, dignity and ego. The man whose soul is prey to selfishness, desire and enjoyment is forever a slave in this world. You spurned self-interest and all your happiness in coming here. You adopted the most difficult but shortest path available to man to attain God ... the path of sacrifice. You are truly an ascetic, not a maid. Sharmishtha, I am aware that a younger sister would not like her elder brother to bow to her; but if you are younger in age, you are by far greater in sacrifice. Therefore... .'

While still talking, he folded his hands in a bow.

I lost all sense of where I was and what I was doing. I quickly went up to him and held his hands. The next moment, I thought he would resent the intimacy and shake my hands off. I remembered how particular he was in the cottage to avoid Devayani's touch. I blushed and was confused. I tried to pull away my hands from his. He must have realised it. Without letting them go, he smiled and said, 'Sister, there is a difference between one touch and another. If my mother was here today and wanted to stop me from going to the Himalayas, would she not have held me back just thus, with the authority of her love?'

Then he let my hands go and called me, 'Sister!'

I kept looking foolishly at him. He had called me sister twice. Kacha calling me sister. I was Kacha's sister. What reason was there to be unhappy?

Kacha added, 'Sister, you have become a mother before being a wife. Mother to the whole demon kingdom! The inner strength which prompted you for this sacrifice, may it ever increase. That is my only blessing to you.'

Every word of his was engraved on my mind!

~

While Kacha had been in Ashokavan, a kind of spiritual intoxication, brought on by his earnest words had overflown in me. But as soon as he left I came down to earth.

I had revived my interest in drawing when at the palace. Even here in the first few days, I sketched every tree, every creeper and everything else I saw. But in a few days, even the variety in Nature ceased to inspire me.

Memories which I had deliberately discarded into the oblivion of the subconscious stealthily crept out and took possession of my conscious mind... . The red *tilak* that I had put on His Majesty's forehead when he was setting out for the battlefield ... his passing touch ... I had also touched Kacha's hands. But what a difference there was! Remembrance of Kacha's touch was a reminder of some beautiful, serene hermitage of a sage in a forest. His Majesty's touch reminded me of an enchanting bower in a lovely garden.

151

It was not as if that touch alone came back to me from the subconscious.

Every night was I reminded of that first night. It made me quite restless. I could not sleep long into the night. Something like the longing with which the river rushes to merge into the sea seared through my blood. And I was like a heady calf. Every part of the body was crying out for love.

One night, I just could not sleep a wink! So, I sat down to draw. I naturally remembered the story of Pururava and Urvashi. I wished to sketch one of the scenes in it. I concentrated on Pururava. The figure that stood before my eyes was that of His Majesty. I found a good model for Pururava. I then thought of Urvashi. All at once, Devayani appeared before my eyes. I was glad that I had found an angel of beauty to represent an angel. But then I visualised Devayani talking disparagingly to His Majesty, like Urvashi herself, 'King, remember one thing. It is not possible to be friendly to women all the time. Because their hearts are like those of wolves!' I imagined Devayani warning His Majesty in a similar tone.

I shrank from making that sketch. But I could not put away from my mind the image of His Majesty as Pururava. In the end I decided to sketch His Majesty alone. I spent some very happy days sketching. At last, the picture was finished. I placed it in a corner and looked at it from a distance. I was by no means a skilled artist, but how lifelike, how much like the original that figure of His Majesty looked.

When I was a child, mother was so proud of my long jet black hair. No matter how busy she was, she took time off to plait it herself in a new pattern everyday.

When making up my hair, mother always used to say, 'Shama, how lucky you are. It is once in a million that girls have such long hair reaching to the knees. They say, such girls suddenly strike good luck.'

How foolish that belief of mother's was!

Hair-do was now a bore and I therefore lived like a mendicant with unkempt hair. Is there a girl who does not like to make herself up in finery and good clothes? But then girls make themselves up not for their own sakes!

In sleep when turning over from one side to another, the hands would naturally touch the hair. That would remind me of a poem I had read when I was sixteen.

The heroine in that poem was awake like me. The hero, however, was fast asleep. Across the window, the moon was shining. In order to ward off the evil eye of the moon from her husband, she wished to cover the window. But her husband could not bear to draw even a thin covering. That day she had worn her hair in an attractive coiffure. Her love had admired it. She quickly undid it. Her ample hair was now loose. She bent over her husband with the hair loose. Naturally, the hair shielded the face from the moon. There was then no danger of the moon casting an evil eye.

After reading that poem, the sixteen-year old Sharmishtha often said to herself, 'I shall also protect him in the same way.' How tickled I used to be at the thought! Now, however, the memory of that poem gnawed at my heart. Where is a lover? Where is my husband and his face?

I tried to recall over and over again everyone of Kacha's words. That would help occupy the day, but the night...

In the lonely solitude of the night, the picture of His Majesty now kept me company. I would sit in front of it, in meditation. With eyes closed, I would listen to the conversation between him and me.

One day I placed a garland round the picture. I felt that His Majesty was annoyed with me and was not speaking to me. To make up I kissed him on the lips — only to realise that it was his picture!

I was ashamed of that kiss. What would Kacha say if he knew about it? Sharmishtha, his sister, his favourite little sister! That she should have no self control. It is difficult but not impossible to close one's mind against all temptation. I had been particular to do so. But

153

from some opening, temptation like moonlight, filtered in stealthily. My kissing the picture was one such stealthy ray of the moon.

I realised how difficult it must be to follow in the footsteps of Kacha, but he is a man. Sharmishtha is a woman. How different are a woman's body and a man's body. Her mind and his! Her life and his.

What a world of difference there is between the two. Man naturally pursues the intangibles, fame, soul, meditation, heroism, God. Such things readily attract him. But not so easily does woman get caught in their lure. To her love, husband, children, service, household and such concrete things are a greater attraction. She will observe a rigorous code of conduct, make a sacrifice but only for something concrete. Unlike man, she is not drawn to the intangible. To worship with her whole being or to bathe in her tears, she needs an entity. Man is a natural worshipper of the abstract, woman prefers things earthly.

I could not make out how this boring life was going to end. Is it possible she hopes that I would get tired of it and commit suicide? I shuddered at the thought.

One dark night, I was toying with the idea. Vaguely, I heard the wheels of a chariot come to a stop on the gravel outside. Who could have come in a chariot to me, a poor maid? Devayani must have sent someone here. How am I concerned? The servants will put up whoever it is in the guest house.

A servant brought an ascetic to me just as I was thinking of all this. It is true that Kacha used to come to these quarters at the back and sit and chat. But he was different! It was not quite right for the servant to bring this sage, whom I did not know, here.

I said to him quite harshly, 'Why did you bring this sage here?'

'I was asked to bring him to you by Her Majesty. She will take him to the palace a little later. She wished you to see him... .'

I looked at the sage. I thought I had seen him somewhere before. The sage was a very imposing figure; he had a presence befitting a king. The *rudrakshamala* round his neck shone like jewels. But on the whole, he gave me the impression of being shy and timid. He had condescended to come so that I could pay my respects. But I did not know how to set about it. If our eyes met, he would look away.

I offered him a seat in the centre of the room. But he would not take it. He said in a hoarse voice, 'We are ascetics! We live in caves. I shall sit in that corner.'

I put the seat in the corner for him. I was puzzled. In that very corner was the picture of His Majesty. I had just placed a garland on it. If the sage saw all this and spoke to Devayani about it, conveying the wrong impression...

I broke into a sweat because he was staring at it. But he did not say a word about the picture. He sat in contemplation for a while and then started talking. How hoarse his voice was. And how weird! But he did look greatly pleased.

When I made my obeisance, he said with a smile, 'You have fallen in love with someone. He is very near you, but you feel all the time that he is very far, that he is unattainable. What are you prepared to do for him whom you love?'

Involuntarily I blurted out, 'I would give even my life!' Unconsciously, I bit my tongue. But what use was it crying over an arrow which had been shot?

A little later he said, 'You still have no confidence in me. Close this door and I will show you how great is the power of my penance!'

He got up, seeing me standing there in bewilderment. He came near and putting his hand on my head said, 'Go and close the door. The golden moment in your life is near. Go.'

That touch of his had in it something to bring me courage, to inspire confidence, to bring peace of mind. I closed the door.

He pointed to the picture of His Majesty and asked, 'Are you in love with Yayati?'

I stood there with my head hung. He again said, 'You still have no confidence in me. We know everything by inner knowledge. Wait. I

155

shall demonstrate it to you. Is there an underground passage leading from this room?'

'No.'

There was a catch in one wall of the room hardly visible. He put his hand to it. A central piece nearly six feet in height moved out, the entrance to an underground passage. But there was none in Ashokavan who knew of it. How did this sage have knowledge of it?

He put his hand to the catch again. The gap closed, restoring the wall.

'I know that you are in love with Yayati. True love is always blessed by us. Sometime Yayati will come to you... remember. He will come through that underground passage. He will call to you. He will call to you in the affectionate singular your parents did.'

'Shama.'

'Yes, he will call you "Shama". Do not be frightened or scared. Press this catch to open the door. Make sure that only maids in your confidence sleep outside the room.'

I could hardly believe my ears. I gazed steadily at the sage. He immediately looked away. He got up to open the door of the room. I thought I recognised the step. I was reminded of the drama portraying Pururava and Urvashi. Might not Devayani have deputed him to make fun of me and to ensnare me?

Then he opened the door of the room. In no time, all the servants had gathered in my room to see the sage. The ascetic was giving all of them his hearty blessings! Devayani's chariot also came up.

She called out to me as in our childhood, 'Well sister Shama, what is the sage like?'

It was many years ago that Devayani had called me 'Sister Shama.' I said, 'He is very nice, I will serve him all my life if Your Majesty agrees!'

Devayani just laughed. The laughter was drowned in the crack of the charioteer's whip!

All through the night — not only that night but every night thereafter, I spent in the shadow of expectation, fear, curiosity and anxiety.

But I was always particular about sleeping alone with the door closed and two dependable maids, from those who had come with me, outside. I would keep awake till midnight to see if anyone called. Man lives in hope, however unfounded it may be.

I was disturbed when I heard that Devayani was leaving to see her father in three or four days.

The day she left was very sad for me. I was very restless thinking of father and mother. I felt better when night came. The restlessness had given place to expectation. I lay down on the bed, looking at His Majesty's picture in the corner. I did not know when I dozed off. I was half awakened by the words, 'Shama! Shama!' For a moment I thought I was dreaming. I was wide awake now. The voice came from across the wall. My legs were shaky. Somehow I got to the wall and pressed the catch; the opening was revealed. On the step below His Majesty was standing. I could not believe my eyes. My joy knew no bounds. I felt faint. His Majesty came forward and supported me as I was falling. The next instant his arms were round me.

In a moment, the river had merged into the sea.

I opened my eyes. Where was I? In the seventh heaven? On a bed of white flowers, brought in on the waves of the river Mandakini? On the swing of a gentle breeze, wafted in cool and fragrant from the Malayagiri mountain?

I did not know. Realisation came only after a long, long time. The mischievous moon was peeping at me through the window and laughing in her sleeve. I blushed. His Majesty lifted my chin up and said, 'How would it be if at the time of the wedding the bride blushed on seeing the priestess?'

I said, 'Renowned poets have in the past imagined the moon in different forms, but I am not aware of her having been made a priestess yet !'

His Majesty said, 'For ages now, love marriages like yours and mine have been celebrated with her alone as witness. She is truly the priestess of lovers!'

I gazed at the moon with my head on His Majesty's shoulder. The moonlight seeped through every part of my body. No, it was not moonlight. It was the fragrance of the dreams of requited love, experienced by the sleeping world. I was soon absorbed in that fragrance. I was just a woman in love.

Many nights after that first one — the innumerable hours of those many nights — the countless moments in the many hours were each one of them a fountain of pleasure.

That pleasure, that joy, that eternal happiness defies description. A woman does not split hair over a word. She is concerned only with the feeling that lies behind it. Mother Parvati underwent arduous penance in sun and rain, to demonstrate to womanhood the path of love. Following in her footsteps...

Yes, I truly followed in her footsteps. I loved King Yayati. Knowing that he was the husband of Devayani, I nonetheless loved him. No one except my two trusted maids outside were aware of my love. It was a very sweet secret. It was the secret of the night, eternal friend of lovers. It was a secret known only to the four walls of my room. It was the secret of the underground passage which spent its lonely days in eternal darkness.

Even before I had recovered from the intoxication of the happiness of the previous night, the intoxicating prospect of the next night was upon me. But even in that trance, somebody was trying to shake me awake. A sharp voice said, 'Sharmishtha, awake; even now take heed! Where are you going? What are you doing? It is a terrible sin.'

As His Majesty's touch thrilled my body, so did the thought of the sin make me shiver with fright. I kept repeating to myself love is a sacrifice, sacrifice of one's all. How can there be sin in it?

158

I tried to console myself, oppressed with the thought of sin thus. But sometimes, the prick of the conscience remained. Then I would fold my hands before the image of mother Parvati and pray to her, 'Mother, give me the strength to love His Majesty as you loved Lord Shiva. She alone is a true lover who can sacrifice anything for her love. I shall never forget it myself and, I hope, I shall not then be considered a sinner!'

Sometimes the prick of conscience caused me uneasiness. But when its thorns did not prick, I was on the peak of happiness. Not unlike the butterfly with its tiny wings, flitting from flower to flower I spent the day from morning till night. The day sped away in planning for His Majesty's entertainment. How quickly followed the night. She appeared like the dancing girl hastening to the appointed place of tryst. But as the night progressed my impatience mounted. I was distressed at the thought that something might crop up to prevent His Majesty's coming.

I had read many love lyrics. I had myself composed some in utter ignorance of the true nature of love. But the joy of reading and composing them was but a faint shadow of the genuine experience. Like the child imagining the image of the moon in a mirror to be the moon itself and playing with it. It was the play of imagination of the sweet adolescent.

True love? What is it? To understand it one must be a true lover. One must fathom the lover's mind. The soothing moon and the glaring sun, life-giving nectar and life-taking deadly poison are mingled — no — it is impossible to describe the nature of love.

One day His Majesty was in conference with the Prime Minister till midnight. So he could not come early. It was past midnight. I was frantic. Sharmishtha has a place in the heart of His Majesty but she cannot go near him! Fate had given me love; but how miserly it had been.

That night I could not rest. I pressed the catch in the wall and bravely descended the steps. But I could not move a step further. I was not afraid of the dark, I was afraid of something quite different. If I step into His Majesty's room at the end of the passage would not our secret love be exposed? Fate, at one moment in one's favour, may turn against one the next moment. I would go to His Majesty's room by this secret passage only to find that Devayani had just returned. What would happen if Devayani came to know? I could not bear the thought. No, never must she know this secret.

Quietly I returned from the passage. God had denied me the right to love openly. That Sharmishtha, a princess, should be denied the right enjoyed by the meanest maid in Hastinapur!

When His Majesty came, my pillow was wet with tears.

That night I was still awake when he fell asleep. I was blissfully happy in his arms but only for a while. Then all haunting fears came back. Sheltered by love I thought of death. I wished that there might be an earthquake, to engulf Ashokavan and everything else there, while we were in each other's arms! Centuries later, some archaeologist would dig it all out. But nobody will comprehend that it was the one golden moment snatched by an unfortunate beloved, who dared not be with her lover openly, from the hands of cruel fate without its knowledge.

The next moment I was angry with the thought! How helpless I was. How selfish! Thinking of my own pleasure, His Majesty...

I shuddered at the idea. Even in his sleep he must have felt me shudder. Drawing me even closer, he murmured, 'You timid!' Half asleep he pressed his lips to mine. As darkness vanishes with the rising of the moon, my fears were dissolved in love. They all came back in even more frightening forms with the next morning's sun. On getting up I felt sick. My two trusted maids were knowledgeable. They looked significantly at each other, while holding my head. Without being told, I also knew. I was going to be a mother. Joy, fear, shame, anxiety, expectation and curiosity were all there strangely mixed up.

Every mother is pleased to know that her newly married daughter is expecting a baby. My mother also would have been overjoyed to know of my secret.

160

Sharmishtha who as an innocent maiden dreamt of being a queen had to be a maid. Nature is not cruel like man; so even as a maid she was going to be a mother. But even this kindly blessing of Nature now looked like a cruel curse.

I was both glad and confused. I was afraid. If Devayani gets to hear of my secret what will she do? What will my parents say when they hear of it? Will they hate me as a fallen woman? How could I explain to them that I had not sinned?

My two maids were also baffled. Devayani had not yet returned from her visit to Maharishi Shukra. But when she did...

I was dazed. I suddenly thought of Kacha. He should have been here now. He would have given me courage. If he thought his sister had sinned, he would have staked all his penance to wash that sin off her. But in this word I was alone — all alone and helpless.

No, I was not helpless. How can a beloved of the King of Hastinapur be helpless? How can the favourite wife of King Yayati be helpless? I laughed at my own timidity...

I resolved every morning to tell His Majesty the secret. Every night the resolve would make me tongue-tied. I just could not bring myself to speak.

Eventually one day I plucked courage and said, 'I ... I ... I am soon ... going to be a mother.'

I could not complete the sentence. Like a child tired from playing, rushing to her mother's side, I buried my head in His Majesty's shoulder.

He lifted my chin and gazing at me said, 'How beautiful you look, Shama! The ruffled hair; there is greater beauty in it and it is more inviting than the made up. That beauty should be at its best in being natural... .'

I wished to be reassured not flattered. Disappointed I said, 'I shall not remain thus pretty all my life!'

'Why not?'

'I shall soon be a mother. Then... .'

His Majesty's amorous playfulness vanished. His face was clouded with care. He again drew me close. But the embrace was not that of an impatient love. It was more like that of a frightened child.

I could not understand his silence and the uncertain anxiety evident in his touch. In the end, the cause of his fear was apparent from his broken words. As in the case of his father, the fear of Maharishi Shukra pronouncing a curse on His Majesty.

I knew well both Devayani — jealous and vengeful — and Maharishi Shukra, short tempered and impetuous! His Majesty's fear was not unfounded.

If His Majesty should be prey to Maharishi Shukra's anger Sharmishtha would have to hang her head in shame all her life. In future all maidens in love will laugh at her and say that she had sacrificed her beloved to preserve her own good name and happiness.

True love is selfless. My haunting doubt of sin had been stilled by the thought that I was following in the footsteps of mother Parvati. Even now I was resolved to follow her, I would bear myself so Devayani will never suspect His Majesty! I would face the situation alone.

Mother Parvati's path — I reminded myself over and over again — led as far as the sacrificial fire. Remember, I told myself that it was only by jumping into her father's sacrificial fire that she became a goddess.

Two or three days later, Devayani returned. I realised that His Majesty must be sticking to his room all night so as not to rouse suspicion. But having been denied the happiness of his sight and touch, my mind felt starved and sleep would intervene at intervals.

Night after night passed in lonely helplessness. Like the eyes, my lips too were thirsty. One day I could not contain myself. I got up and showered innumerable kisses on His Majesty's picture. They say love is foolish. Time raced by like an agile, frisky horse. Devayani was in her ninth month. So, she did not come the way of Ashokavan. Once she purposely sent for me. I went to the palace. I was relieved that she had no inkling of my condition.

That same day, my grief at the separation from His Majesty got over.

I was standing at the window of the room, admiring the beautiful evening. Suddenly, I saw the tiny crescent of the moon smiling from the sky, behind a tall tree. I was happy at the thought that I also had a tiny crescent inside me — invisible today but a very heartening crescent. I would fondly talk to the little one. While His Majesty used to be with me occasionally and only for a short while at night, the tiny life was with me all the time. I could forget all my sorrow absorbed in it. The pain of separation from His Majesty, of the body hankering for his touch; the pointed arrowheads of all this pain were blunted in the company of that tiny life.

Is it possible that the presence of God is revealed to ascetics like Kacha in just this manner? If otherwise, would their minds be ever calm and cheerful?

What a great happiness is motherhood! No matter how beautiful the leaves, the creeper is incomplete in its beauty without flowers! A head of leaf is the glory of the creeper. But the flower creates a new world. There is nothing in the whole world to compare with the joy of creation. Was it for nothing that Maharishi Shukra was so proud of his achievement of Sanjeevani?

I was very happy talking to the tiny life in our privacy. I would ask him: 'Would you like me for a mother? Your mother is a maid but she became one for her country. Will you make your mother happy? Your father is the King of Hastinapur! Even so, he cannot keep me happy. Now you are my only hope. My little prince, my baby moon, there is nothing in this world except you that is mine.'

I spoke to him endlessly like this. Occasionally, I thought he responded. That must have been my imagination. But talking to him dispelled my gloom and misery. As the sky clears after a shower, my mind would clear up. I started craving for things. If I had been with my mother she would have fondly granted every wish of mine, and elaborately too! But...

163

Also, my hankering was rather unusual. I would want to wander in the forest, hunt the wild beasts there, climb the taller trees at night, and gather all the blue flowers on the creeper at the top of the trees for a braid for my hair. If I met a lion, I wanted to open his mouth, holding him by his mane and count his teeth.

Devayani had a boy. I was present at the naming ceremony. My body looked different now.

I somehow consoled myself that Devayani would be so happily engrossed in the ceremony that she would have no time to notice me. I tried to keep out of her sight. But she called me near to see her Yadu. She stared at me and said, 'Ashokavan seems to have rather agreed with you, Sharmishtha! Are you not rather lonely there?'

'I was in the beginning. But two maids who looked after me in childhood are now with me. We spend lots of time talking and reminiscing about childhood.'

'I see! Who else visits you there?'

'Who can come? Occasionally sages come there and time flies waiting on them.'

When I got away from her, I felt relieved, as if I had escaped from the cave of a tigress.

I talked to acquaintances among the maids. Devayani's old maid followed me and I was frightened. I decided to return to Ashokavan, without delaying anymore, when Devayani herself sent for me. Trembling I went to her room. She dismissed the other maids, closed the door and asked me harshly, 'Are you expecting? This illicit affair... .'

'I am not a wanton. By the grace of a great sage... .'

I spent that whole night tossing in bed. I had not sinned in my love. Why did I not summarily say to her, 'Please do not involve Kacha for nothing. He has nothing to do with this.'

What else was open to me except to beg in silence for forgiveness of Kacha? His affectionate figure stood before my eyes. I knelt before

164

it, folded my hands and said, 'Dear brother, forgive this helpless sister of yours.'

~

I was almost dying with labour pains. I was baffled by this strange pairing of life and death. I would close my eyes when the pain became unbearable, but I doubted if I would ever open them again. I thought I would never see this beautiful but cruel world again. Will it be a boy? God, if I am destined to die, let me see my child first — let me at least cuddle it in my arms.

I felt everything turn pitch dark and I do not remember what happened. When I opened my eyes again, I felt as if I had woken up from eternal sleep. My two maids were whispering something in my ear. In no time, those words were like the strains of music pervading the earth. I listened — listened with my heart in my ears. The maids said, 'It is a boy. A boy... a boy... fair skinned chubby little boy.'

There were only three of us present at the naming ceremony — my maids and myself.

My boy was the son of a king. But he had been born to hapless Sharmishtha. Who was going to celebrate the naming ceremony? I wished to name him Pururava after His Majesty's great grandfather — a renowned warrior. But I was afraid that undesirable suspicion would arise. I named him Puroo. The ceremony was held in the garden outside the apartment, with my hands for a cradle, the moon above for the toys hung on the cradle and the trees and creepers around for garlands.

Puroo brought unending happiness into my life. He had at birth a lovely head full of hair. If Puroo was hungry and tugging at my sari for my breasts, it was the height of heavenly bliss. Sometimes he would blow the milk away with '*Phuh*.' The drops would fall on his cheek. I would then kiss those cheeks to his exasperation. His eyes gazing at me steadily were like two little stars. His lips breaking into a gentle smile at seeing me contained all the splendour of spring.

Puroo grew day by day. In due course of time he could turn over, crawl, sit up and soon he made friends with the birds, flowers and the moonlight.

Puroo's first birthday was at hand. Devayani had left with her son to see her father. That day, I was impatient like a new bride. In the evening, Puroo played about with my carefully and eagerly done up hair and ruined the coiffure. For the first time, I was angry with him. When he persisted, I even got rough with him. The next moment, I relented and bathed him with tears. How pleasurable such tears are!

It was well past midnight but the door of the passage had not opened.

It was more than an hour later the secret door creaked and slowly moved open. My heart was in my mouth. The next moment like lightning in the clouds, I was in the arms of His Majesty.

We had come together after a long parting — how the union overflowed with joy. We had lots to talk about. But try as we would, the words would not come and yet we did talk a lot, not with our eyes, with touch and tears.

His Majesty sat for a long time gazing at Puroo sleeping. Then he took both my hands in his and said, 'Shama, you must forgive me. Today, I can do nothing for our dear Puroo. But tomorrow... .' I stopped him.

Devayani had arranged to spy on me. So I was content with seeing him once or twice a week.

One night Puroo was awake when he came. He had learnt to pick flowers in the garden. In a little while the sky was glowing with stars. Puroo was fascinated with their splendour. He must have imagined, he could pick the stars as well. He beckoned to the maid to lift him higher and higher. Puroo insisted on picking them. He cried till his eyes were red and swollen. When feeding him, I called all his friends the sparrow, the crow, the cat and so on. But he would not eat. I was patting him in my arms till after midnight but he had obstinately kept awake.

That was the only time His Majesty saw him awake. He stretched out his arms to pick Puroo up. He turned his back on His Majesty. His Majesty looked admiringly at the back of that slight figure on my shoulder.

Puroo wanted to show me something and took my face in his hands. In the corner was the picture of His Majesty drawn by me. He was all the time pointing to it and to His Majesty.

His Majesty kissed him very lovingly with the words, 'You rogue!' I kissed Puroo on the spot where His Majesty had done. And a thrill went through me! That one kiss bathed me both in love and affection.

Devayani's return put an end to all my happiness. By now Puroo had broken into monosyllabic speech, I started sitting before the picture of His Majesty with Puroo every evening. I would make him fold his hands to it and say 'da, da'! I often wished that he should quickly learn to say 'da, da,' that sometime when His Majesty was here he should so call him. Then I wondered if it was good for man to fly thus on the wings of imagination.

I was so engrossed in bringing up Puroo that I had no time to brood.

Once one of my maids started talking about my own doings in childhood. I could not help comparing my carefree childhood with my present slavery.

One after another, the old wounds opened and bled.

When I was thus restless I would think of Kacha and his heartening words. If that was not enough to bring me calm, I would have a bath and wear the red sari which had come to me, after I had worn it by mistake on the day of the spring festivities — that beautiful piece of silk — the soft red sari.

I did the same one morning. Unexpectedly, Devayani sent for me the same evening. The message was urgent and she asked me to bring my boy with me. I was baffled and did not even remember to change my clothes.

Had Devayani got scent of our secret love?

I was in a flutter when I got there. Devayani saw my red sari. I was glad she did not raise her brows. She had purposely sent for Puroo! The old palmist had returned to the capital.

This time Devayani had thought of a way to test his knowledge. She gave Yadu and Puroo similar clothes as if they were real brothers. She gave them a heap of toys and the children were playing in her room. While the children were engrossed in their toys, the palmist was sent for. He looked at their right hands, carefully over and over again. He looked at their left hands also. In the end, turning to Yadu, he said, 'This boy is unlucky!'

He lingered long over Puroo's hand and said, 'This boy will be a great king.'

To ridicule the palmist, she said, 'You see they are brothers. They are both princes. How can their lives be so vastly different?'

The palmist calmly replied, 'Your Majesty, Fate is a mysterious power!'

Just then His Majesty came in. Seeing His Majesty, Puroo started saying 'da, da' and was straining to go to him. Fortunately nobody understood the monosyllable of Puroo's!

When the palmist was gone, without saying a word to His Majesty, Devayani said, 'I have something for you. Let us go to His Majesty's room and talk in peace.'

Devayani herself closed the door when we got there. I was rattled. Sitting on the sofa, she asked me in a harsh tone, 'Sharmishtha, I hope you haven't forgotten that you are my maid!'

'I have not.'

'I am the queen. If you defy me, you will have to bear whatever punishment I give you. I am going to hold court tomorrow. There, I am going to charge you with having an illicit liaison. There you will have to establish your innocence and purity.'

I was terrified and my insides turned. I resolved not to listen to another word of Devayani and leave, come what may. I ran to the door clutching Puroo at my breast.

'Where are you going?' These words of Devayani had me rooted to the spot. They had the uncanny power of an unscrupulous hypnotist.

I wanted to shout to His Majesty, that the secret which we had kept with such great difficulty would be exposed. I swallowed my pain and fear and stood still like a stone pillar.

Devayani beckoned to me to follow her. I followed her. She went to the east wall of the room. There must have been a secret door in it, as in Ashokavan! Devayani pressed a catch and a door opened. She ordered me to precede her in.

Like one spellbound, I descended the steps to the cellar. She herself came down slowly.

I did not know where she was taking me along the underground passage and what she had in mind for me. But it was not far to go. At the end of the passage was a cellar.

Devayani turned to me and asked me to go in. She added, 'There is privacy in this cellar. You must make up your mind tonight whether you are going to divulge the name of your lover or not. Otherwise, there will be a proclamation in the town and a court in the evening at which your illicit liaison will be enquired into, and... .'

She paused and smiled. Her smile was full of the essence of deadly poison. 'But don't forget one thing. There is very little time now. Tell me the truth, tell me how your son came to have the markings of a future king on his palm?'

I calmly replied, 'By the blessing of the sage.'

'Then perhaps by another blessing of the self-same sage you will be able to disappear from this cellar!'

I retorted, 'Why not? What is so improbable about it?'

169

I said what I liked, firmly determined not to yield to Devayani, come what may. But all my strength ebbed when she locked the door of the cellar.

I felt as if I had been in that cellar for ages. Puroo was frightened of the darkness and was crying. I covered him with my sari. Knowing that he was near his mother, the poor mite fell asleep in my lap, comforted.

Every minute was gnawing at me. Slowly, the darkness in the cellar lightened a little.

Suddenly a bright light flashed across the room. It must be the lightning outside. The flash through the window. The flash brought me courage. I was reminded of Kacha. In this encounter with death, I had his red sari on me, to remind me of him. I thought I was lucky. I calmed down. I lay down with Puroo by my side. Gradually I fell asleep.

I woke up at the creaking of the door. Somebody had opened the door of the cellar. I was torn between hope and fear. Could it be someone come to release me or... ?

Might it not be Devayani bringing me a cup of poison?

There was another big flash. In that light, I saw it was His Majesty.

We quickly came up to the room. His Majesty pressed a catch somewhere in the south wall. He went ahead and I followed. In all this bustle, Puroo had woken up. He was calling 'da, da' to His Majesty. I put my hand on his mouth to stop him.

In silence and swiftly we walked through the underground passage to Ashokavan. His Majesty opened the door leading into the room. He said, 'Do not stop here a moment longer. Don't mention this even to your maids. Get onto the chariot which is waiting outside. Madhav, my friend, will drive you in it. Go quickly. Hereafter I do not know where and how we will meet. But go quickly.'

170

Tears came to his eyes while talking. He kissed me with wet eyes. A few tears dropped on my cheek. He patted Puroo's head and quickly shut the door of the passage.

My maids were scared. They had been looking for me. Without saying a word, I went to the chariot waiting outside. Immediately the chariot was on its way.

Before we were out of the town it was pouring. Soon, the earth put on a grim appearance. The chariot was still on the move. In the end, it stopped near an old dilapidated temple.

Madhav, sitting next to the charioteer and dripping wet, was calling me, 'Your Majesty.'

I was thrilled by that word. Madhav said, 'Your Majesty may get down here!'

'Is that the order of His Majesty?'

'Yes. I am taking the chariot straight back to the capital so that there maybe no suspicion anywhere of anything. Your Majesty should on no account return to the capital; there is danger in it.'

I got down with Puroo. The queen was being anointed by rain. Lightning was waving tufts of peacock hair before the future sovereign.

I asked Madhav, 'Will you take a message to His Majesty?'

'What?'

'Sharmishtha will always worship His Majesty with all her heart. Even in face of death, she will always bow to his command and wherever Puroo maybe, the blessing of His Majesty should always be with him. By the blessings of His Majesty... .'

I could not speak anymore. I drew Puroo, who was dripping wet, closer to me and said, 'Come, my little prince, come. Rain which brings new life to earth is your attendant. Lightning which lights up the sky serves for a light in your mother's hand. Come, you must be cooler than rain and more luminous than lightning.'

YAYATI

D evayani's first dance was over. Before it died down, there was a thunderclap. Even on our way from the palace to the dance hall, the sky had been overcast with dark clouds. I said to her, 'Why didn't you detain Sharmishtha for your dance?' She smiled saying, 'I did press her to stay, but she was not well. So she returned to Ashokavan in the evening.'

But my suspicions were not quelled. I could see a demon-like gleam in her eyes.

I whispered into Madhav's ears. He rushed to Ashokavan with the chariot and made enquiries from Sharmishtha's trusted maids. She had not yet returned. I was convinced that Devayani was planning something diabolical and would do away with Sharmishtha by treachery. Suddenly, the thought of the cellar where Alaka had been poisoned occurred to me. Every queen must, by tradition, be told about that cellar. How to set Sharmishtha free?

Devayani's spring dance was beginning. Some of the great artistes present there had performed in the demon kingdom. King Vrishaparva himself had said: 'If Devayani were here, none of your troupe would have dared to take the floor!' Naturally, all were very keen to see her dance. At first she avoided it, but in the end her pride was aroused. It was now clear that Devayani would be in the dance hall till late into the night.

How beautiful, how delicate and how innocent Devayani looked, performing her spring dance.

Devayani gave an excellent exposition of a creeper bursting into leaf with the first whiff of spring, then blossoming into flower, and in the end, intoxicated by her own flowers, dancing to the tune of the spring breeze. In the end, the creeper twines round a tree nearby, rests her head on its shoulder and falls asleep in the bliss of love. How delicately she had delineated this last episode.

Devayani was immersed in depicting the many hues of the sentiment of love through her spring dance. She was a woman in love. But I had never experienced this sweet side of her. I had rarely experienced in her embraces the intensity of Sharmishtha. Even in her kisses, I felt as if she was hiding something.

As an artist, she made a perfect lover, but she could never assume that role as a wife. Why should that be?

After the spring dance, she was going to do a piece from the life of Uma. In it, beginning with Sati* in Daksha sacrifice, to Parvati posing as a tribal and wooing Lord Shiva who had gone away in a fit of temper, there were many scenes. She was going to depict all the situations in her dance.

I went in and told Devayani how exquisite her spring dance was. She smiled like an innocent maiden. At that time she was living in the world of art, a dedicated artist.

I stole out of the dance hall. Madhav was waiting with the chariot. He left me at the palace and went straight to Ashokavan. I bribed Devayani's old maid and she talked. Sharmishtha was in the cellar. And not alone. Puroo also. I shuddered.

There was no time to think. Every passing moment skirted the border between life and death. I hastened to take Sharmishtha out of the cellar and to Ashokavan. My heart broke when bidding farewell to Sharmishtha from top of the stairs.

And that little infant. My son, what was your sin in the previous birth that as the scion of a king your lot should be that of an orphan born to a criminal? Only earlier this evening the palmist had said

* Wife of Shiva. Unable to bear her husband being insulted by her father, Daksha, she killed herself at the great sacrifice held by her father.

that the lines in your hand pointed to your being a king. And barely two hours later, you have to leave town like the child of a roving beggar!

I yearned to pick Puroo up once. But then parting would have been even more difficult. I steeled my heart and bid farewell to Sharmishtha, not with words but with my lips, eyes and tears.

On my way back to the dance hall, I selected a lovely gem encrusted necklace from my bedroom.

To give Devayani some rest, minor recitals had been interposed. Later, Devayani performed another dance. The spring dance had embodied budding love. Intense love had now to be shown which, Devayani did to perfection. I was troubled again with the same question. Where does all this intensity disappear in privacy with me? Like a live stream freezing, why does she turn cold in my arms?

Although the audience were carried away by the dance, I was unable to enjoy it. I was anxious for Madhav's return. Why had he not come back? Had he perhaps been stopped on the way by somebody? No, that was not possible. He had the royal signet with him. Then why should he be so late?

A servant quietly brought back the royal signet and gave it to me. It was clear that Madhav had left Sharmishtha near the old temple far out of town. I was calm.

The monsoon dance was over. There was a thunder of applause. Devayani bowed with pride. I got up, put the necklace round her neck and said to the audience, 'This is not a husband's tribute to his wife; this little trinket is a token of appreciation to a unique artist on behalf of all of us.'

The dance hall echoed for a long time with applause and shouts of joy.

Devayani got up very late the next day. She got ready and came to my room. Standing at the window she said, 'What a lovely morning.

174

Come and see. I was very happy last night when you put the necklace on my neck.' She added, 'But I was not satisfied with the necklace.'

'You can command any jewel you wish from the treasure of Kuber.'

'I do not want that sort of a thing at all.' She again gazed at the flowers in the garden and said, 'Men do not understand women.'

She threw an enchanting smile and said, 'There is one thing I would like! There are many lovely flowers in the garden. Your Majesty should gather them yourself. Masses of them. I will make a braid and a garland from them. Your Majesty, then shall I put the braid in my hair and I shall garland you. It is a childish wish, perhaps.'

I knew why she was sending me away. When I returned to the room, Devayani was not there. She had sent for the old maid and was closeted with her.

Later Devayani came to me. She looked downcast and bitingly asked me, 'Did Your Majesty visit the palace during the dance last night?'

'Yes, I thought of the bejewelled necklace after seeing your spring dance.'

'Do you know that Sharmishtha has disappeared?'

The tables had been turned on Devayani. But I was to realise later in the day how transitory the joy of getting the better of her was.

The sun set and night was on its way. It was not stormy like yesterday. Night had given up the role of a raging fury and was entering her palace in the sky, like a coy maiden blushing with love. On her way, she was lighting starry lamps one by one.

Last night, I had felt happy in the belief that I had done something great in freeing Sharmishtha. That feeling was gone. The memory of the same night was troubling me over and over again with the question: 'Where is the Sharmishtha in whose arms you found bliss? You cruel man, lying on a feather bed, have a thought for her. Open your eyes and see. That unfortunate one is sleeping on the floor, in a barren uninhabited place, with a stone as hard as your heart for a pillow. Her pillow is bathed in tears. You, her lover, who held her in an embrace, asking her if she was his, did not melt when deserting her in a storm. Her delicate lips and tender cheeks, which you kissed thousands of times with burning passion, are now exposed to the biting cold wind. Look, look carefully. How she is struggling to keep Puroo warm. And you? You are lying in your warm bed. Is this what your love of Sharmishtha amounts to? Is this your affection for Puroo? In your place, Kacha would have taken her to the Himalayas himself.

'If Kacha was in your place?'

The reference to Kacha set me thinking of him. I was going to shoot at that beautiful bird. But Kacha stopped me.

My Puroo. He also is a tiny and beautiful innocent bird but last night I...

That little girl in the hermitage. She was going to pluck a half open bud to give it to him. But Kacha stopped her.

My Shama. She was also just such a fragrant, half open bud. And last night, I...

I was very restless. I drank some wine hoping to feel better. I did feel a little better. After sometime I calmed down and fell asleep.

But I had a horrible dream, making me feel that it would have been better if I had not fallen asleep:

In my dream there was nothing to see. It was just two voices. The first was mine. I knew that, but the second I did not know whose it was till the end. For a moment I thought it was Kacha's. It was very harsh.

The latter was asking the first, 'Did you love Sharmishtha? Did you really love her?'

The first said boastfully, 'There is no doubt. If I were not in love with her, I would not have ventured to free her from the cellar last night.'

176

'If you had followed her into the jungle, there would have been some sense in what you say. Love is a state of mind in which you are willing to lay your life down for your love. Get up, even now it is not too late. Leave the palace. Go and find Sharmishtha, bring her back. Make her stand in front of Devayani and tell Devayani. "She has given me the love which every heart yearns for. She will remain here as my favourite queen."

'With a storm raging in pouring rain, without the slightest care for the dark future, Sharmishtha had the courage which ... You profligate. Selfish coward.'

They were not simple words. They were like hammer blows. I could not bear their impact. I sat up with a start.

If Devayani notices in the morning that I have been drinking? As it is, she is annoyed. It would add fuel to the fire. With difficulty, I controlled myself.

Devayani came in the morning with bad news. Madhav had suddenly been taken ill last night. He had a high fever now.

'Don't you know how your friend got ill?'

'No, I don't. He was with me the day before at your dance. He went away in the interval. I myself went looking for him, but could not find him.'

'How could Your Majesty see him? They say he returned very late dripping wet.'

I arranged for the royal physician to see Madhav at once. Within the hour, I also went to see him. But I felt very depressed on the way. Is life just a circle of happiness and misery?

We stopped. There was a girl standing in the doorway. It was Taraka. How she had grown! She was no longer a mute bud. She looked like a bud blossoming into youth.

177

She blushed on seeing me and looked down. No more in the abandon of childhood, she was now on the threshold of youth. A moment later, she looked up. Her attractive eyes were like stars — pale blue like Venus — so near each other.

She quickly turned away and went in. Madhav was tossing about in his fever. The physician was sitting by him, feeling his pulse. He looked despairingly at me. I was taken aback.

A young woman came in with some medicine. I could not see her face. With the help of the physician, she gave him the medicine. I saw her from the rear, bending and sitting down. I thought I knew her, but there was no young woman in Madhav's house. Madhav's mother was old and Taraka's mother had died sometime ago.

Madhav was delirious. She changed the cold compress on his forehead and turned to go into the house, when I saw her clearly. She was Mukulika.

Mukulika! Mother had driven her out of the town. But what had come to pass was not her fault alone.

With solicitude, I asked her, 'How are you Mukulika? All is well with you, I hope.'

She came forward and bowing to me, said, 'By your grace, Your Majesty, I am well.'

I remembered that night of father's impending death. Mukulika showed me the oasis. When our lips met, my fear of death just vanished. I was ashamed of myself, reminiscing of a love affair by a sick bed. Mukulika enquired after me and the prince which reminded me of Puroo.

Where will Puroo be now? What may Sharmishtha be doing? Sharmishtha, who as a child used pearls for sacred rice at her doll's wedding, would now be begging at somebody's door to feed the offspring of her flesh and love.

Noticing my silence, Mukulika got worried. She asked softly, 'Have I said anything wrong?'

In an effort to hide my distress I said, 'No, no, you are not in the wrong, I am. I have seen you after such a long time. I saw you tending a very dear friend. Even then, I did not enquire about you except formally. Tell me, how did you come here?'

She said, 'I am in the service of a great sage. He was passing through here during his pilgrimage.'

She added, 'In less than two hours after contracting a temperature Madhav was in a delirium. His mother lost her nerve. She beseeched the sage and he gave her sanctified ashes to put on Madhav's head. Knowing that there was no one else in the house except Taraka he sent me here.'

'I must see your sage sometime. If his dissertations bring peace of mind, I am greatly in need of it.'

Mukulika did not reply. She just smiled.

In bidding farewell I said, 'Mukulika, Madhav is my second soul. Such a friend is not to be found anywhere in the world. Look after him as well as you can. I shall not forget your obligation.'

That night also I was unable to sleep. First I kept thinking of Mukulika. What a great difference there was between the Mukulika of Ashokavan and the person she was now. That infatuated Mukulika and this one dedicated to service. I must see the sage for whom she is working. Who knows? He maybe omniscient. If I can find out from him about Sharmishtha and Puroo... .

I wondered where could Sharmishtha be? What could Puroo be doing? Would she return to her parents? Where would she go? Or would she, in her disappointment, hurl herself down a precipice clutching Puroo to her breast?

I began to see before my eyes the mangled bodies of Sharmishtha and Puroo. The kites were tearing at them. I closed my eyes to keep out the ghastly scene and yet I saw it. From the mangled bodies seemed to arise flames of fire, dancing weirdly as much as to say,

'Where is that treacherous lover? Where is that passionate sex-ridden husband? Where is that irresponsible father? Where is that irresponsible drunkard?'

That picture of flames oppressed me all day and even at night. I did not get to sleep till midnight. In the end I took a little more wine than yesterday. I wanted to take even more but I controlled myself with great difficulty.

But restrained in one direction thus, the mind ran amuck in another. I spent all that night thus tormented. I desired to go to Devayani but dared not.

I went to Madhav everyday to enquire after him and returned depressed and dejected.

The royal physician did his best. Madhav's mother kept a sharp vigil to keep off death hovering round the corner like a snake poised to bite. Mukulika was ever in attendance on him without a moment's rest. Poor innocent Taraka was sitting at his feet, comforting him and staring at everybody around, like a frightened deer.

On the fifth day, it looked as if Madhav was regaining consciousness. He was groaning. There was a shade of satisfaction in the royal physician's face. Mukulika was happy and I was heartened. I sat near him at his head. He muttered groaning, 'Your Majesty, those are the King's orders.'

That day for the first time, he had spoken a whole sentence. But that seared through my heart like a saw. I knew Madhav's gentle nature. As he was physically unable to weather the storm, he was also unable to bear my abandoning Sharmishtha.

And I felt nothing in giving up that guileless emblem of love, Sharmishtha, who found bliss in laying her head on my shoulder, who had boundless faith that in my arms even death could be defied.

That night I was reminded again of the two voices. They were scrapping loudly. I woke up with a start and picked up the jar of wine near my bed. It was not a jar. It was the sea. The fire in my heart could only be drowned in that sea.

A week had passed and yet there was no sign of Madhav recovering. But no one had any inkling, not even the royal physician, that he would pass away the next day.

That day, he perspired profusely. There was now hope that the fever would come down. He regained consciousness and asked, 'Shall I recover?'

The physician said, 'It will take time but you will definitely get well.' Madhav asked 'Where is she?' I realised that he was referring to Sharmishtha, but his mother thought he wanted to see his betrothed and sent for Madhavi.

'Your Majesty, I do not want to die yet. Who will look after Taraka if I do? If I die now it would mean that I have betrayed Madhavi and her love. Your Majesty, shall I live? Promise me that you will save me at any cost.'

What he said was not irrelevant. But I thought he was in delirium. For his consolation I gave him my word, 'I shall save you at any cost.' That moment the physician looked at me with queer dejection. He took out some medicine from his bag and asked Mukulika to give them to Madhav.

Madhav, uttering broken words in his delirium, was now talking fluently to Madhavi, 'Have we not agreed that if our first child is a girl, I shall have the privilege of choosing the name and if a boy you will name him. Do you agree? Make up your mind. Otherwise you will quarrel later.'

What could the poor thing say? The music of that ethereal dream of privacy sounded like a terrible nightmare in the face of death.

Mukulika brought the medicine. But he refused to take it. The physician beckoned to Madhavi to give it to him. She took it to his mouth. He clasped her hand tightly and said, 'We are married, are we not?' He talked in that strain for two or three hours and suddenly stopped. He was gasping. The physician kept trying one remedy and another. Nothing availed. No one even knew when life left him.

Madhav who had taken his Madhavi's hand and said, 'We are married' earlier in the day was now lying on the funeral pyre. I could not bear to see his lifeless body. Where was that cheering smile of his?

The pyre was lit. Madhav's body slowly burnt to ashes. I was looking, first with tears in my eyes, then I stood still like a statue.

Life and death. What a cruel game it is! Is man born only to take part in that game? What does he live for? Why does he die?

Death. What a great mystery it is. Children build castles in the sand on the seashore. One sweep of the tide and the castle disappears. Is life any different from such a castle? What is man whom we glorify as the image of God on earth and whose achievements we worship? A tiny leaf on the huge tree of the world.

A tiny leaf which may fall at anytime with one gust of the wind. And I, Yayati, the King of Hastinapur, who am I? A mere human, a tiny leaf which may fall anytime.

I paid my last homage to Madhav and returned. That night. No, it was not a night but a hissing black cobra setting at me every few minutes. I kept thinking of death. I could not emerge from the whirlpool of thought.

I stood looking out into the darkness with a blank mind for a long time:

In that darkness, I suddenly saw a chariot on the road. The chariot was headed straight towards me But the wheels made no sound, neither did the hooves of the black horses yoked to it. I could distinctly see the horses even in the darkness. I gazed intently at them. I could not believe my eyes. The chariot advanced straight across and over the trees and bushes in the garden, trampling them down and came and stood directly under my window. The charioteer softly said, 'Are you not coming, Your Majesty?'

182

I said, 'The queen is sleeping and so is little Yadu. Without taking their leave... .'

I myself could not hear what I said after that. Before I knew what was happening, the charioteer stretched his hand, reached the window, picked me up as one plucks a flower off a plant and put me in his chariot.

The chariot was on the way. We were leaving the marks of Hastinapur behind. The temple, the dance academy, Madhav's house, the sports stadium where in my youth I had tamed a wild horse.

The chariot was flying like the wind. There was Ashokavan going by.

I could no longer contain myself. When I asked the charioteer, where we going and when we would return, he said he knew naught except only two names. 'First, Your Majesty's. And the second my own.'

'What may that be?'

'Death!'

What a terrible nightmare it was. I clutched at the window bars with both hands and still felt that I might fall to the ground, shivering with fright.

With difficulty I walked to the bed and sat down. But my heart was palpitating and my legs were trembling. I could not calm myself, even for a moment.

I drank wine, glass after glass. After an hour or so, I felt better. Gradually I dozed off.

But in that disturbed state, I had a terrible dream:

In it, a funeral pyre was burning in front of me. In that blazing fire, one after another, my limbs were being reduced to ashes. Before my eyes, the ears, the lips, the hands and feet were burnt to ashes. As I would never again experience the fragrance of the green *champak**and the ripe pineapple, I would never enjoy the fragrance of the abundant hair of the beloved.

With these visions, I came to. I sat up in bed. My heart was palpitating as if death was hammering away at it and I was hearing the echo of those blows.

Like the deer running for life with the hunter on its trail, my mind ran amuck. Wine was now its only recourse.

For many years now, I had not taken so much wine. Gradually it made me intoxicated. I was now being put in mind of another kind of intoxication. Mukulika, Alaka, Devayani and Sharmishtha in their desirable forms passed before me, rousing my desire.

I stretched my hands to take Alaka in my arms. But I opened my eyes and looked again and again. I was alone. 'Alaka, Alaka,' I shouted.

Someone responded but it was not Alaka. It was Mukulika. I was kissing her. But what is this cold feeling against my lips? Was this something cold against my lips the hand of death?

I opened my eyes again. I was alone. Maybe death was hovering round me — invisible. Maybe this is the last night of my life. Who knows? Let me make the best of it, let me enjoy it to the full. This draining cup of life — once, only once, let it be filled to the brim with the wine of a woman's beauty. The last cup — this very last cup.

'Sharmishtha ... Shama ... Shama!'

I got up on shaky legs. I was unsteady, yet I got up, opened the door and strolled out.

---

* A light yellow coloured ornamental flower native to India. Scientific name *Michelia Champaca.*

The maid outside Devayani's door was dozing. She was taken aback on seeing me and got up with a start.

She almost ran in. I thought I would wait until she came out. It was only proper that I should go in only after the queen had sent me word. I realised it but the body would brook no delay.

Excessive liquor had made me very unsteady. Even so, I went in. I do not remember what exactly transpired. I was walking as if in a deep fog.

One thing I remember though. I wanted Devayani. But she knew at once that I had taken wine. She lost her temper. She was angry, furious. I also was annoyed, angry. One word led to another. Once, by mistake, I mentioned Sharmishtha. In the end, she made me swear to one thing, by Maharishi Shukra...

'I shall never touch you.'

Defeated and unrequited, I came out of her room. I would never see Devayani's face again. I would spend my days thinking of Sharmishtha.

I took a chariot to Ashokavan. Devayani and Sharmishtha were alternately before my eyes. I wanted both but one had discarded me. And the other? I had sent her away.

Mukulika. Her preceptor, the sage. He was staying in a *serai** near the dance academy, I remembered. I thought instead of spending a restless night at Ashokavan, I would go and see him. See if he could bring me peace of mind.

Mukulika was startled at seeing me there at an odd hour. Blushing, she took me to the sage.

He looked a great sage. I thought I had seen him somewhere before, but only for a moment. I could not remember where.

I told him of my unhappiness. I begged him to forgive me for having come to his sacred place drunk. He smiled and said, 'Your

---

* An inn.

Majesty, you have already gone half the way to achieve peace of mind. Life here is beset with much unhappiness. There are only two remedies to counter it on earth'.

I eagerly asked: 'Which are they?'

'Wine and women!'

I was stunned. I took courage to ask, 'Drinking wine is a great sin... .'

The sage intervened. 'Good and evil are imaginary concepts put out by clever men and fools. In this world, only happiness and misery are real. Everything else is delusion. Good and bad are appearances ... the play of the mind. To my disciples I always give wine as sacrament.'

I wondered if I was dreaming. The sage said, 'Your Majesty, you seek peace of mind? There are many deities at my command who can bring peace of mind to you. Pray for anyone of your choice.'

He got up and walked away. I followed him like one hypnotised. But all the time I could not help feeling that I was falling off a mountain peak, hurtling down an endless dark precipice, which light had never penetrated.

SHARMISHTHA

I was returning to Hastinapur after eighteen years. The same way I had fled. In a similar troubled state of mind. Nothing has changed in the last eighteen years. Am I the same Sharmishtha of eighteen years ago? No, this is a different Sharmishtha.

Sharmishtha then was a wife and a lover, even though she was a mother. Today, only the mother in her survives with only one care, 'Is my Puroo safe?' She has no thought for anything else.

Sages like Kacha, Yati and Angiras are haunted by the fear of the penance undertaken by Maharishi Shukra. But such fears do not touch her. She is obsessed only with one fear. Where will Puroo be? Will he go to Hastinapur with the victorious Yadu? He looks so much like His Majesty. If Devayani recognises him...

There are guards with me and Alaka also is there. That golden-haired girl has fallen in love with Puroo though she never shows it. But flowers in bloom, even hidden from the eye, give themselves away by their fragrance. She insisted on coming with me. But when the brave girl loses her nerve at the fall of night and wipes her eyes I am moved. Then I cannot sleep till after midnight. All the memories of the last eighteen years come to life. Right from that terrible night...

That night, the night Madhav went away. I was all alone in the blinding darkness and pouring rain. Alone? No, my Puroo was with me. But Puroo was dripping wet. What if he got ill... ? I was angry with the elements. This biting wind, this black sky, the lightning, the thunder — why should they have mercy on me?

When man can be heartless like a stone, why expect a stone to have a heart? Devayani was out for my blood. If His Majesty had not dared, Sharmishtha's life would have ended in the cellar. It is true His Majesty saved my life. But how did he reconcile himself to leaving his beloved Sharmishtha to fend for herself? 'Sharmishtha, I do not prize this kingdom or its splendour. I want only you.' If only he had said this, I would have been greatly heartened.

I would not have permitted him to come with me. But that life-giving message of love, couched in sweet words, would have remained with me through the thunder of clouds and the crash of lightning. But such good fortune could hardly be Sharmishtha's.

I do not know how long and how far I walked that night, from where I got the strength to do so, with Puroo in my arms. But Sharmishtha, a princess, who had grown up as a spoilt child, who went about in a palanquin and was used to walking on a carpet of flowers all her life, was now footing her way, hour after hour, through a forest strewn with thorns. She was running away from Hastinapur, her cellar of death. She was no daughter of King Vrishaparva. She was not the beloved of King Yayati. She had only one bond in the world. She was the mother of an infant. That shivering tiny life clutching at her had inspired her. She meant to live to see his greatness before facing death.

Next morning I stopped by a temple in a small village. Where to ... was question that troubled my mind. Shall I go to father? He will be happy to see his grandchild. But all that will ebb away when he gets to know that I am Devayani's co-wife and that she is after my life.

I thought to myself, how lonely man is in this world. The whole earth stretched before me, but I had no one on it except my child.

Early in the morning, a kindly woman came there. With solicitude she took me to her house. She treated me like her younger sister. I spent four happy days there. The fear that Puroo might be taken ill after that dreadful night's discomfort had passed.

It was the fifth night. Puroo was sleeping by me. I was floating in pleasant dreams.

I woke up with a start. Did I feel somebody's arms round me? No, but I did feel a strange rough hand touching me. I saw the figure of my host with his lustful look. I was startled by the touch and screamed, 'Sister.' The lady hastened into my room with a light. She patted me and asked, 'What is the matter, sister?' I said that I had felt something like a snake crawling over me. She called out to her husband and they both looked round the room. But how could they so find the snake who was there in the form of a man?

I learnt a lesson. So far I had been sheltered in the palace where my beauty was safe from molestation. Now in the open world it was likely to cause trouble. I had not only to protect Puroo but myself too.

Next morning, I made many excuses and reluctantly took leave of my sister. I was sad at leaving and tears came to my eyes, wondering if I would ever see her again. Is life nothing more than a mixture of meetings and partings?

I passed village after village. I took to unfrequented roads avoiding large towns, to get as far away from Hastinapur as possible, never staying at one place for more than a day, never confiding in anyone and never disclosing my real name. If somebody was persistent, I would say that I had set out in search of my husband who had deserted me and my infant and gone to the Himalayas. This aroused pity in some and suspicion in others.

I had thought that Puroo would tire from the discomfort of the journey. But not at all.

I was well away from Hastinapur. I was tired of walking and was forced to camp for a few days in a village. I was taken in by a rich widow. She harried me with questions about my identity. I had my set answer. She said sympathetically, 'Your husband left such a beautiful wife to turn an ascetic? How strange destiny can be in some cases!'

All day she kept staring at me. I was restless when I lay down but I could not sleep for a long time. I went over all the happy moments I had spent in the company of His Majesty — the very intimate ones in the hope that I would fall asleep. In the end, sleep herself took mercy on me.

I woke from the disturbed sleep with a start, by a light shed on me. Someone was peering at me. I opened my eyes just a little, to see. The old woman was whispering something to a young man. I listened with my eyes closed. Wicked broken words, Hastinapur, proclamation, a fat reward and so on, distressed my ears, like drops of poison. I was scared.

The young man was saying, 'No, it is not possible that this is Sharmishtha.'

They went out arguing. My heart was in my mouth. I got up then and left the house at dead of night.

Like a hunted animal without exposing myself, avoiding large towns and taking shelter only for the night, in a temple or *serai*, I went on. Sometimes, I was depressed. I thought it was no use continuing with such hide and seek in which one day I was bound to be discovered.

Whatever the hardship I must live for Puroo. Whatever the odds, I must till he grows up. I must be prepared to cross the mountain of unhappiness.

A few days later, I came to a village temple. It was evening, so I decided to spend the night in the adjoining *serai*. I washed Puroo at a well nearby and left him in the front of the temple to play. Everyone who came into the temple first rang the bell. Puroo also wanted to ring it himself. He was dragging me to the bells. I put him off for sometime but a mother has to yield to the wilfulness of the child! I lifted his hands to the bell with glee, when before the temple an announcement was being made promising a big reward to anyone who would present me and my child to Devayani.

I shuddered at the first few words of it and my legs began to shake. I was holding Puroo high and thought I would drop him. I was terrified and collapsed to the floor.

How happy is a child's world. How blissful his ignorance! Puroo did not understand a word of the announcement. He was absorbed in reaching up and ringing the bell. He was annoyed because he had not been able to do so. He started crying when I pulled him away. The announcement was still ringing in my ears. My heart was beating fast. A middle-aged man, seeing Puroo crying, walked up to me saying, 'The child is crying. Take him and soothe him. See what he wants.' The next moment, he was peering at me.

The announcement upset me greatly. I was convinced that I must never again be seen in public places like a bazaar, a temple or a *serai*. I must disguise myself. I knew that it would be easier to effect a disguise if I left Puroo somewhere. But the thought was heartbreaking. Separate from Puroo? No, that was quite impossible. Puroo's eyes were like the sun and moon to me. All the treasures of Kuber could not equal the joy of a kiss of his. I had to live for his sake alone.

I set out with Puroo inspite of the darkness. I decided that I must not stop with anyone. For rest I must look for a place somewhere outside the village, maybe even out in the open. That must be an inflexible rule even at the risk of life.

The next four or five days were without incident. Kacha's memory was heartening. So far, I had put away the red sari given by Kacha. For the first time one day I wore it.

That day, I stayed at a deserted temple away from a village. Outside and about was a dense forest. For a moment I was frightened. I was putting Puroo to sleep on my lap when an ascetic walked in. He went straight to the idol. Puroo must have noticed him! He got up and started prattling 'da, da.'

The ascetic turned quickly and walked away past me. Puroo was crying, saying 'da-da.'

In the hope, that Puroo might sleep in the cool breeze, I took him outside. It was moonlight. The whole world looked like a white lotus with a thousand petals open. The forest in front and around was bathed in moonlight. What was otherwise a dense forest, now looked gently inviting, like the flowering shrubs in a garden. The world was sleeping soundly in the lap of mother earth, to the tune of the lullaby sung by the moon.

By now the moonlight was going to my head. What beautiful patterns it made under the trees! I was not in a mood to hum a tune to myself since leaving Hastinapur. But now gladdened at heart to overflowing, I broke into song. I was in a trance. They say, that moon is a friend of the God of Love. That realisation dawned on me now. The fascination of the moonlight was akin to that of love.

I had covered some distance. Suddenly, the forest seemed to end. Before me, a huge black rock was spread out like a tortoise. Beyond it was a sheer chasm.

I was drawn to it. I wanted to walk right up to its end and peep into the chasm. After all did we not play at the same game as children?

I said to myself, today the moonlight is really wonderful. This beautiful view is unique. I wanted to drink in all that beauty. The rock was jutting out a little too far, but what did it matter? What was there to be afraid of? Does not man find pleasure in living surrounded on all sides by death? Who has time to reflect on other things, while enjoying silvery moments such as these?

I walked courageously ahead. I was getting near the narrower end of the rock. Someone shouted, 'Stop, stop.' I was taken aback.

I saw him heading towards me. He was coming nearer every moment. He was probably an ascetic. The thought that somewhere at hand there must be the hermitage of a sage heartened me. I could see him distinctly in the clear moonlight. From hope I had again fallen into despair.

The ascetic was Yati!

Yati was peering at me. I was in a cold sweat remembering his weird behaviour at court, the terrifying experience of Ashokavan and his hatred for women. I felt helpless. Yati was looking closely at me and at Puroo sleeping on my shoulder. I bravely met his gaze.

I thought his earlier insane look had changed to a softer one. He paused for a few moment and asked, 'Sharmishtha, how do you happen to be here?' His tone was affectionate and kindly. I sobbed. I did not know how or what to tell him.

He was bewildered at my sobbing. But I pulled myself up and, trying to smile, said, 'I came away from Hastinapur on purpose for Puroo to see his uncle. I knew you would not come to Hastinapur to see him, so I decided to bring this jewel of your family to show you.'

The words helped to relieve the mounting tension between us. Yati came nearer and said, 'Is he my nephew? Yayati's son? I was wondering if the nephew would give his uncle a kiss. But Prince is asleep. It will be the first kiss in my life and I must find an auspicious moment for it.'

I looked at him stunned. Was it Yati or had Kacha disguised himself as Yati? How did this miracle happen? How did a beautiful lake take the place of a barren desert?

I followed Yati to the hermitage which was run by one of the disciples of Maharishi Angiras.

Is life a chain of coincidences? At least at that moment I thought so. I had put on the beautiful sari given to Devayani by Kacha only because of the mistake of a maid. A princess had been reduced to a maid. Later, the king came into her life by the passing whim of Devayani and brought her a lifetime of love. Still again, the maid was turned into a refugee. But she soon found someone to lean on. And of all the people, an ascetic who had been dubbed by the world a lunatic.

I told him my tale. I mentioned how Kacha had given me heart by adopting me as his sister, and how he had earnestly pleaded with Devayani to release me from bondage. I broke down during the narration. But these were tears of joy at the thought of my good fortune in having found such selfless and noble love. I paused to wipe my eyes.

Yati must have been prompted to open his heart after hearing me. He spoke quite calmly, as if he was talking about someone else's life. He was almost off his mind when he left Ashokavan. Kacha had directed the hermitages on the way to bring him to Bhrigu Mountain if anyone should find him. One of the disciples persuaded him to accompany him to Kacha's cottage. Kacha tended him like his own brother.

Yati had taken a mistaken view of life and started to detest everything sweet, ranging from sweet fruit to woman's love. He formed a firm idea to which he stuck that pure bliss and self-knowledge could be reached only through such hatred. He had set out to find God but was caught in the snare of black magic, hypnotism and occult powers. He had no friend or disciple. He had never come across selfless love. Yati's life had become like that of a leaf which drops from a tree and is carried up swirling through the air in a whirlwind.

I heard of the whirlwind and the leaf for the first time when Yati was speaking. He talked at length. I cannot recall today all that he said. I wish I had carefully made a note of every word of his in the diary of my mind. What he said was born of bitter experience. Like the fragrance wafted on the breeze, like the silver streak of lightning, I have now only the memory of his words. But even the mere memory is inspiring.

The Queen Mother was on the Bhrigu Mountain. Under her loving care Yati recovered his balance a little. Kacha himself strove to guide him. They had debates for hours. The outcome of it all was that Yati found the golden mean of his life. He told me on that moonlit night of the philosophical maxims contained in their debates. I remember very few of them today and those also in odd bits.

Yati said the body and the soul are not enemies of each other; they are the two wheels of a chariot; if one of the two breaks down, the strain has to be taken by the other and it is borne down!

To torture the body for the uplift of the soul or to deaden the soul for physical pleasures are both wrong. The varied beauty broadcast by the Almighty in this world cannot be impure or tainted. The relation of man and woman is just like that of the body and soul. Not by hating each other but rather by intense love for each other, love so great that each one forgets self, man and woman attain heavenly bliss in workaday life. That is why keeping the household is regarded as sacred as making a sacrifice. To the common man, that alone is religion.

Sages like Shukra and Kacha bear the cares of the world's well-being; Lord Indra, Vrishaparva and Yayati, the great kings must tend to the happiness of their subjects and the common householder must carry the burden of property and well-being of his family, friends and relations. They must at all times beware that their happiness does not impinge on others to make them unhappy. Individual duty, social obligation, royal duty and the duty of an ascetic are all on par. None bound by any of these duties may deprecate life or transgress the fundamental restrictions laid on it. It is a sin to violate one's religion or duty. But everyone must determine for himself which duty to take upon himself. In its pursuit, everyone from the ascetic to the husband must remember that selfless love is the king of all religions and the highest form of duty.

Hearing all this, Kacha rose greatly in my estimation. How unfortunate Devayani was! She had been loved by a great man who combined in himself heavenly and earthly qualities. But in the end, she had pronounced a curse even on him. With her own hands, she had felled the tree with the power to grant all one's wishes.

Yati knew many tribals at the foot of the Himalayas. He said, 'They are a brave and honest people. They will look after you and Puroo.'

I wished to build a cottage at the foot of the Himalayas where the three of us could stay and I would have the opportunity of looking after my brother-in-law, who had all his life neglected himself. In the end, I took courage to say so. Yati smiled and said, 'Dear Sister, that just is not possible. Kacha is going to undertake grave penance.

'He is an exemplary man. He has no trace of jealousy in him or desire for fame. He does not even wish to be the preceptor of the gods. But since he lost the power of Sanjeevani, Maharishi Shukra has taken it upon himself to acquire an even more potent power and to make the demons more powerful than the gods.'

I timidly asked Yati, 'What is this potent power Maharishi Shukra aspires to?'

'By the power of Sanjeevani the dead can be brought back to life. Now, Maharishi Shukra is determined to acquire power by which the living can be killed by merely wishing it.'

'And, is Kacha too after the same?'

'Kacha is greatly distressed at that. He sincerely believes that an ascetic should not go after destructive power. But the only check to Maharishi Shukra's destructive power is the possession of an even more potent power. Nothing less will do. So, Kacha is sitting down to penance. God knows how long it will take. But while he is in penance, it is necessary that his co-disciples and friends like me should, in our own way, undergo penance for peace on earth. True asceticism requires it. I propose to do my duty.'

We reached the foot of the Himalayas in a few days. Yati arranged for my comfort and then prepared to set out. Bowing to him, I said, 'Brother, when shall we meet again?'

He smiled and said, 'When? The Omniscient alone knows!'

I said, 'May your blessing be the only hope of unfortunate me!' He turned to me and said, 'Sister have no care. Puroo may be in the wilderness today but he is destined to be the King of Hastinapur tomorrow!'

Puroo was growing up. Puroo by now was also taking aim with a tiny bow and arrow. My joy knew no bounds at his infallible aim. Puroo grew a little more and started learning the *Vedas* at the hermitage of a sage some distance away. By the time Puroo was ten or eleven, I was proud of his valour but afraid of his adventurous spirit. It was wonderful that those little fists should clutch a bow and arrow and kill such big animals. Puroo, who as a child was frightened of his own shadow on the wall, was now nonchalantly facing the wild animals of the jungle.

The river is negligibly small at the source. A thin stream no bigger than a finger flows down the hillside and enters the plains. It broadens and meanders. As other streams join in, it grows in volume. Puroo also grew up like that. Even in exile, he made many friends, some ascetics, some tribals. His blossoming mind was engrossed in local festivities, the merriment, the happiness and misery, and generally the course of life there!

I had a strange feeling that one moment Puroo was as close to me as he was when he was in my womb. The next moment I thought that he was going further and further away from me. His contact with me now was no more than that of the bird, who soars all day in the sky singing merrily, and returns to the nest only at night. His was a different world now. I hoped that the unfortunate mother would have a space in the fullness of that world.

Such thoughts were very depressing. Puroo would fondly say, 'What is the matter, mother?' I could say nothing. Is it the rule of Creation that fundamentally man must be lonely at heart?

When I was thus depressed, I would come out of the cottage to look at the snowclad peaks of the Himalayas. These peaks rising high to the heavens gave me much forbearance.

And not only the Himalayas. Everything around me heartened me in its own way. The ultimate essence of life was being revealed to me. I learnt that the easiest way to be happy is to cheerfully live the life given to us, to find pleasure in it, experience the beauty and fragrance of it and to share it with others.

The meandering stream similarly brought cheer to my depressed mind. Seeing its swollen raging waters in the rains and the havoc caused by it, I would feel that after all, youth is not completely a blessing, it also carries a curse. There is no knowing how much a man might lose his head in the flush of youth, what rocks he will crash on in his pursuit of pleasure and how many pure, innocent gentle things he will trample on in his wild chase.

I understood from my exile why sages and ascetics take to the jungle for their penance. Nature and man are inseparably linked together from the beginning to the end. In fact, they are twins. That is why life reveals itself in its true form only in the presence of Nature. Man then begins to understand the content and limitations of life. When he drifts away from Nature, his life becomes one-sided. In that artificial one-sided existence, his thoughts, feelings and desires assume unreal and distorted forms. My misfortune had in one way turned out to be good luck. That is why I came here. I was able to see clearly the truth underlying life.

It was not as though I was thus thoughtful and balanced all the time. Sometimes I felt lonely from a sense of separation. At night, on my bed of straw the body ached and the mind hankered for His Majesty.

I strove hard to stop such fancies which were heartrending. I would remind myself of the renunciation of Kacha and Yati. But my mind was like an unbridled horse. It could not be checked. It would fly to Hastinapur and Ashokavan and wait at the door of the underground passage. No, it is not possible for man to dissociate himself from his body all the time.

Such sentiments, repressed with great difficulty, would unexpectedly burst out. It happened once when Puroo was seven

198

or eight. Puroo was sitting with ascetics. A lady sitting by me had a girl of four or five in her lap. Her eyes were very beautiful. But I was attracted more by her hair than her eyes. The abundant hair with occasional streaks of gold was fascinating. They were like fine golden threads drawn through a black mass of cloud. The girl was not only sweet but daring. When I stretched my hands, she came to me and sat in my lap without demur.

I bid farewell to her, hoping that we would meet again and returned to the cottage. But I could not sleep thinking of that sweet little girl. I longed for His Majesty's company and the memory of that pleasure was disquieting. I wished Puroo had a sister like her.

Even in this peaceful life, I was troubled by much agony. One day Yati came and gave me the news of the death of the Queen Mother. She had been good to me. I wished I had been able to serve her in some way. But I was sorry the opportunity had never come my way.

I once met an ascetic who had come from Hastinapur. According to him His Majesty had ceased to look after the affairs of the state. Devayani was attending to them. Was it possible that there were differences between Devayani and His Majesty? Even if so, a man cannot neglect his duties. Like flowers some persons cannot live except with the dewdrops of love. Without it, they just dry up. If the differences are material and lasting, what will happen to His Majesty?

I was very depressed that day. I felt like going to Hastinapur, even at the risk of my life, to beg of His Majesty to come with me to my humble cottage. But Puroo was still small. I wept bitterly. As usual, I said in my prayers before going to bed the words, 'Lord, make him happy.'

As a child, Puroo, repeated after me whatever I said in my prayers. But now he had grown up a little. He asked me out of curiosity, 'Mother, who is him? Tell me the name!'

'I shall tell you when you are sixteen.'

But before he was sixteen, Nature was beginning to reveal to him who the 'him' in my prayer was. Until the age of twelve, he looked like me. But in the next one or two years, he shot up and filled up. He was now looking more and more like His Majesty. To add to it, the occasional visits of the ascetic from Hastinapur would bring news which worried me. His Majesty had dissociated himself completely from the administration of the State. For months on end, he was away from the capital. Even when in town, he did not stir out of Ashokavan. There was now no limit to his indulgence in luxury and excesses.

I did not know what to do. That I should be helpless to save from degradation a dear one for whom I would cheerfully and without hesitation have laid down my life! How frail man is.

In an effort to forget this new turn of unhappiness I turned to drawing again. One day, I felt like making a sketch of Puroo. I thought over it a great deal, and I realised that in his adolescence he was growing up in His Majesty's likeness.

Puroo was now sixteen. I told him the secret that he was no ordinary youth but a prince of Hastinapur. I consoled him by saying that I had to leave Hastinapur because of Devayani's jealousy.

It is very difficult to make children understand. The first flush of youth is not only adventurous but blind. It cannot perceive the problems of everyday life. It is constantly surrounded only by the fragrance of the flowers it dreams of. I explained to him over and over again that it would be better to stay where we were until the time His Majesty sent for us. He would not agree. When I made him swear that he would not divulge the secret of his royal birth without my permission, he impudently said, 'Not even to His Majesty.'

I comforted him by saying, 'I am not asking you to do that. You are free to tell His Majesty that you are his son. But remember never to tell anyone else who you are. I enjoin you upon my life.'

As they grow up, children drift from their parents. Love and achievement are the inspirations of the young mind. These draw young boys and girls from the sheltered existence of their childhood.

The parents, however, continue to dwell in their old world, anxious for their children's well-being.

As fear left him by one door, love entered by another to find a place. Budding, youthful, blushful, innocent love. Love like the delicate pink tones in the eastern corner of the sky just before dawn!

But he never gave away this secret of his. That sweet girl Alaka with the golden hair. Her mother was now a dear friend of mine. Naturally the children also became friends. But when Puroo was sixteen, there was a subtle change in their behaviour. The two no longer played together with their earlier abandon. There was an imperceptible coyness in their approach. If others were not looking, they looked stealthily at each other. They would blush and look away and Alaka would hang her head and ply the ground with her toenails. When she was very small, and asked to do something for Puroo, she used to say, 'Why should I do anything for him? He never does anything for me.' But now whenever she came, she was more concerned about his comfort.

All this dawned on me gradually. There was nothing wrong in it. But sometimes I wondered if it was right, if that first incipience of love should be allowed to grow.

On second thoughts I would reason, 'You were once a princess. Were not you later reduced to being a maid? Alaka may not have blue blood. But her love is genuine. Is the love of a maid and that of a princess vastly different?'

I was bewildered by the conflict in my mind. But I did not have the heart to speak to Puroo or Alaka about the matter. Like the young, the elders also feel constrained to say anything in such cases.

~

Three more years went by. Puroo was nineteen now. One day he returned very perturbed from his hunt. He had heard that the tribals called Dasyus had organised a very big rising in the North. They had

201

set out to march on Hastinapur. There were rumours of Prince Yadu leading a large army to put them down. I could not sleep a wink that night.

It constantly occurred to me that if Yadu was leading the army, where was His Majesty?

Like me, Puroo also was tossing in bed from side to side. I asked him once or twice, 'What is the matter? Why can't you sleep tonight?'

He said, 'Nothing at all, mother.' He did not say a word more. I laughed. I thought he was thinking of Alaka. It is a difficult age. Who knows, he may have kissed her for the first time today.

Next afternoon, I knew why Puroo was restless that night. He set out for a hunt in the morning and did not return till nightfall. I enquired about his friends who had accompanied him. None of them had returned. It was a nightmare. I was stricken with terror that night. God forbid such a night falling to the lot of a mother!

Till noon next day I was restless like a fish out of water. Puroo and his friends had gone out on a campaign against the Dasyus. They had left their houses on the pretext of a hunt for fear that the elders might not give them permission. On the way lay Alaka's village. Puroo had gone on, entrusting Alaka with a letter to be delivered to me the next afternoon. Alaka gave me the letter with trembling hands. I opened it.

It said:

> The kingdom of Hastinapur has been attacked. Need I tell you where my duty lies in such an event? I am going away without your permission. Forgive me, mother, and don't worry about me. Your Puroo will soon return to you, after meeting the challenge to the Hastinapur kingdom with his prowess and skill in war.

Tears came to my eyes while reading the letter. Who can say that the son of a Kshatriya should not go to war? But mine was the heart of a mother. It could not be calmed. It dripped through the eyes.

Alaka wiped my tears. She embraced me and kept consoling me, 'Please don't cry.' The mild sun lit up the gold in her hair. For a moment, my heart bleeding for Puroo was gladdened that I was going to get her for a daughter-in-law. She who would stand out in a million girls.

It was now Alaka's turn to cry. 'Aunt, will he come back safe?' she asked. The question distressed me. I drew Alaka near and patted her head. I said, 'Don't worry dear. Do not others go to war? Fighting is laid on us Kshatriyas as a duty.'

Yet, we both cried together. It was only then that we calmed down a bit.

We talked and thought together a great deal. News of them would necessarily take time to reach us. So it would be better to go to a village eight or ten miles from Hastinapur. We would thus be able to get news from passing soldiers and messengers. Alaka's mother reluctantly permitted her to go with me, saying, 'After all, the daughter belongs to another home. It is a debt which might as well be honoured on time.'

Two brave elderly persons, from among those detailed by Yati to look after me, prepared to go with us. We two set out on our way, imagining a hundred things. Sometimes repressing our tears and sometimes stealthily wiping them, sometimes dreaming of Puroo's heroism and at other times, waking up with a start, seeing him injured in our dreams.

~

I was returning to Hastinapur after eighteen years, the same way I had left. Equally frightened at heart. I was going on dreaming of the future, dreams sometimes golden, sometimes black!

When I had passed this way eighteen years ago, I was worried about protecting little Puroo from harm. The same Puroo had today gone to battle leaving his mother in a sea of anxiety. I was all the time, at every step, distressed whether he was safe. Are anxiety and shadow twins? Is it the will of God that these should be constant companions of man?

At last we reached a village some ten miles from Hastinapur. It was a day of ill-omen. On that very day, bad news had just come through stunning us both. In a skirmish, Yadu and some of his brave soldiers had been captured by the Dasyus. It was their custom to behead the enemy and carry his skull on a spear in procession.

But our misery went much further than that and was more poignant. Puroo must almost certainly have been among the brave soldiers accompanying Yadu. In fact, he might well be a prisoner himself.

In what condition then were we likely to see Puroo? As a victorious hero? Or at the end of a spear?

What had I done in my previous birth that God was punishing me thus?

DEVAYANI

The pitch darkness of the new moon night seems poised to pounce on me. Looking at the sky through the window, the stars are twinkling as if in derision. There are so many retainers in the palace, but they are dumb. I am in a state as if flames are ablaze all around and there is no escape.

This evening the messenger brought the evil tidings. My Yadu is defeated. The Dasyus have taken him. Oh no. I just cannot believe it. How did such a fate overtake him? Queen Devayani's son vanquished. Maharishi Shukra, acclaimed as the world's most illustrious ascetic, his grandson defeated?

No, the words ring false. They seem like ghosts.

How enthusiastic he was when setting out for battle! I put the red *tilak* on his forehead. How eagerly I waited for news of his victory. But, like the *chatak* bird expectantly looking up to the sky for a drop of rain and getting struck by lightning instead, I am stunned.

Devayani has not had to hang her head down so far. She has not so far submitted to anyone. But today? What can I do now? Whom shall I supplicate?

It is nearly time for father to end his penance. I have not seen him these eighteen years. I never told him about any of my unhappiness. He is short tempered. I bore my unhappiness, repressed it, lest he should thoughtlessly give up his penance halfway. He had, at my insistence on bringing Kacha back to life, lost the invaluable power of Sanjeevani. Now he is again on the point of achieving some such power. In these circumstances, how can I go to him and say, 'Free my Yadu!' What right have I to break his penance?

No, I shall not be so thoughtless. Not even for one of my own flesh and blood. Many bitter unhappy recollections are piled up in my mind. I am going to wreak vengeance on everyone of those who have offended me. That Sharmishtha, her brat aspiring to be King Emperor and His Majesty, but not yet. After father has successfully completed his penance and achieved the new power.

I want my Yadu! I want nothing else. I do not want this kingdom nor father's new power.

No, this is not Devayani talking. This is the weakling of a mother. But Devayani is Maharishi Shukra's daughter and the Queen of Hastinapur. She must not weaken thus.

What shall I do? How can I free Yadu? I suddenly thought of His Majesty. Can a brave father sit quiet knowing that his son has been taken captive by the enemy? Yadu is not only mine. He is as much His Majesty's. Is it possible that he has not yet heard of Yadu's defeat and capture by the Dasyus? How can that be?

The Prime Minister brought me the evil tidings and said, 'I shall inform His Majesty about it. Knowing that the entire state is in jeopardy, he will not keep quiet. The situation now is grave. He will himself lead an army to free the Prince. The Queen may rest assured.'

It has been nearly two hours since the Prime Minister left to see His Majesty. My son is in captivity, his life is in danger. It is a blemish on the fair name of Hastinapur. I am a mother. I am the Queen. How can I keep quiet and not act?

Why has His Majesty not come to me yet? 'I shall free Yadu and bring him back. Be ready to welcome us with lights.' Words such as these would have dispelled the gloom in my heart. Steeped in wine and women, has he forgotten even his duty as a father?

It was an evil day when I was tempted to be Queen of Hastinapur. It was not my wedding but my sacrifice. I have been scorched by the flames of that nuptial sacrifice for the last eighteen years.

I am reminded of that stormy night eighteen years ago when renowned artists lost themselves in the beauty of my dances. Spring dance, a piece from the life of Uma, autumn dance; all of them had reached great heights that night, but there was something the artists who greeted me with thundering applause did not know. Each one of those dances was tinged with the blood oozing from my wounded heart. There was a big gash in Devayani's heart. A wound mercilessly inflicted by her husband. It was in an effort to forget her agony that Devayani had poured all her life into her dances that night.

That night the sky was overcast. It was like my heart in agony from deception. But I had agreed to dance for those artists. I had not forgotten the nuances of my favourite art. I went on the stage for my first dance and in an instant left behind the agony of my mind. The world of art transcends transient things like thought, sensibility and passion. I was engrossed in my dance. As engrossed as I often was in my beauty before a mirror.

Sharmishtha is palpably a liar. The lines in Puroo's hand pointing to his sovereignty were unmistakable evidence of their love affair. I was still in a trance when His Majesty presented me with the necklace. I went to bed in that trance.

I woke up the next morning as the Queen, but I also as a deceived wife and an affectionate mother dedicated to the well-being of her son.

I sent His Majesty out and went down to the cellar. She was not there. I saw red. Everyone from the old maid to His Majesty denied all knowledge. But truth cannot remain unrevealed.

Under the horsewhip, the old maid soon talked. I went to Ashokavan and I came to know of Sharmishtha having gone away, in a chariot somewhere. I could not find out who the charioteer was, but in a day or two learnt of Madhav's illness. As a matter of formality, I went to see him. Madhav's bride-to-be, Madhavi, was standing there. The child was bewildered and tears kept coming to her eyes! I patted her to console her. When she calmed down, we talked and she soon told me how Madhav had been taken so ill.

Madhav had returned home that night, drenched to the skin a couple of hours after midnight. I knew how loyal a friend Madhav was. He had gone on His Majesty's errand. He went to leave Sharmishtha far out of the town. Why, otherwise, should he have got drenched in the pouring rain? In the town, he could have taken shelter anywhere.

With this thread, I started unravelling the mystery of Sharmishtha. I purposely visited Madhav frequently. Madhav was in a delirium talking. A lot of it was irrelevant. But from one or two of his sentences, I was convinced of His Majesty's conspiracy. Once he said, 'On with it, driver!' Another time, 'Your Majesty must get down here.' Eventually it dawned on me. He must have been calling Sharmishtha, 'Your Majesty!' The whole mystery was revealed to me by that one word. He was bent on making her Queen. He had designs on my life. He must have intended to keep Sharmishtha and Puroo safe somewhere until he could bring them back.

I resolved to nip the poisonous growth in the bud. I immediately made a proclamation throughout the length and breadth of the State, announcing a big reward to anyone apprehending Sharmishtha and her son. I felt that sooner or later someone would present himself with them. But it was not to be.

For the first few days, I had a watch kept on Ashokavan for any surreptitious communication between them.

~

I was wondering why even after news of Yadu's capture His Majesty had not come to me. Why should he come to me? We had drifted so far apart in the last eighteen years. In the eyes of the world, he and I are husband and wife. But at heart we are sworn enemies. I took upon myself the administration of the State, taking the powers away from him. But he has thoroughly avenged himself, by indulging in animal pleasures and making himself quite oblivious of the fact that Devayani was his wife and Yadu his son or that he owed a duty to them.

I have often wondered if this is not the perverse result of my turning him down that night, insulting him and making him swear that he would not touch me again.

One night he came to my rooms. They say that a man excited with liquor desires a woman. I had only heard of it. But that night I myself had that experience. He begged me to give myself to him. Worse than a beast. I was unable to bear the foul smell of his mouth stinking with liquor. I stood far away from him. He ran after me and grappled with me. I asked, 'Have you remembered me today because Sharmishtha is not there?' He laughed a ghostly smile and said, 'I am the son of King Nahusha. I want Sharmishtha. I want Devayani. I want every pretty woman on earth. Everyday a fresh woman.'

I was unable to stand it. He was talking like one who had gone out of his senses. I was reminded of his elder brother coming to court. He had gone off his head because of his hatred of women. Was His Majesty going to be unhinged by his lust for women?

He said, 'My father could not get Indrani. But I will. I am going to take all the pretty women on earth. Pluck one flower, smell it and throw it away. Again pluck one, taste it and throw it away.'

I closed my ears. He was laughing hysterically and coming nearer. I collected all my strength and shouted, 'Keep away. Keep away. Don't you know who I am?'

He replied, 'Yes, you are my wife.' Spiritedly I retorted, 'I am the daughter of Maharishi Shukra. You know what a great ascetic my father is. I am going to him now to report your behaviour. You will not come to your senses except after a terrible curse.'

He stood still on hearing the word 'curse.' For a moment, I also melted and felt like pleading with him to mend his ways — for my sake and for Yadu's sake. After all he was my husband. If friends and relations do not forgive one's failings who else will? I was a wife. Even if he failed in his duty as a husband, was it not enjoined on me to do my duty as a wife?

Is love something one can buy? Value for value is the rule of trade. But life is not trade. If His Majesty was going astray, I should have pointed it out to him. I should have convinced him of it. I should have stood by him if he lost his balance.

For a moment, maybe only for the moment, I melted at this thought. I was fidgety when His Majesty asked me, 'Where is Sharmishtha? You devil, you have taken her life.'

He was coming forward. I was afraid that he might strangle me. Soon His Majesty was very near me. His intention to strangle me was quite evident. I shouted from mortal fear, 'Keep off. Don't forget I am the daughter of Maharishi Shukra. Step back. Go away. Get out of my room... .'

His Majesty began trembling and went back a step or two. He mumbled, 'No, I won't come any further.'

The reference to Sharmishtha had enraged me. I said, 'First swear to me that you will never touch me again.' I do not want even to be touched by that defiled body of his. I warned him, 'Swear to me that you will never touch me. Swear in the name of my father.'

His Majesty swore and left my room. That day the fine silken cord of our relation as husband and wife, the most beautiful tie in life broke. We were thenceforward to go through life turned away from each other.

How am I to blame for the unfortunate incident that day? The daughter of Maharishi Shukra, the mother of Yadu and the Queen of Hastinapur every single one of them has consistently confirmed that what I did was right.

But then who is it that occasionally whispers to me, 'You were wrong. You did not live up to your duty. You failed to realise your responsibility.'

Who is this creature torturing me with her pricks, for the last eighteen years? This woman has no name, no complexion and no form. I first thought, she was the wife of King Yayati. To stop her nagging, I said, 'Why should a wife love her husband who has trampled upon the sanctity of their marriage and who is known to be a deceitful rascal? My resolve that night was the only right one. Knowing full well, that I would thus be deprived of marital happiness I came to that resolve.'

That foolish woman was never convinced. So many years have gone by but she still protests, 'You did not truly live up to your duty. You failed to realise your responsibility. Does love depend on such exterior attributes? The day a person becomes a near and dear one any arithmetical count of his good and bad points ceases. What remains is just selfless love. Love which gropes, stumbles, struggles up only to fall again, a love which aims to rise to the peak of devotion, inspite of the many falls. Do we ever sit down to reckon what God has given us or denied us when we bend in worship to him? Love is the worship of one person by another. You violated that worship, you are a blemish on womanhood. You will never, never be happy.'

Today was the same. I was stunned by the news of Yadu's capture. Drawing on my distraught condition this woman was dinning into my ears, 'You did not live up to the duty of a wife, to the responsibility of a woman. This is the fruit of that sin.'

No, it is not true. Yadu's defeat is the fruit of the sins committed by His Majesty.

Who has not had to taste the bitter fruit of his sins? Poor Madhav, his dear friend, lost his life in taking Sharmishtha out of town. His bride-to-be was in the likeness of Rati, the goddess of love. What beautiful eyes she had. They say her body was found floating on the Yamuna one day.

There were only Madhav's old mother and niece left in his house. Taraka soon grew up and granny was worried about her marriage. A few days later I learnt that Taraka had gone off her head. I could not bring myself to believe it and went to Madhav's house. There was Taraka sitting in the doorway making a braid. She carried the lovely bloom of youth, but her eyes were vacant. They were frightening. She stared at me a long time, but did not recognise me.

Just then her granny came out. She said, 'Taraka don't you recognise her? She is the Queen. Bow to her.' Taraka said, 'What queen?' Granny said, 'Don't you know, you silly? She is the Queen of our King Yayati?' Suddenly she looked at the braid in her hand and screamed, 'Lord, what a big snake! Snake! Snake!'

Taraka had nothing to do with His Majesty. She was only his friend's niece. But even she did not escape misfortune.

Eighteen years ago I had made His Majesty take the oath. Even as Queen, I have lived like an ascetic. For nights on end, I was restless.

Sometimes, my firmness was on the point of giving way. I would go to Ashokavan but even after getting there, I never went in.

His Majesty, however, kept his word. He started a life of indulgence in animal pleasures. First, when I heard of it, I was stung to the quick. I was disgusted with the love affairs of men and women. I felt the world would have been a happier place if God had not created this attraction.

Occasionally, a chord somewhere in a corner of the heart would pulsate. It would come alive with the words, 'You silly woman, forget your pride. Go straight to His Majesty, wherever he maybe. He maybe drunk. He maybe in the arms of another woman. Fall at his feet and bathe them with your tears, saying, "What are you doing? Lord of my heart, where are you going? A blemish on you is a blemish on me. I fall with you. I am your wife. Must not the husband protect the good name of his wife? You may squirt liquor on me. I shall not turn a hair. Crush Devayani for the sake of your pleasure as you might a flower. But stop this sacrilege of your duty. Wake up to your duty as a husband. Remember your duty as a father. Do not forget your duty as King." '

I did quite often feel like falling at the feet of His Majesty and saying all this and more. But it was a passing thought. The next moment, I would think of Kacha. How dearly he loved me. He gave up love from a sheer sense of duty. He returned to heaven with Sanjeevani. All the beauties of heaven must have laid their beauty at his feet. But he was not moved or tempted. He did not stray from his undertaking.

Remembering Kacha's austerity and renunciation, the indulgence of His Majesty was disgusting. I was ashamed to submit to him. Kacha used to say: 'Why do we lay flowers on a stone? Has the fragrance of flowers ever permeated the stone?' A lover should be in Kacha's image. A woman should worship such a man.

Married to Kacha, I would have been happy. The happiness which I would have had in his cottage has not come my way, even for a day, in this palace.

But, would I in fact have been happy? I certainly loved him; but is the attraction of blind love enough to make one happy? Was my love of him selfless? No. Even that was a kind of self-indulgence. If I was truly in love with him, I would have hesitated in pronouncing a curse on him. My lips would have turned black with those poisonous words.

What is love? What a puzzle it is. Is the disgusting indulgence of His Majesty over the last eighteen years love? Was he genuinely in love with Sharmishtha? To flirt with another woman deceiving one's wife...

Sharmishtha! Her mere memory makes me burn. It must have been an inauspicious moment, when I decided to make her my maid. Because of her, I was separated from His Majesty. On the one hand, I am denied even his touch. On the other, he has fallen to abysmal depths. Today, Prince Yadu has been defeated. What a calamity! But His Majesty is not paying any heed to it.

His Majesty should have rushed to me. If he had set out to free Yadu, my eyes would have filled with tears, worshipping him. He would have tenderly wiped those tears, saying, 'There is nothing to

213

worry about, you silly one. Inside of two weeks, I shall bring Yadu back to you.'

'You silly one.' How sweet the words are. No, that is not to be. Is loneliness forever going to be my miserable companion?

Memories of the last eighteen years haunted me. I was disheartened. The Prime Minister had not returned. It was clear that His Majesty was not prepared to do anything to free Yadu.

~

A maid brought news of the Prime Minister's return. He came in, hung his head and was quiet. I asked sharply, 'Why were you so long?'

'I could not get an audience with the King for sometime.'

I asked, 'In the end, did you or did you not see him?'

'I did. After hearing me, he merely smiled.' The Prime Minister went on with his head hung low, 'I gave him Your Majesty's message. At that he laughed and said, "Tell Her Majesty that I am deeply indebted to her to be remembered after so long." '

Angrily, I asked him, 'What more did he say?' With great hesitation and a tremor, he repeated the impudent words of His Majesty. 'The enemy might capture the Queen also. I would not mind at all. I have nothing to do with the Queen.'

Those venom-laden words pierced my heart. The last chapter of the war between us, which started on our wedding, will soon open. Let father finish his penance. Then there will be time to show him.

A maid rushed in. Her face was lit up with pleasure. She breathlessly said 'There is a messenger outside come on the gallop. Your Majesty, his horse vomited blood and died as the rider got off.'

I rushed out. He humbly made an obeisance and said, 'Your Majesty, I have come with very happy tidings. The Prince has been rescued from captivity.'

My joy knew no bounds, I was very proud of Yadu's valour and adventure. I asked impatiently, 'How did the Prince free himself? How did he escape? By killing off the sentries?'

'No, Your Majesty. Someone risked his life to free the Prince.'

'Who? The army commander?'

'Not he. He is a youth of about the same age as the Prince.'

'His name?'

'I do not know the hero's name. He is not of our army. The army commander sent me post-haste to give Your Majesty these glad tidings. The Prince is on his way to the capital to present the hero to Your Majesty. They will reach Hastinapur in two weeks' time.'

I was still thinking of a present to be given to the messenger, when another maid brought news of a second messenger.

I recognised the messenger as he came in. He had come from King Vrishaparva. Father had successfully completed his penance. The demon kingdom was festive. Father was coming to take me to the festivities. The message said that he would be here in two weeks.

A happy Devayani was consoling the unhappy Devayani now. She said, 'Today your penance has borne fruit. You suffered very badly for eighteen years. Now the worst is over. You shall inform Maharishi Shukra about Sharmishtha, he will immediately set up Yadu on the throne and punish His Majesty... .'

I was in a trance:

I had visions of Yadu being crowned as king. The sacred waters of all the rivers in Aryavarta were being sprinkled on him; and yet all the priests and ascetics felt that there was a flaw somewhere. In the end, Yadu bows to me. My tears of joy bathe his head. Father smiles and says, 'Now the coronation is sanctified!'

In a moment, His Majesty is on his knees before me saying, 'I am in a hundred ways guilty of neglecting you. Forgive me.'

215

YAYATI

Where am I — in heaven or hell? Am I really Yayati? The husband of Devayani? Devayani! What Devayani? Devayani is nothing to me. How can that be? She is my sworn enemy from an earlier birth. She has thrown me into this hell.

Am I in hell? Oh no, for many years now I have been enjoying heavenly bliss.

How many years? Eighteen? No, I have been in heaven for something like eighteen hundred years. I am forever drinking nectar from the lips of beautiful maidens. Under the tree which grants every wish is my bed. I loll in bed night and day, on a mattress of delicate white flowers. Now, I am going to take Indrani in my arms.

Indrani, it was on Indrani's account that King Nahusha was cursed. Who is that whispering in my ear? 'The children of King Nahusha will never be happy.'

But I am the son of King Nahusha. I am happy. My brother Yati ran away to the jungle and lost his reason. But I am sailing in a sea of happiness. All my sorrows have been drowned in this sea. Except only one, the memory of Sharmishtha. No, this agony of mine will never get drowned in wine. I cannot wipe out that memory even with blood drawn in a hunt. No maiden in my bed, tending to my physical pleasure with her embraces, can crush that poignant memory.

No, Yayati is not happy. He is unhappy.

Am I unhappy? I really do not know if I am happy or unhappy. What is happiness? What is misery? There cannot be two more difficult questions than these.

Am I still Yayati or someone else? Where am I going? Why? What for? Where am I? Where am I headed for in this pitch darkness?

Darkness! Where is the darkness? Am I going off my head?

Here is my cup of wine. My only friend, since the death of Madhav; a companion who does not leave me day or night. My dear friend, who tenderly removes the bristles and the thorns in my side. Here is my cup of wine. The empty glass, once filled for drowning me in heavenly bliss...

What is this here in this empty glass... ? Am I off my head?

What is this queer sound emanating from the empty glass? Who is this emerging from the cup? It is not just one figure. But — one ... two ... three ... seventeen, eighteen. Eighteen naked witches emerging from this cup...

What a weird dance they are doing. What are they dancing on? They look like the corpses of inexperienced beautiful young maidens. This sweet girl baffled by the first stirring of love; this budding sweet girl who blushes to herself with the first imprint of love in her heart; this bold maiden, thrilled by the sacred experience of love; this charming young woman bursting with youth, preparing to enter the golden temple, cherished in her dreams, of love, with a salver stacked with flowers and other articles of worship; these ugly witches are dancing on the corpses of all these.

They join in song with their dance. Their notes are like the furious hissing of a cobra.

Oh God! The twinkling lamps of heaven are going out one by one with every note sung by them. In no time the sky is dark and inky. These witches have put out all the lamps in heaven with every breath of their song.

What song, heralding the end of the world, are these witches singing?

One of them danced up to me and with a grotesque smile said, 'Do you recognise me? How foolish. You still have not recognised us sisters! We have striven so much for your pleasure, you ungrateful wretch! You have failed to recognise us, after all the pleasure you derived to your heart's content in our company?'

Another tall one came very close to me. She laughed fiendishly. I closed my eyes, terrified by her intimacy. She put her arms round me and said, 'Come and play with me.'

I opened my eyes. She took her hands off me and closed her fist. When she opened it, there were *cowries** in it.

Cowries? No, they are eyes. These, these are Madhavi's! These are Taraka's!

They were not *cowries*. They were eyes. How much had I kissed them. They were like little boats out to exploit love with eyelids for their oars. In those tiny boats, I have often been as far as the fringe of heaven.

The witch said, 'Come, let us play with these *cowries*.' I shuddered. For fear of life itself, I pushed her away with difficulty.

Was all this fiction? I had never indulged in it in the last eighteen years. Then why should it come to me now? Was it fact or fiction? Before me is only an empty glass. An empty glass. A blank mind. A vacant heart.

The feeling of emptiness burnt inside me. Like a bird caught in a forest fire, flapping its wings and screeching, my mind was flapping in a void of loneliness. There was nowhere it could rest. In the end, I jumped into the ocean of wine. I said to every wave in it, 'Take me

---

* Shells.

far, far down. Take me to the bottom of the dark sea of forgetfulness. Hide me in the chasm of some huge rock. Let me sleep there in peace. Let me sleep there in peace for all time.'

One day, I was fast asleep. But I woke up suddenly. I could see nothing. I could perceive nothing.

'It is evening.'

Who was talking? What did he say? It was evening? Did he mean the evening of my life?

This celestial messenger must have been mistaken. You silly, this is the Ashokavan in Hastinapur. I am King Yayati. How can the evening of my life come yet? I eagerly look forward to every night. Go away celestial messenger, try and remember the name of that senile old King on his deathbed for whom it was intended and give him your message.

'It is evening, Your Majesty. It is time to get ready.'

I laughed to myself. It was only Mukulika talking to me. How terrified and upset I was, believing her to be a celestial messenger.

'It is a beautiful evening. Shall I set your things out?'

'Pour me some wine and get my things ready if you have been able to find a nice fresh flower.'

I went to the window. It was indeed an inviting evening.

I thought all poets are slaves of portents. They have set ideas on beautiful evenings such as this. This intriguing pink of eventide in the west — is this the hue of eventide? The sun took a sip of wine and put the same cup to the lips of the evening. She demurred and was coy but while protesting mildly, that she did not want any, she suddenly put her hand out for it. With that the cup fell down and this is the wine that was spilt.

This gorgeous red of the eventide! This is the joy incarnate of the pleasures of a hunt. This day, the quarry which had escaped at dawn from the hands of the tribal, was now within range. The arrow has dug deep into its heart. It is the blood spurting from that deep gash that has coloured the western horizon.

I thought I might cast an evil eye on the exquisitely beautiful panorama before me and closed my eyes.

In life there are only three abiding realities — wine, women and hunting. Man forgets his unhappiness in their pursuit.

Wine stimulates the imagination and frees the inhibiting shackles. All thought of morality, duty and good and evil melt in the tempting warmth of wine.

In this life, one who does not want to be a quarry oneself must prey on the others. There is nothing like hunting to bring home to one this ultimate truth of life. The truth jars and smacks of cruelty. But that is the most important, all pervading hymn in the lyric of life. Purity, beauty and innocence are mere words conjured up by the upright and weak. The holy sacrificial fire is nothing more than the funeral pyre of the sacrificial goat. A beautiful woman is no more than a living doll catering to the transient impulse of passion. The carefree harmless deer is just food, provided by creation for the hunter.

And in the company of a woman are combined the pleasures of wine and the hunt.

I opened my eyes. All the hues of eventide had vanished. Darkness held sway over the sky, the interstellar space, the earth. It was Time! All-consuming Time! It was He who had made short shrift of the beautiful hues of eventide.

I did not dare to stand there, I turned away and lay down on the bed. Mukulika had already laid my things out. She was aimlessly hovering round me. I could not bring myself to believe that this was the Mukulika in whose company the mystery of the attraction of man and woman had been first revealed to me.

She was now middle-aged and tomorrow she will be old. I also...

Yesterday, today, tomorrow. No, what do yesterdays and tomorrows matter? Man has only one concern — the present moment. I have lived for the present for the last eighteen years. I tried to drown the swift wheel of racing time in a cup of wine and bring it to a standstill. I tried to ensnare it in the glances of beautiful women and hold it in their embraces.

No, I refuse to heed the past or the future.

Get rid of Mukulika? Can she easily be put away? No, her existence and my pleasures are inevitably linked together!

~

That terrible night eighteen years ago. I came out of Devayani's apartment, taking an oath that I would never again go near her. The poisonous darts of disgrace were gnawing at me.

In the end, I turned to the cottage of Mukulika's preceptor. I thought I had seen him somewhere before. The mystery was soon cleared. He was Mandar.

Mandar posed as a great sage. He had made up very well. His speech had a lure about it. His discourses on religion had the power to bring peace to troubled minds. There were as many disciples of Mandar as there are nuances of misery in the world. On the other hand there were many among his following who were there merely to achieve pleasures, not easily available otherwise. But there was a handsome sprinkling of beautiful young women also. Mandar made skilful use of them. He had captivated me eighteen years ago by just this device.

That night I longed for indulgence which would enable me to forget everything. I wished to forget Devayani's insults, I had no time for good and evil or morality and immorality. It was Mandar who showed me the way that night. I cannot even bear to think what would have happened if that night Mandar had not shown me this easy way of escape, if he had not piloted the bark of my life, heading for suicide.

Seeing Mandar that night in his hermitage, I was reminded of Yati. Yati strove with implicit faith towards attaining God by torturing his body.

Yati and Mandar? — What a contrast! Mandar's philosophy was very different from Yati's. The ordinary man believed in it — it was more acceptable to him. I fell a victim to his teachings just because of that. The essence of Mandar's philosophy was life is transient; it is like a flower which blooms today and fades tomorrow. One must taste as much of its fragrance as one can; the means are immaterial. There is no sin in it.

Treading this unfamiliar path, inherent inhibitions sometimes made me uneasy. As much as to say harshly, 'Fool, where are you going?'

On such occasions Mandar would persuade me, sometimes by quoting from the ancient tenets of the sages. At other times he would recount the unbridled indulgence in pleasure of renowned men and women. Yet again, he would impress on me the transience of life from examples in everyday life.

Once he and I were driving round the town in a chariot. We turned off the highway. Alongside was a potter's shop.

Smiling cynically, Mandar said, 'The Almighty also is a potter.'

I asked, 'In what sense?'

'He also makes similar earthen vessels ... like you and me. When earthen vessels break, they return to earth, as does man one day. If the potter's earthenware were imbued with life, I would say to them, "Listen Ye! Do not be content with drinking water only for your life. Drink wine. Drink nectar. Drink today whatever you can get. On the morrow, when you are in pieces, not a drop of any drink can you have." '

Once on our stroll, we passed by a cremation ground. There on the funeral pyre was burning the body of a young man. Mandar told me the history of his life. He had taken a vow of celibacy for attaining God. He had thus broken the heart of a girlfriend of his boyhood.

222

She was unhappy all her life. Till that day he had never tasted any physical pleasure; after that day he would never again be able to do so.

Looking at the blazing pyre, I imagined myself in the place of the youth.

Mandar put his hand on my shoulder and said, 'Your Majesty, in the running account of life, there is no place for deferred consumption. He who does not draw on pleasure today may not be able to get it tomorrow. In life the next golden day will dawn. The fragrant flowers will bloom. But he may not himself be there on the morrow to enjoy them.'

One day we happened to visit the house of a man of learning. Madhav had taken me to that very house. Now he was senile. He could remember nothing, see nothing and was barely able to walk. But the pleasures which he had spurned in his youth, had now turned on him in revenge. His unrequited passions were rising to the surface in strangely distorted forms. He would stand on the road and try to ogle at young girls passing by. His children would take him back to the house and lock him up. Even there he defaced the walls with obscene sketches in black. The women in them were half naked and in the presence of his grandchildren, he would kiss them.

In Mandar's cottage, I saw many young and middle-aged men and women. It all added up to this — religion, morality, duty, soul and goodness — all these pious words are sacrosanct to man. But it is only a blind.

Life is transient. Death is uncertain and may come any moment. Therefore, every moment of life is worth its weight in gold. Man must accordingly assuage his desires wringing from life all the fragrance, sweetness and happiness he can. Such was the philosophy given to me by Mandar.

I started on this new life like the whirlwind. For eighteen years, one season followed another. Spring, summer, autumn and winter seemed to be chasing each other around. The wheel of time had covered eighteen milestones. Night and day played hide and seek. Night found the day and the day in turn found the night. Year after year rolled by. But there was no break or change in the routine of my life.

Beautiful young maidens tended to my pleasure one day and were gone the next. My one concern was to ensure that the cup of my happiness was full. Mandar and Mukulika did keep it filled and filled to overflowing for eighteen years.

There are two nights in this orgy which I cannot put out of my mind. They are gnawing at me. They are nightmares.

One evening, Mukulika brought to me for a companion a beautiful young girl. I took her to bed. All I knew at the time was that she had lovely eyes. The girl in my arms muttered, 'Madhav, Madhav.' I was gently trying to put my hands round her, when she hugged me closer and murmured, 'Am I not yours? Don't Madhav, don't leave me like this!'

I was stunned. I peered at her. I recognised her. She was Madhavi. Mukulika must have doped her or maybe Mandar had hypnotised her. They alone knew what they did in replenishing my cup of happiness.

Gradually, Madhavi came to. She looked steadily at me. Then she screamed and ran out of the room, pushing open the door. Her body was found in the Yamuna the next day.

Another night, Mukulika brought to me a coy young maiden. Only next morning did I find out it was Taraka! She woke up as I was looking at her. She was in terror, as if bitten by a snake. The next moment she was screaming, 'Snake, snake!' and running out of the room.

I heard later that she had gone off her head. Some years later, someone told me that she mistook the sparks from a fire for flowers, went near to gather them and was burnt to death.

The bride-to-be of my dearest friend! His niece! Both lives were laid desolate because of me. I had ruined the life of Madhavi and had been guilty of the cruelest act towards Taraka whom I had seen playing with her dolls. 'Will you be the husband of my doll?' Those lisping words of hers. I brought her living death!

On these two occasions, I was upset for a long time. But I did not know of any way other than Mandar's. I thought I was secure and fulfilled under the influence of drink, the excitement of the hunt, and the heavenly bliss in the arms of a woman. Away from them, I was obsessed with being lonely, unhappy and insecure.

The seasons followed one another and the wheel of time kept turning. The course of my pleasure was uninterrupted.

I heard Mukulika saying, 'It is almost midnight, Your Majesty.' I opened my eyes.

I smiled at Mukulika. She came forward quickly and dressed me in no time.

~

I stood before the mirror. I was happy looking at my full-length reflection. I was handsome enough to be attractive to any young woman. I looked as young as Yayati bending over young Alaka to kiss her.

I had a good look at myself in the mirror. In a few moments, the image dimmed and became hazy. Behind the vague outline, I could see the forms of innumerable young maidens, grinding their teeth at me.

I stepped back a little and the haziness disappeared. I looked at my reflection again. My hair was tousled. I looked more carefully. The next moment I was stunned as if by a blow. One white hair was peeping through an otherwise black mass. That white hair seemed to me like the ashen hand of a sage pronouncing a curse.

225

The banner of old age had been planted on Yayati's head! Old age? The most unsavoury part of the drama of life. I would soon be old. I am still hungry and thirsting for pleasure. No, I shall not get old!

But that white hair? It maybe my imagination, as were those forms of young maidens a little while ago. I looked into the mirror again with great hope. The white hair was still there. It was a clear manifestation of what was coming.

I closed my eyes. I kept impressing on myself that the only real Yayati was the one who had kissed young Alaka. The white hair was the precursor of the cruel inevitable. I did not want to heed its message. I tried to escape from it into the past.

In doing so, I got back as far as Alaka. The Alaka of that glorious evening — with her golden hair — I had not yet had one with golden hair.

Mukulika quietly opened the door of the bedroom. The girl got up from the couch. She cast a luring glance at me and sat down.

The maiden was beautiful like the sculpture of an angel. I spread my arms...

Just then I heard Mukulika's tremulous hoarse words: 'Your Majesty.' I asked in irritation, 'What is the matter?'

'The Prime Minister is here.'

'I have no time to see him.'

'He has been here sometime and he will not take no for an answer. He says, the Prince has been captured.'

The Prince ... captive ... Alaka ... golden hair ... white hair ... old age ... death.

The Prime Minister talked at length. He prattled on and on. But I did not want to hear for a moment his idle talk about court matters. My mind was hovering round the girl near me.

Devayani was crying because Yadu had been taken captive. Devayani had deputed the Prime Minister to remind me of my duty as King and as a father but how far had she honoured her duty as wife? Did she once think of her husband in the last eighteen years? Did she ever feel that she ought to have forgiven him? Did she ever wish to rescue him from being carried away and drowned in the stream? Was she afraid of the huge flood? Sharmishtha would never have kept quiet in those circumstances. The fact is that she never loved me. What is the use crying now? She feels today that I should be true to my duty as King and as father. Only he who honours his duty has the right to expect others to honour theirs. Where did she leave her duty as wife for the last eighteen years?

The Prime Minister talked away. He was trying to persuade me to return to the palace.

Go on a campaign to free Yadu, take to the battlefield. What if I am killed! No, my life is yet to be lived. I am yet unfulfilled. My youth is still unsatisfied. The golden-haired girl ... golden hair ... white hair ... old age, death. No — I shall not set out to rescue Yadu. I had by then lost control over myself and did not care what I said.

'Please tell Her Majesty I am grateful to her for remembering me after so many years.'

The Prime Minister returned to the attack. By now, I was exasperated and lost my temper. I added, 'Let alone Yadu, I shall not move my little finger even if Her Majesty were captured.'

As soon as I returned to the bedroom, my unknown bedmate stood up. But my white hair was bothering me. What if she sees it? No, the shadow of old age creeping over Yayati must not be noticed by anyone. Yayati is ever young! Yayati was going to *remain* ever young!

I stood before the mirror. What great hope I had that the white hair would have disappeared. But the wicked thing was impudently jeering at me.

I remembered the golden hair of Alaka. I was taken aback to find the girl standing close to me. She had put her hand on my shoulder. Seeing me inactive inspite of her intimacy, she put her arms round me.

I looked at her hair and shouted, 'Go away.'

She did not know what she had done. She looked at me a little scared. I called angrily to Mukulika.

'Take this flower of yours and throw it away. Don't you know my taste?'

She went to the girl and lifted her head a little. She was crying. I bent her head gently, saying, 'Look and see. Is there a single golden hair in this? I want a girl with golden hair! When can I get her ... tomorrow?'

'How can I find one by tomorrow?'

Mukulika begged of me with folded hands, 'If Your Majesty will kindly give us fifteen days?'

'All right, I will give you the time. But if you do not succeed, the sixteenth day you and your preceptor will be publicly disgraced. What is today?'

'It is new moon today.'

'All right. If by full moon day, a girl with golden hair is not presented... .'

Mukulika stood there with folded hands. I shouted at her, 'Get out.'

I woke up next day well after sunrise. Immediately on rising, I went to the mirror and looked carefully at myself. I was stunned. Not only was the white hair of last night mocking me but by its side was another white hair.

Distressed, I went and lay in bed. I tossed about from side to side. The tumult of thought, enough to split the head, would not stop. I was again and again reminded of Sharmishtha. I could have told her without reserve my fear of old age, death and lack of contentment with life. Her tears would have assuaged the unnamed fear in my heart. But I was alone. In this whole world, I was all alone.

I began thinking. Why should I not feel contented even after eighteen years of licentious pleasure?

What is the content of life? Why is man born? Why does he die? What is the purpose of life? What is its significance? Are life and death, youth and old age, the two sides of the same coin? Are they pairs as natural as day and night? Why then is man so afraid of old age and death?

What does man live on? Love? But what then is love? Are love, kindness and affection mere masks? Man lives only for his own happiness, only for the satisfaction of his ego.

The love of the parents, the love of man and wife — all love is pretension. It is mere playacting. At heart, man only loves himself, his body, his happiness and his ego. Even in that wonderful, tender and mysterious attraction between man and woman, this element of self does not change. Do a few hours of physical pleasure measure up to love? Momentary satisfaction of violent passion — does it amount to love?

No. Love is apart from desire. In the love of man and wife also, desire burns but that is sacred like the sacrificial fire. It burns within the bounds of the morals of life.

I did not keep the sanctity of it. My profligate life has been nothing short of a forest conflagration. Many innocent birds were scorched in that fire. Many tender fragrant creepers were reduced to ashes in it.

Is this repentance? Is this premature renunciation brought about by the sight of those two white hairs? To achieve pleasure, I spent every moment in indulgence. Why then am I still unsatisfied? Why am I unhappy? How is it that the stream of countless momentary pleasures does not produce even a drop of eternal happiness?

Really — what is happiness?

Pleasure is a butterfly. It flits from flower to flower, tasting honey. But can the butterfly aspire to be an eagle? If you wish to bring a jug of nectar from heaven, a butterfly is unequal to the task. Only the eagle can attempt it. The butterfly and the eagle. Momentary pleasure and lasting happiness are things apart. I pursued pleasure but getting it did not bring me happiness.

What constitutes happiness? Has it no relation to any physical pleasure? No, there was nothing wrong with the libertine's life which I had led for eighteen years. I loved myself. I sought my own pleasure. Was I to blame for it?

Is man's love confined to the love of his own self? Alaka's love, Madhav's love, Kacha's love, were all these loves selfish? Were they not selfless?

And Sharmishtha — her love for me? There she is in the jungle eating roots and herbs, worshipping me at heart. And I? I am all the time mocking her sacred love steeped in wine. The lips sanctified by her kisses are sacrileged with kissing other tainted lips.

Why should it be so? Why should I not be capable of loving as Sharmishtha did? Why should I be unable to live a restrained life like Kacha?

Desire — desire in any form — is it man's fault? No, desire is the very basis of life. Then what wrong have I done? That my desire was uncontrolled? That I did not realise, that in life the smallest happiness of any individual is circumscribed by his temperament, circumstances and the incompleteness of life?

Like me, Kacha also could have been steeped in pleasures when he brought the Sanjeevani to the gods. But he was unaffected. Where did he get the strength to do it?

Kacha was not born a recluse. He loved Devayani with all his heart. He put duty to his community before self. In honouring that duty, he renounced love. That sacrifice did not make his life futile, miserable, or idle.

I had the happiness of a household in the company of Devayani. I experienced a glorious, noble love with Sharmishtha. But I was not satisfied. I am still not satisfied. And yet, Kacha, who is unaware of

230

the nectar of a maiden's luscious lips, is satisfied. Why should it be so? Where did I go wrong?

Kacha wrote to me from this very Ashokavan. I very much wish to read that letter once again, but it is at the palace. Both the things are there. The golden hair of Alaka and that letter of gold of Kacha.

Shall I get peace of mind by reading that letter? But Devayani will not give it to anyone else. What if I go to the palace and fetch it? I shall never go there as long as I live.

But am I happy at least in Ashokavan? Why is my mind straining to drown the fear of death, roused by the white hair, in the infatuation of a golden-haired maiden?

Are desires akin to ghosts? My desire for Alaka in my youth remained unsatisfied. How has that desire, repressed in the subconscious for many years, come to the surface now?

Why should I not be able to conquer it? Is it the rule of the universe that unless the pursuit of pleasures is renounced, the ultimate truth of life is not revealed? Devayani had taken care to keep Yadu away from me all the time. My instinct of affection was unsatisfied. Would the void in my mind have been filled in Yadu's company? If not Yadu, Puroo? Where is he? How heartless I have been. I have completely forgotten him in the last eighteen years. Do sensuous pleasures dull the mind? Do they lead to lack of humanity? How did Kacha acquire his restraint? Why could I not have it?

To all appearances, I was lying down quietly on the bed. I looked as if I was fast asleep. But inside I was shaken by blow after blow. Things which I wished to forget were stealthily peeping through the subconscious. They were tearing at my heart. I dared not look at my past life without trepidation. There was only one way out of my misery — suicide.

I shuddered. Then I laughed to myself. If I had the courage to take my life would I not have done so eighteen years ago?

I had another long familiar way of emerging from my queer depression. That was to go over the sweet moments of past indulgence.

Many figures who had served to keep my cup of happiness ever filled to the brim passed before my eyes. Here is one. What a beautiful head of hair she had. Not a head of hair, but a mass of bees attracted to her lotus face.

Here is that dark but lovely maiden. If you just touched her lips with yours, a thrill of ecstasy ran though your body. What utter delight her mouth was! Here is that vivacious maiden. She could teach a thing or two in the art of making love, even to the god of love.

Innumerable such figures passed before my eyes, I gathered a rich harvest of happiness in alluring glances, tender embraces and silken heads of hair. But even so, a golden-haired girl...

'Is Your Majesty not feeling well tonight?' Mukulika standing by the bed, bent over to ask me.

I opened my eyes. I said angrily, 'Where were you so long?'

'I had gone to the palace very early.'

'What did you find out?'

'The Prince is free. There is great rejoicing at the palace.'

I asked in surprise, 'The Prince is free? How?'

'Some brave youth freed him at risk to his own life. The Prince is on his way here with his friend.'

My heart should have leapt at Yadu's being released from captivity, but what I said was, 'Yadu has been freed? Good.' Was Yayati living a fuller life day after day in the last eighteen years or was he dying by inches? How much of Yayati was dead? Who, who was that whispering, 'Yayati is alive only physically!'

Mukulika hurriedly told me, 'Now that his penance is over the father of Her Majesty is soon coming here.'

232

Maharishi Shukra coming here? In which case should I go out of Hastinapur? Mukulika went on, 'Kacha has also been invited by Her Majesty!'

She was by now very near me and whispered, 'The Queen has decided to crown the Prince. In order to get the blessings of both Maharishi Shukra and Kacha... .'

Whatever happened I would not relinquish the throne of Hastinapur. I said, 'Kacha also is sitting in penance.'

'Yes, but they say that also is over.'

I smiled and said, 'It looks as if generally the time for penance is up. So be it. My penance can also end now.'

'What does Your Majesty mean?'

'Fill the cup and I will tell you.'

'In the morning... ?'

'A maid has no business to ask questions. Your duty ends with giving me even a cup of poison, if asked for it.'

I put the cup to my mouth and said, 'Wake me up when the golden-haired girl arrives. Till then let me sleep... sleep.'

During those fifteen days of waiting for the full moon and the golden-haired girl another realisation kept recurring. It said, 'Yayati, you fool, where are you going? This is the way to hell.' I would sip a little wine and say, 'Is it not true that Heaven and Hell are near each other?' It would say, 'Yes ... they border one another.' I would reply with a smile, 'Then why are you so afraid for me? Tomorrow, in a moment I shall quit the way to Hell and go on the way to Heaven.'

It would say, 'You fool, there is a barricade every inch of the border between Heaven and Hell. In man's childhood, it is all taken down. But as he grows up man himself raises them one by one. And once closed, none of the doors can ever again be opened. Unfortunate one! Now there is only one door open to you. Don't close it with your own hands. Listen to me, heed me!'

This pricking consciousness I would drown in the cup.

233

But the nightmare I had could not be drowned:

I would first see an enormous chariot. It had six horses tethered to it. All of them appeared to be spirited animals. The charioteer of my dream was staking his life to rein in the steeds. But they were beyond his control. They were running at will, careering madly over pits and potholes, shattering loose the chariot in their mad rush.

Every night I dreamt thus. But on the fourteenth night:

The chariot went down a difficult bypass. On one side were towering hills. On the other a deep chasm. The finest and most spirited of the six horses took the bit between his teeth and ran amuck. He headed for the chasm. The reins broke, the whip lashed the back of the air and in no time the chariot crashed. From the abyss came a deafening roar as if the heavens had fallen.

I got up screaming 'Shama, Shama.' Why did I call to Sharmishtha in my dream? I felt the dream was an evil omen. Perhaps Sharmishtha was taking leave of this cruel world somewhere. I could not sleep. All night I lay in bed dead drunk, like a corpse.

The sun was setting. The full moon was coming up. The sky appeared to be thrilled with happiness, drinking from the cup of the moon. The cup in its hand tilted a little and the wine overflowed as moonlight on the earth.

Soon, Mukulika gave me the good news. With great difficulty, Mandar had found a girl with golden hair for me. Shall I find the joy of taking Alaka when I crush her golden hair in my hands?

I told Mukulika, 'I shall not be deceived. If her hair is not golden, then you two will be beheaded. And where did you find this golden-haired doll?'

234

'Here itself.'

'If she was found here, why was she not brought to me before? That Mandar is a fraud. You are cunning.'

'Forgive me Your Majesty, but she is not from Hastinapur. She only came to the town today looking for her lover.'

She continued, 'Her lover is a youth who has gone to war. Someone told her that he was coming to town today with Prince Yadu. She left her escort, an elderly lady, and came to town this morning, only to learn that the Prince was returning tonight. She was disappointed. She is very naughty. She started screaming, so we had to give her a little dope. She should come round by about midnight.'

'Must I wait so long? Why did you give her so much dope?'

'She was very violent, Your Majesty. There are many visitors today in the hermitage. What if some of these strangers got wise to what is happening? Also, the courier has brought word that Maharishi Shukra will arrive at the palace at about nine. The Prince is also arriving about that time. So the preceptor thought that your Majesty will be otherwise engaged till almost midnight... .'

'You are a fool and your preceptor is worse. I am not concerned with the Prince returning to town. Make arrangements to bring the golden-haired girl in a palanquin straightaway, without rousing suspicion.'

Looking at the girl lying unconscious on the bed, I could not make up my mind whether I was dreaming or it was in fact my Alaka that I was seeing again. She certainly had golden hair. The intervening twenty years had rolled away. I had regained my Alaka!

I was getting impatient for her. I was angry with Mandar and Mukulika. Who had asked them to give her so much dope? How can one make love to a corpse?

I did not know how late it was. I had now no desire to sip wine. I wanted just to forget everything. God knows what tomorrow will bring? Maharishi Shukra, Devayani...

Today, here — now was the moment, the golden moment!

I could not wait. I went and stood near the girl. I bent down to kiss her golden hair. I was back again in my youth. Alaka was going to be my love tonight. That golden dream hidden in my heart for years was going to come true today.

But before I could put my lips to the golden mop of hair, Mukulika screeched from behind the door, 'Your Majesty, please come out ... come out quickly!'

I resented the interruption but raised my head and asked, 'Why?'

'The Queen and Maharishi Shukra are coming. Maharishi Shukra is in a rage and is asking everybody where Your Majesty is!'

My legs gave way. The tongue went dry. Like one lying ill for a long time, I stumbled into the outer room dragging my feet.

Seeing me come in, Devayani, who was sitting on a couch, turned her head in disgust. Maharishi Shukra was pacing the floor in a rage. The room was going round and round. I leaned against the wall mirror and held myself up with difficulty.

Maharishi Shukra suddenly stopped, fixed me with his eyes for a few seconds and then in great anger said, 'Yayati, I have not come to you in the role of a sage. Do you recognise me?'

I nodded with trepidation.

Jeering at me, he said, 'You are under the influence of drink and not in your right senses. I am Shukra, the invincible Preceptor of the Demons, who having acquired Sanjeevani brought even the gods to their knees. I have again acquired a power as potent as Sanjeevani. I have come to inquire about my daughter's well being and have had the misfortune to see my daughter steeped to the neck in misery. You irresponsible creature, I gave to you for safe keeping a matchless jewel, invaluable as the earth, and you threw it away as a piece of flint.'

I was scared by the wrath of Maharishi Shukra. No words would come out. In the end, I gathered all my courage to say, 'Sire, I am guilty; I have offended against you in a hundred ways. But Devayani is equally to blame for what has unfortunately come to pass.'

On hearing this, Devayani turned round and seething with rage, said, 'Father, did you bring me here to see for yourself how at every step insults are hurled at me? You are tired. Let us go back to the palace. Persons steeped in vice are worse than the devil.'

My anger knew no bounds and I blurted out, 'And what about persons steeped in selfish egoism?'

Devayani got angrier. She put her hand on Maharishi Shukra's shoulder and said, 'Father, Yadu must by now be entering the town in state while you are with a libertine, drowned in wine and women.'

Maharishi Shukra brushed her hand away and said in anger, 'Devayani, you are my all. But you are a fool. You do not know the right time to do a thing. Once before you lost me the power of Sanjeevani by insisting on my bringing Kacha back to life. I shall not spare Yayati as a son-in-law. I must punish him with something which he will remember all his life... .'

Devayani said to him sweetly, 'Setting Yadu on the throne will open his eyes. I have now no mind for any other happiness in life.'

I was burning inside at her melodrama. But Devayani intended to insult me which hurt me. I said harshly, 'I am the King. How can Yadu be crowned without my consent?'

Maharishi Shukra intervened calmly, 'King, I grant you your rights as the King. Has Devayani no rights as the Queen? When you accepted her hand in marriage did you not swear on oath that you will not violate the sanctity of marriage?'

'I was unable to keep it. My youth was to blame. I fell a prey to temptation.'

'If you were young, was Devayani old?'

'I beg to be forgiven, Sire. I am guilty in a hundred ways.'

'Forgiveness is only for the first offence. A confirmed criminal will not mend his ways with light punishment.'

He fell silent and was absorbed in thought. I was like one chained to a huge rock, at the mouth of a rumbling volcano!

With a disparaging look, Maharishi Shukra said, 'Your Majesty, is it not true that you spurned Devayani and took to yourself Sharmishtha?'

'I did not love Devayani,' I wanted to say.

Sage Shukra raised his voice. His words sounded like the thunder of black clouds. He said angrily, 'Had I not warned you to be careful of Sharmishtha? You broke my command ... the command of Devayani's father ... the command of Maharishi Shukra. You must take the consequences of disobeying my command.'

'But, Sire, youth is blind.'

'I only wish to cure you of your blind spot. Youth is blind. It was youth that tempted you. Was it not? Then I am only going to ordain that you shall from now on lose your youth. I pray that the sinner before me, sinful Yayati, immediately turn into a decrepit old man.'

The curse left me staggered, as if I had been struck by lightning. The world swam before my eyes. My mind became a blank. When I looked into the mirror with trepidation, my face was wrinkled. My head was all covered with white hair. Standing before the mirror was a decrepit old man.

I was reminded of the golden-haired girl in the bedroom. It must already be past midnight. The girl must have come to by now. A little while ago, I had not even kissed her golden hair. Now, now — I can never kiss it again. That glamorous girl with Alaka's face...

I was agonised by my thoughts. Devayani was sitting at the feet of Maharishi Shukra and moaning, 'What have you done father?'

A ray of hope arose in my heart. I folded my hands and pleaded, 'Sire, have mercy on me. My mind is still young. I very much want to live happily with Devayani. But what pleasure can she get in living with a decrepit old husband like me?'

Devayani intervened with a pitying look, 'Father, I cannot bear to look at him. Make him young again.' Maharishi Shukra said, 'Your Majesty, the arrow of a warrior and the curse of an ascetic never go in vain. You must suffer my curse. You wish, even if belatedly, to live happily with Devayani again. I shall, therefore, pronounce a counter curse. If some young man of your own flesh and blood comes forward to exchange his youth for your old age, at your wish your old age will pass to him. His youth will come to you. But remember one thing. This borrowed youth of yours will only return to him at your death. And in no other way. You must think of me and repeat three times, "I am returning your youth" when you fall dead... .'

Devayani screamed, 'Father what kind of a counter curse is this? This is even more terrible than the curse itself.'

Maharishi Shukra was overcome with anger and shot up from the couch. He looked angrily at Devayani and said, 'My girl, I rushed here immediately on arrival to resolve your domestic affairs. That was a mistake. I have fondled and spoilt you a great deal since childhood. What did I gain? Insults! Nothing but insults! So far I have done what I could for you. Now I have nothing to do with you and your husband.' Maharishi Shukra left the apartment with those words.

The two of us remained behind, a senile decrepit and a beautiful lady. Devayani was afraid to look at me. I was ashamed to show my face to her. What a queer and unseemly plight. We were in one room. But we lived in different worlds.

I heard vague sounds from the bedroom. The beautiful girl must be coming to. That golden hair of hers...

I heard a maid saying from the doorway, 'Your Majesty, the Prince is coming to see you.'

I saw two youths walking in. I quickly turned away. If Yadu were to see my old haggard self...

But Yadu was my son, Yadu was of my family. He was my flesh and blood. He could take on my old age and give me his youth.

239

Yadu was talking to Devayani. Hearing that she had suddenly gone to Ashokavan, he had rushed here. With him was the brave youth who had freed him from captivity.

Every atom of my body was contemplating the beautiful girl in my bed. At that moment, I wanted youth. I wanted the pleasure I could get in her company only with youth. Suddenly like lightning, a thought struck me.

The two youths were taken aback on seeing me. I calmly called Yadu to me and said, 'Yadu, do you recognise me? I am your father Yayati. Do you love your father enough to make a sacrifice?'

Devayani suddenly screamed, 'Yadu, Yadu!'

Devayani had avenged herself on me for eighteen years. Now was my golden opportunity to wreak vengeance in return. I wished to take over Yadu's youth and go into the inner room and come out arm in arm with that beautiful girl.

I said to Yadu, 'I have no more wish to continue as King. You could be crowned but not only because you are my son. You see this old age on me? I came by it as the result of a curse. I am looking for a youth of my flesh and blood who is prepared to take it on himself in exchange for a kingdom. On the day of my death, he will regain his youth. Maharishi Shukra has granted me a counter curse to that effect. If you want, ask your mother if it is not true.'

Yadu was startled at my words. He drew back a little and hastened to Devayani. She took him in her arms and said, 'Yadu, your father is off his head. Come, let us return to the palace. Leave him alone here, to admire his white hair in the mirror.'

I was furious with Devayani. But I was helpless. His refusal was reflected on his face. My hopes had died!

Devayani said looking at Yadu's companion, 'Yadu, you have not yet told us the name of your companion. This skeleton in our cupboard should not have been exposed to an outsider!'

The youth said to Devayani in all humility, 'Mother, I am no stranger.'

'You have saved the life of Yadu, my son. How can I now look upon you as a stranger?'

'Mother, I am willing to do what the Prince is frightened to undertake.'

Hope sprang in my heart. I went near the youth and said, 'Are you prepared to take over my old age?'

'Gladly.'

'But, but how could you? It cannot be taken over except by one of my flesh and blood.'

'I owe every drop of my blood to you, Your Majesty. I am your son.'

Devayani trembled like an ashen leaf at those words. She looked at the youth and said, 'His Majesty has only one son, who alone is heir to the throne.'

'I am not laying a claim to the throne. Mother, I wish to abide by my duty as a son. I want to grant father's wish. I am His Majesty's son. None can deny me the right to take over his old age.'

'You, you are the son of Sharmishtha?' asked Devayani in agony.

He replied, 'Yes, my name is Puroo.'

Every atom of my burning body said, 'Remember, such an opportunity for revenge will never recur. You are getting your youth back. Do not forgo this opportunity for vengeance.'

I looked at Puroo. He stood still. There was not an iota of fear in his face.

I was begging Puroo, now on the threshold of youth, for his youth. I was set on giving him my old age. No, no, can I even bear to see Puroo, whose mop of hair I had fondly caressed, standing before me as a haggard old man with white hair? I was shaky in my intentions.

Devayani was aflame with the strange happenings of the last two hours. In measured steps she walked up to Puroo and said, 'You are Puroo? Truly Puroo? The son of Sharmishtha? Why are you hesitating

241

then? She is said to have been deeply in love with him. What is there to think of? Give your youth to him! And, and take on his old age.'

All the lurking desires were drumming in my ears: 'There is that beautiful maiden waiting for you in your room. For the last fifteen days, you had set your heart on her. Are you going to throw away this opportunity without even putting your lips to it? Then why did you not turn an ascetic eighteen years ago? What, after all, does Puroo stand to lose by taking over your old age for three or four years? On the other hand, in exchange, he stands to gain a kingdom. For a few years, enjoy life to your heart's content; assuage all desire and then return to him his youth.'

Whether it was because of Devayani's nagging, Puroo immediately stepped forward. He put his head on my feet and said, 'Father, I am the son of a Princess who agreed to be a maid for the sake of her people. I am willing to take on your old age.' And all I could say in reply was, 'So be it!' Realising the implication of those words, I immediately closed my eyes. A few moments later, I opened them to bless Puroo. The Puroo standing before me was decrepit and old.

Devayani was nonplussed at the miracle. She left the room that instant with Yadu.

Puroo stood before the mirror and scanned his appearance. For a moment, he covered his face with his hands. I did not know whether he was sorry for his sacrifice. But soon after he calmly went to the couch and sat there. That calmed me a little.

When leaving the town, Sharmishtha had sent a message, 'Let the hand of His Majesty ever bless Puroo!' But today, I had crashed a thunderbolt on his head. I wished to go to him, draw him to me and console him, but that was only momentary. I did not have the courage. How timid sin is!

In a couple of hours, the world had turned topsy turvy. Liquor does make one subject to hallucinations. Was this one? In the whirlpool of thought I became numb; I felt choked.

242

Hard fact stared me in the face in the haggard form of Puroo. I saw myself in the mirror. I was looking even younger. My desire for Alaka — with her golden hair — the unsatisfied longing of twenty years was the one and only desire, that fired my mind now like the great fire at the destruction of the world! I turned to the bedroom.

I went in. The girl was sitting up. She could not fathom how and when she had come into the bedroom. She looked at me and smiled. I felt that my youth had been rewarded. I stepped forward. She showed fright on her face. She got up and retired into a corner. I stepped forward to take her hand when I heard someone sobbing in the outer room. My hand went limp.

First, I thought it might be Puroo sobbing. He must be repenting his thoughtless sacrifice. But the sobs were those of a woman.

The sobbing outside continued. It grew louder. I did not want such distraction at my happiest moment. I came out in anger.

Puroo was sitting on the couch like a statue. Sitting close to him, with her arms round him, was a woman weeping and sobbing. Her whole body was racked with emotion.

That a maid should be so intimate with Puroo? I lost my temper. I stepped forward and said, 'Puroo, you are now King. And a King must keep his dignity. Who is this lowly maid, with her arms... .'

The remaining words stuck in my throat. At the sound of my voice, the woman had turned her head. I wished that mother earth would open up and swallow me.

She was Sharmishtha. She was weeping bitterly at Puroo's condition. I could not bear to look at her. Her sobs were unbearable. I hung my head in shame.

Eighteen years ago, while bidding Sharmishtha farewell from the top of the underground stairs, I had said, 'God knows where and in what circumstances we shall meet again.' That our meeting had taken place today. And in such a setting. I was numb. I closed my eyes. I was rooted to the spot.

243

Sharmishtha, my beloved Shama. I was dying to draw her near me, wipe her tears and console her. But how was I to lessen her grief? Can the hunter who has killed her young one console the deer?

By ourselves, I had often said to her, that Sharmishtha and Yayati were not two but one. But today I had turned her enemy. He whom she had worshipped all her life in her heart had today consigned her to the flames.

Sharmishtha's tears were bathing my feet. But every single tear was branding my heart. I was ashamed that an angel like her should fall at the feet of a devil like me. But I did not have the courage to touch her, even to lift her up.

She looked up once. In her eyes was crowded the pathos of eternal death. With trembling lips she said, 'Your Majesty, what has happened to us?'

I had wrought it all with my own evil hands. With all consciousness, I had exchanged my old age with Puroo's youth. Deliberately, for the momentary satisfaction of the desire for sex!

I had trampled underfoot my duty as a father. I had spurned parental sentiment and forgotten common humanity. For momentary selfish pleasure, I had sacrificed the offspring of my flesh and blood. For eighteen years, I had been raising a temple to the demon of desire. What a terrible dome I had set on it today!

Sharmishtha was mine. She had given me unflinching love. It was my duty to lay my life down for a tear of hers. It was not just a duty; in such death lay seas of happiness. I began thinking. To make Sharmishtha happy, I must return to Puroo his youth. And that, without a moment's delay. But except with my death there was no returning to him his youth.

Death, from constant fear of which I had succumbed to physical pleasure, the unknown, unnamed death. Without a thought, was I to embrace it?

I turned to Sharmishtha. How expectantly she was looking at me? Had she grumbled when she went into exile eighteen years ago? She had gone through that ordeal only to save me from Devayani's wrath.

The love of Sharmishtha, of Madhav, of Kacha. Should I also not love thus? A corner of my heart, which never in the past had been revealed to me, was now coming into view. There was a gentle light in that corner. Slowly it grew bigger.

The joy of dying for someone else is a hundred times greater than the joy of living for oneself. What a great and noble truth this is! But, for the first time today, it was revealed to me.

Maharishi Shukra had changed my exterior, now Sharmishtha was changing my heart. A Yayati I had never seen before was now standing before me. He placed his hand on the shoulder of death and said, 'There are only two things real in life, Love and Death. Come my friend. I have come to keep you company in this darkness. Fear not, fear none. Have you seen this lamp in my hand? What did you say? This is the star of Venus? No, my friend, it is Sharmishtha's love.'

I raised her up and said, 'Shama, don't worry. By the grace of God, everything will turn out all right.'

She asked pathetically, 'Will Puroo be restored to his old self?'

I replied smiling, 'Yes, here and now.'

She said with tears in her eyes, 'No, Your Majesty, you are deceiving me. Puroo will not be his old self.'

Wiping her tears I said, 'Calm yourself Shama, calm yourself. Your Puroo will be restored to his old self. Maharishi Shukra did not curse him. It was pronounced by the wicked man known as Yayati. This licentious, profligate, inhuman Yayati is your culprit. He has sinned against Puroo.'

She looked blankly at me. She did not believe my words. I was touched with her faith in me. Truly, how good man is. He lives on the strength of confidence, faith, attachment, love, devotion and service. He has the courage to face death on the strength of those. But all

245

these sentiments are not attributes of the body. They are attributes of the soul.

During the last eighteen years I had lost my soul. Sharmishtha, on the other hand, had preserved hers. With the strength of her faith, it had blossomed. I must embrace death, with the same ecstasy as of love, and return Puroo's youth to him.

Knowing that I must accept death for the sake of Puroo, Sharmishtha was bewildered, and she lost her nerve and began sobbing, 'Your Majesty, as I am a mother, I am also a wife. I want both my eyes ... both of them, Your Majesty.'

She could not say more. I melted seeing her devotion. But this was no time to take love; it was time to return in full measure the love received.

I said to Sharmishtha, 'It is late in the night now. We can think more clearly tomorrow. In any case, I promise, that your Puroo will be restored to his old self. Go and sit with him. You have given birth to a selfless son. You are truly the mother of a hero. Go and comfort him.'

As soon as Sharmishtha's back was turned I closed my eyes in meditation of Maharishi Shukra. I kept saying, 'I wish to return this borrowed youth to its owner. In doing so, I am willing to accept death.' I repeated it twice. I started saying the words silently to myself, with Sharmishtha's back turned to me. Suddenly I felt the room going round like a top. Simultaneously, I heard the words, 'Kacha has come.'

At that, I collapsed on the floor.

I do not know how many days later I came round. It was probably evening. Someone was chanting in a sweet voice. The chanting stopped. I could see a vague form approaching me. It put a mark of sacred ashes on my forehead. I peered at the figure and saw that it was Kacha.

He did not say a word, just smiled. In response, a faint smile must have appeared on my face. He smiled again. Truly, how sweetly communicative a smile can be.

When I woke up again, it was morning. You could see the dawn in the east. I lay quietly with my eyes closed. Someone was chanting hymns. I opened my eyes. Kacha was praying to the ball of fire in the east.

I could hear his prayers distinctly:

Oh Sun God. Welcome to you. You are the epitome of the power of the soul over the senses. You have conquered darkness. As much as you are the soul of the universe; you are also the soul of the spiritual entity of man. Although your charioteer maybe lame, you never fail in your duty. Let your sacred light penetrate our minds as it does the caves and hollows of the world. There also wild beasts live. Oh you, of the thousand rays, welcome to you.

Morning and evening, Kacha would chant hymns like this. Even otherwise, when he visited me, it was his habit to chant hymns. But these hymns would transport me to another world. There, flowers had no thorns to them and the stones oozed fragrance.

Many hymns from Kacha's recitation have come to be engraved on my mind:

The fragrance of flowers cannot be seen but is felt by the nose. The beauty of the soul is something like that.

All kinds of passion are death. This death is very different from the ordinary one because in them the soul itself perishes.

Oh eagle! Flying in the direction of the high peaks, you know how deep the valley on the other side is. Come and tell man, blindly pursuing transient pleasure, of that valley. Bring him this nectar.

Conscience, feeling and body: the triple confluence of these constitutes life. How can any one of them, attain the sanctity of the three together?

Do you wish to understand the grief of the deer, which in pursuit runs till it bleeds from the heart? Then hunter let the deer be the hunter. Give it your bow and arrows. And you? You be the deer.

Do you wish to know how to love? Then make the river, the tree and the mother your tutors.

The senses are never satisfied by indulgence. As the fire blazes with an offering, so do the senses get incensed the more by indulgence.

I could recall a whole lot of hymns to this effect. They were my friends in my sick bed.

Gradually, the royal physician permitted me to talk a little. In this intervening period, not only was I reborn but apparently Devayani also. She had acquired considerable restraint and love of service.

I tried to piece together the incidents from the time I collapsed to the floor that night. In my mind I tried to weave into a fabric the clues provided by Kacha, Sharmishtha, Devayani, Puroo and Yadu.

That night with Maharishi Shukra in my mind I had said twice the words which would return Puroo's youth to him. I had started on the third time but did not complete it. It was interrupted by the words, 'Kacha has come.' I then collapsed to the floor.

Kacha also had acquired by his penance a power as potent as that of Maharishi Shukra. On the strength of it he restored Puroo's youth to him.

Only when talking about ascetics, their penance and the powers achieved by them would Kacha be very disturbed. Then he would say, 'Your Majesty, man is no beast, but at heart, man remains much like the beast pursuing life by the blind instinct of self preservation. Talking ill of the preceptor is a sin, but concealing the truth is an even greater sin. I must, therefore, talk a little about Maharishi Shukra. Seeing him falling a prey to anger at every step, who can guarantee that the superhuman powers achieved by man, after prolonged penance, by a man who has been unable to gain mastery over his passions, will always be used for the well-being of all? What sense is there to a life in which, with the two sides equally matched, strife continues? Is this how the world is to go on? No, if man desires happiness he must first conquer his passions.'

Kacha would talk thus. I would listen. I was distressed by his sincerity. I was convinced of the truth of his words. But I did not know how to comfort him.

On my sick bed, we two came even nearer. Immediately after his penance, on hearing of my degeneration he had set out to come here. He had got Devayani's invitation on the way. As soon as he entered the town, he heard that I was staying at Ashokavan and came straight to me.

How timely his arrival was! My death was averted by his coming. Puroo got back his youth. And I was saved from an overwhelming sin!

That golden-haired girl ... Is it possible that in her last moments Alaka had prayed to God, saying that her desire to serve Yayati had been left unfulfilled? How could it have been ordained that she should return to Hastinapur to be my daughter-in-law?

Sharmishtha also had come in the nick of time. She had come to live in a village near Hastinapur, so as to keep in touch with news of Puroo on the battlefield. She was afraid that Puroo might also have been taken captive with Yadu. Hearing of Yadu's return to the capital, she and Alaka decided to come to Hastinapur early in the morning; but in the night when Sharmishtha woke up Alaka was not there! She looked for Alaka all night in that village. Heavy at heart, she somehow reached Hastinapur in the evening. She saw Puroo entering the town with Yadu. The crowds were hailing Puroo as the saviour of Yadu and Puroo received more cheers and greater ovation than Yadu. Her heart was full. She wanted to see him at closer quarters but did not succeed. Suddenly Puroo and Yadu went away somewhere. Later an old man told her, 'They have both gone to Ashokavan for an audience with the Queen.' She was terrified. Would Devayani bless Puroo as the saviour of her son's life or would she avenge herself on him as the son of a co-wife?

She did not know what to do to ensure the safety of Puroo. She just ran for Ashokavan. But it was only when I saw Yati again, that I realised, that miracles greater than the most miraculous do happen.

Yati came on purpose to see me, knowing that I was ill in bed. I wanted to get up to bow to him, but he would not let me. He drew me in close embrace. The hard-hearted, harsh Yati that I had met in the forest and this loving Yati — what a contrast it was. I wished mother was here to witness this meeting of her two sons.

I said to Yati, 'You are the elder brother. This kingdom is yours. You must take the throne.'

He smiled and said, 'A deer skin is a better place to sit on than a throne. Try it and see.' Yati had said it casually, but his words sank deep. They germinated and grew into a big tree.

In life, I had gone the limit in sensuality. It was only natural that I should now turn to renunciation. I resolved to renounce the household. Kacha agreed with me and it was no wonder that Sharmishtha should follow me into the jungle. What astounded me was Devayani. She also resolved to go with me.

That night I was just coming round. For a few moments, I was fully conscious. It first seemed as if Alaka was sitting by my bed. But I realised the next moment that she was Devayani. She was fanning me.

I looked down and there was Sharmishtha massaging my feet.

I pondered over this great change in Devayani for a long time in bed. Kacha must have talked to her at length. But that was nothing new to her. In the end, I brought it up before Kacha. I asked him in jest the cause of this reformation in Devayani. Seeing that I believed him to have worked the miracle, he said, 'You are wrong, Your

Majesty. What I had been striving for years happened that night; but not because of me but because of Puroo.'

I said in astonishment, 'How?'

'When Puroo took over your old age, you gave him the kingdom in return. But as soon as he got back his youth, he ran to Devayani. He fell at her feet and said, "Mother, Yadu is my elder brother. Father has given me the kingdom. But I will not take it. I shall not take the throne insulting Yadu. Let Yadu be king. I will take his orders. I swear by you mother. I swear by my mother Sharmishtha, I want you as mother, I want Yadu as brother. I do not want a kingdom. I want a mother and a brother." '

Devayani who had never before yielded to anyone or anything melted at this love, affection and sacrifice of Puroo. She hugged him and bathing him with tears said, 'Puroo, as to who is to take the throne, that is for the king and his subjects to decide. But you have today given me something which is beyond all kingdoms. A selfless warrior like you has made me his mother. Puroo, who taught you so much love? It would have been far better if I had been taught that in my childhood. I am now going to learn it from you. You gladly took over your father's old age. From love for your brother, you were prepared to relinquish your kingdom. Puroo, I want nothing more than the strength to love like you.'

Puroo had relinquished his right to the throne, but the subjects to the last man wanted him to be king. Yadu's defeat had lowered him in their estimation. The Dasyu rebellion to the north had to be put down. It could only be done by a brave king. Devayani also bowed to the wish of the people.

On the day of Puroo's coronation we retired to the jungle. Immediately after the ceremony, Kacha asked all three of us, 'Does any of you have any residual wish?' Devayani and Sharmishtha immediately said, 'No.' I however kept quiet. Kacha said, 'Your Majesty... .'

I said, 'Now, I am not to be called Your Majesty, but Yayati. We are friends, right from the days of the sacrifice in Maharishi Angiras's

251

hermitage. Today again, we are friends as in childhood.' Kacha said, 'All right. Yayati, is there anything more you wish for?'

'Yes, two of my wishes are yet unfulfilled.'

'Which are they?'

'Madhav's mother is now very old. I wish to take her with us, so I can be of some service to her. And that we three should tell our story to the whole world without any reservations.'

King Puroo came to receive our blessings. I blessed him with, 'May this family attain fame in your name. Like your valour, may your spirit of sacrifice grow.'

'What else Your Majesty?'

'I am no Majesty!'

'What else father?'

'I have no household now.'

'What else... .'

'In happiness and misery, remember one thing. Sex and wealth are the great symbols of manhood. They are inspiring symbols. They sustain life. But they are unbridled. There is no knowing when they will run amuck. Their reins must at all times be in the hands of duty.'

Oh man, desire is never satisfied by indulgence.

Like the sacrificial fire, it ever grows with every offering.